KILLER FLOCK

SHANNON BAKER

Copyright © 2025 by Shannon Baker.

All rights reserved.

No part of this book may be reproduced in any form or by any electronic or mechanical means, including information storage and retrieval systems, without written permission from the author, except for the use of brief quotations in a book review.

Severn River Publishing
www.SevernRiverBooks.com

This is a work of fiction. Names, characters, businesses, places, events and incidents are either the products of the author's imagination or used in a fictitious manner. Any resemblance to actual persons, living or dead, or actual events is purely coincidental.

ISBN: 978-1-64875-655-9 (Paperback)

ALSO BY SHANNON BAKER

The Kate Fox Mysteries
Stripped Bare

Dark Signal

Bitter Rain

Easy Mark

Broken Ties

Exit Wounds

Double Back

Bull's Eye

Close Range

Taking Stock

Killer Flock

Michaela Sanchez Southwest Crime Thrillers
Echoes in the Sand

The Desert's Share

The Nora Abbott Mystery Series
Height of Deception

Skies of Fire

Canyon of Lies

Standalone Thrillers
The Desert Behind Me

To find out more about Shannon Baker and her books, visit severnriverbooks.com

To all the readers who've made it possible to keep riding this trail.

1

A few months ago, if you'd told me I'd be huddled up on a stormy afternoon in my little bungalow with my sister and niece, planning how to extract my boyfriend's ex-fiancée from a South American country, it's a fair chance I wouldn't have believed you.

Sure, I'd seen plenty of unlikely situations in the last few years, ever since my former husband and sheriff had been accused of murder, and I'd ended up being sheriff, and then three years later—in more craziness—left the office. But this, what we were doing tonight, stretched the bounds of believability.

I focused on my niece Carly's phone screen and resisted the urge to stroke the face speaking on the other end of the connection. For all the good that would do, a finger touching a cold surface wouldn't be anything like feeling his warm skin, scratchy with a light scruff of whiskers that he rarely allowed.

Diane, my older sister, was all business. In fact, she sounded impatient. "Have you made any progress at all?"

Baxter looked tired and pale. But maybe that was my worry over him being in Chile and away from US doctors who treated him for weak lungs. I wanted him safe, but I understood why he needed to be there. Whatever our future held, Baxter cared about Aria, who likely still believed they were engaged, since Baxter hadn't had time to talk to her.

I wanted him home. Or home-ish. We hadn't worked out the logistics of where we'd build our nest. Because he ran a news empire in Chicago and I now managed a small herd of Highland cattle in the Nebraska Sandhills, we'd need to do a fair amount of negotiating.

We hadn't had much time to be together, let alone plan our future, since Aria had disappeared within days of Baxter's and my planets colliding in my heart's Big Bang. At least, that's how it felt when we finally admitted we needed to be in each other's orbit from now on.

All that overdue drama had happened as Aria's childhood and security had blown up around her and she'd fled to bury herself in her latest business project, a desalination plant in Chile. Baxter had flown down to talk to her, believing he needed to break off their engagement in person, like the decent person he was. By the time he flew into Santiago, Aria was nowhere to be found.

That had been three weeks ago.

So far, no one had sent a ransom demand. Baxter went to the construction site, where no work had begun. He'd found few people who knew anything about a beautiful American woman, or at least anyone willing to risk talking. Every lead he'd found circled in on itself and left him with no answers. It was as if she'd simply vanished, something that would be nearly impossible for a woman as remarkable and accomplished as Aria. She wasn't the type to fade into the background, unless that background was as dense and dark as a jungle on a moonless night.

Baxter squinted against the tropical sun. "I found the cocktail server the bartender sent me to. She didn't recognize the pictures of Aria. Another dead end."

Carly tucked her blond hair behind her ears and concentrated on Diane. Her face held all the dearest memories of her growing up, a sprinkling of freckles and wispy hair escaping her braids as she mastered roping a calf or digging a post hole. I knew that feisty look in her eye, and a surge of emotions rose in my chest. Hope, because it meant Carly was ready to jump into action. Fear, because even though Carly had skills and experience in dangerous situations I could only guess at, she was only twenty-one, and the memory of me changing her diapers and rocking her to sleep was too close for me to want to send her into harm's way.

Carly's mother, our oldest sister, Glenda, had died of cancer when Carly was only twelve. I'd always spent a lot of time at their ranch helping outside and taking care of Carly. But after Glenda had passed and Carly's father died a few years later, I'd been Carly's guardian.

In the cozy warmth of my cottage, Diane rubbed her forehead in agitation. It seemed she and Carly carried on a silent conversation before she finally blew out a long breath. "Fine. Yeah. I'll make some calls. We can be in Santiago tomorrow."

Baxter didn't look relieved. "Is this the best way to handle it?"

The afternoon was fading, snow starting to stick to the winter-brown prairie outside my window. A bluish tint lit my small house, and I'd be snapping on lights soon. Carly had been home from the University of Nebraska in Lincoln (Go Big Red) since yesterday. How that girl managed to pass any classes remained a mystery, since it seemed she spent more time away from school than on campus. But that was only the least of the secrets she kept.

Diane had arrived a few hours ago from Denver. I didn't know exactly what Diane and Carly did when they disappeared for days and often returned with bruises or unseasonable tans. Always with no explanation.

In high school, Baxter and Carly's father, Brian, attended the same exclusive boarding school, as had Diane's first husband.

In the Second World War, a group of students from that school had become involved in extracting citizens from dangerous situations. All I knew was that Diane, who had contacts in the international banking world, worked with the current Legacy generation. And now Carly was involved. I'd tried not to ask questions and not search for clues. The less I knew, the better.

After the weeks Baxter had spent looking for Aria and coming up empty, I'd acknowledged my need of their skills and called them in. They'd been on the phone with Baxter for an hour. I suspected that Diane had started researching the situation in Chile before she'd begun her drive from Denver to Hodgekiss. Now I was certain of it.

I broke into their conversation, not able to hold my concern in. "Are you okay? Feeling good?"

Carly gave me a half grin. "You've got it bad."

Diane jabbed at Carly. "Leave her alone. She's in love."

You can't win with this Fox bunch. For the last few years, the whole clan had chased me into finding romance, even with the most unsuitable partners. And even though the rest of my seven brothers and sisters weren't aware that Baxter and I finally committed to each other, Diane and Carly had somehow known all along that Baxter and I had an unbreakable connection. You'd think they wouldn't need to give me a hard time now.

The fatigue lifted from Baxter's face, and his smile seemed to shine through the small screen. "I'm fine. Tired and worried, but nothing beyond that. I see a blizzard is heading your way. Do you have Brodgar and the ladies taken care of?"

Of course, despite everything he had to worry about, he'd check up on me. Brodgar was the Highland bull he'd bought at the Denver Stock Show last month because he knew I wanted him with all my heart. "Brodgar's ladies" referred to the forty head of cows that I managed for Aria.

And that brought me full circle to Aria. We hadn't known each other for long, but it was one of those friendships that sparked immediately. She'd probably hate me when Baxter broke the news to her about calling off their engagement. It wrecked me that I'd killed our connection, but more than anything, I wanted her home and safe.

"The storm's not supposed to hit until midnight, and they're saying it won't be too bad. We're fine here." Why were we talking about weather when I wanted to tell him how much I missed him. How worried I was about him. Promise to hold him close when he came home.

There was no way I could actually see his eyes on the small screen, but I knew the brown-flecked gold that reminded me of a lion. They held love for me, and even though we weren't saying the words out loud, the emotion was there.

"As riveting as this conversation is," Diane said, "can we get down to details?"

My phone rang, and I reached for it, moving away from the screen to let Diane and Carly coordinate with Baxter.

Douglas, my younger brother and one of the twins, spoke as soon as I answered. "I'm giving you warning."

Uh-oh. "What's coming at me?"

Douglas ran the University (Go Big Red) research ranch at the northern edge of Grand County. He herded grad students through projects while maintaining the working ranch. I heard a smile in his voice. "Two things. First of all, the storm has hit here way earlier than expected, and it's coming in hard and fast. The wind is howling. Whiteout. So, if you've got to get something in, better do it in a hurry."

He meant if any of my cattle needed shelter, I'd best be getting to it. "We're good. You forget that Highlands are made for this kind of crap." I paused. "Give me the real reason you called."

Even if he was six years younger, Douglas always protected me. "She's on her way to your place."

She could only mean one person. Our second-born sister, Louise. Dang. We hadn't told her Diane and Carly were here, and now she'd find out and be butt-sore. But if Douglas knew Louise was charging here, there had to be another reason. "Why?"

"She's looking for Dad."

That only added another question. "I didn't know he was missing."

Douglas sounded amused. "Louise made chili and cinnamon rolls and called to invite him over."

We all knew that was Dad's favorite meal.

"He didn't answer his phone, so she went over to his trailer. He's not there. She's called all over, and now she's heading out to your house."

Leave it to Louise to overreact. "Why didn't she call me?"

He laughed. "She has the impression if you're hiding Dad, you won't answer the phone. She's trying to catch you in the act."

"I'm not harboring Dad, but Carly and Diane are here. And that's going to blow her up."

"I'd say you've got about five minutes to get them out of there."

I hung up and grabbed Carly's and Diane's coats. "Take this call on the road. Louise is on her way out."

My house hunkered on the edge of shallow Stryker Lake, a ten-minute drive to Hodgekiss, population one thousand souls, give or take. There wasn't much around me except grass-covered hills. Perfect, as far as I was concerned. But I couldn't picture Baxter being content here any more than I'd bloom in the penthouse overlooking the Chicago River.

Not my concern now. If I didn't get Carly and Diane gone, we'd be stuck for hours hashing out why Louise hadn't been invited to the party, and never being able to mention Aria and Baxter for fear there was some international incident going on.

What Louise suspected about Carly's and Diane's activities, I didn't know, but I really didn't want her involved in any way with the Aria situation. And I wasn't ready to tell her about Baxter and me. It probably wouldn't hurt for her to know, but a lifetime habit of keeping my private life from Louise's comments and scrutiny was hard to break.

Carly and Diane must have felt the same as I did, because they jumped up. It was funny to watch two women in the middle of planning a mission to a foreign country panic over facing our sister when she felt left out.

Before Carly could end the call, I stuck my head in front of the screen. "Be careful." *And I love you and please come home.*

Carly grabbed the phone. She and Diane each gave me a quick hug, told me not to worry and that they'd stay in touch. That last part I would believe when it happened, since they would tell me what they wanted when they wanted. They were gone in a flurry of snowflakes.

I stood on the screened porch, my arms crossed against the chill. The temperature must have dropped ten degrees since I'd been outside just an hour ago, taking us from the low fifties into the forties. The sun played hide-and-seek with the low clouds, and snow gave the world a gray tone. The purr of Diane's Mercedes faded with her taillights over the hill, and a cottony silence settled over the hills.

Where was Aria tonight? Maybe in a resort on the other side of the world, taking self-care to the extreme a wealthy woman's indulgence made possible. Maybe she was safe and had no idea we were worried about her. Or maybe she'd been kidnapped and was in serious trouble. I didn't want to think of anything even worse, though I knew bad things could happen.

A swell of gratitude welled up for Carly and Diane, who'd rushed in to help. They were brave and resourceful and loyal. All the best of the Fox clan.

Hopefully Diane could race down my dirt road to the highway before Louise made it to the turnoff. I wasn't too worried, though. Diane drove her car like a fighter pilot flew an F-16. And she was motivated to avoid a Louise who would make their unannounced visit to the Sandhills a monumental insult.

Since Denver was in the opposite direction from where the storm approached, I figured they'd outdistance the worst of the weather. My house was stocked with provisions for several days, and Poupon, my spoiled standard poodle, and I would have nothing but worry and a few good novels to see us through. I wouldn't bet my Wi-Fi or even electricity would hold out if the storm gathered fury, as Douglas had warned. But I had a generator for heat and light. Admittedly, having Baxter snowed in with me would be ideal. But, as Dad was fond of saying, "If wishes were horses, then beggars would ride."

2

While I ran through the storm preparations in my head, the roar of an engine interrupted the still of the snowy afternoon. I stepped outside to wait for Louise to slide to a stop in front of the house. She popped out of her old Suburban and, like a panzer, rolled toward me. "He's been here. I saw his tracks. Where did he go?"

I gave her a puzzled look. "Where did who go?"

Louise had seized the role of leader after Glenda passed away ten years ago. None of us cared if she thought she had authority. My MO was to avoid Louise whenever possible, deescalate if I had to be around her, and love her from a distance. Because, despite her being responsible for me being the only sheriff ever recalled in Grand County, I did love her. She meant well, however misguided her methods.

Now she stomped up the steps of my porch and barreled past me. "Is he here?"

Since two of me could fit inside a Louise suit, I stepped out of her way to let her pass. "No one is here. There's no vehicle parked outside."

She kicked off her fake Uggs so she wouldn't track in snow—always the mom who knew someone would need to clean up a muddy mess. "As far as I know, it could be in the shed along with your rig."

I'd settled my 1973 Ranchero, Elvis, in the old barn across the yard that served as my garage. He didn't need to brave the elements. "Nope. What's crawled up your butt to get you out on an afternoon like this?"

She stopped in the middle of my house. Literally the middle, since it was a tiny bungalow, with one side a living room–dining room combo that led into a spacious kitchen you could hold a barn dance in, as long as you didn't invite more than one other couple. The other side had two shoebox-sized bedrooms. The bathroom, small enough you could sit on the stool and soak your feet in the tub, was tucked off the kitchen.

She planted her hands on round hips and stared at the table, where I'd had the forethought to remove the coffee cups Carly and Diane had used.

She looked troubled. "I can't find Dad. And he's not answering his phone."

"You know he doesn't always keep his phone charged. He's probably fine."

She didn't look convinced. "He's not at his trailer, and the weather is bad. He's not as young as he used to be. He has no business being out in the storm. And you don't seem at all concerned. What if he's had an accident and is freezing in a snowbank?"

Opting against being petty, I didn't point out that none of us were as young as we used to be, and also, it would have to snow a lot more to work up a deadly snowbank. Louise had five kids. Her oldest was away at school at the University of Nebraska in Lincoln (Go Big Red). That should mean she had plenty to worry about at home. "Since there's only an inch of snow, that doesn't seem likely. Maybe he's with Deenie. Did you try calling her?"

Louise flapped her arms down and slapped her thighs. She wasn't at all happy with Dad keeping time with Deenie Hayward, a woman about the same age Glenda would be if she were alive. "No, I did not call Deenie. I don't have her number."

I started for my phone on the round oak dining table. "Let me give her a try." I liked Deenie quite a bit. Baxter had ten years on me, so I accepted the age difference between Dad and Deenie, short for Gardenia, a name I was sure no one but her mother called her. But more than that, Deenie was cheerful and calm, with an easy laugh and a personality that accepted everyone.

Louise lunged to keep me from my phone. "That's just it. I'm pretty sure

Dad's not with Deenie, and it's her fault he's out there somewhere." She choked up on the last bit.

Louise often got notions that made no sense to me. For instance, the reason she instigated the recall against me was because she'd convinced herself that being sheriff wasn't good for me or the Fox family and she needed to save me. She'd also convinced herself that *I* was somehow responsible for Mom disappearing from our lives, a real sieve of a theory.

Whatever crazy story Louise had cooked up about Dad and Deenie, I wanted no truck with it, and I deflected and detoured. "Douglas said the storm is pretty bad up there and heading our way."

Louise couldn't be distracted that easily. "Exactly. And Dad is out there someplace, all because of that…that…that…"

I wasn't sure what term Louise reached for, but I jumped in before she could call Deenie something I'd have to throw a punch to defend. "How about some tea? You didn't happen to bring any cinnamon rolls with you?"

Her eyes lasered in on me. "You know I made rolls? Who called you? Michael? No, it would be Douglas. That's why you're acting so innocent. Listen, I know you think the sun rises and sets with Deenie Hayward, but she's not good for Dad, and now she's gone and done—"

She paused, and I heard the rumbling of an engine as a vehicle pulled up and stopped. We both hurried to the front porch.

We got there in time to see someone halfway across the yard, running through the snow toward the house.

Louise's mouth dropped open, and I shoved her aside to welcome Deenie Hayward inside.

Deenie shouted a hello and raced past me from the porch to the living room, and I followed.

"Whew!" Deenie said, brushing snow out of her blond hair that showed a quarter inch of dark roots. She wore snug Wranglers on a frame somewhere between Louise's comfortable mom and my five-foot-three work-toned, and a barn coat I recognized as an abandoned jacket from one of my brothers years ago. She kicked off her wet tennis shoes next to Louise's boots. "Whoo. It's getting cold out there."

Louise had barely moved, and I considered shutting the door and leaving her alone on the porch. Instead, I turned to Deenie and raised my eyebrows in a questioning way. "Hi?"

She quit hopping from foot to foot trying to warm up. With an almost shy smile that revealed two crooked front teeth that looked bunny-cute, she started. "I'm sorry to drop in like this. I should have called, but I didn't know I was coming here until I was at your turnoff. The roads are getting slick, and I didn't want to head up to Gordon tonight. I was hoping I could crash here?"

Louise had crept inside and clicked closed the front door. A facsimile of a polite smile stretched across her broad face. "Do you know where Dad is?" It probably chapped her to ask Deenie.

Deenie shifted inside the barn coat and looked as uncomfortable as a hairless cat in a sandbur blanket. "I couldn't say. I haven't seen him since yesterday."

The tightness in her voice told me there was more to this story. Since Louise was here, I wouldn't need to be the one to ask.

Louise narrowed her eyes, still standing in front of the door. "So. It's true."

Obviously, I wanted to know if what was true. But I waited for Deenie, who glanced toward the kitchen, where she knew a back door offered escape.

With the courage of a chihuahua cornered by a rottweiler, Deenie lowered her chin and faced Louise. "I don't know what you heard, but I'm assuming some version of your father and me calling it quits."

Tabasco on marshmallows. For so many reasons, I hated to hear this. For the first time in three years since Mom left, there had been light in Dad's eyes. He'd started smiling, laughing, and teasing again. That was a precious gift Deenie brought to him. And there was the selfish fact that as long as Dad was happy and occupied with Deenie, the burden of taking care of him had shifted from my shoulders. Maybe *burden* was too big a term, because I loved Dad, and spending time with him was great. But him being with Deenie took a worry away from me and made me happy for him.

"I'm sorry," I started, wanting to ask what happened, but not wanting to intrude. Still, if Deenie had dropped in unexpectedly to stay with me, that would mean she felt comfortable enough to call me a friend.

But Louise didn't give me a chance to ask. "Norm heard it at Fredrickson's." That was the gas station–convenience store where Norm worked an unreasonable amount of hours to support his big family. Since they served pizza, and hot dogs that rolled on the heaters for hours if not days, and with coffee machines and packaged snacks, plenty of locals stopped in to pass the time at the molded fiberglass tables in the back. Norm caught most of the county gossip and brought it home to release it at Louise's feet.

She continued. "Everyone is talking about it. And now Dad's disappeared, and I'm worried about him."

Deenie wrinkled her brow. Everything about Deenie seemed comfortable, like the best mattress. One that was soft enough to sink into, but firm enough to give support. Her round face, usually full of humor and invitation, looked uncharacteristically sober. "He can take care of himself."

"Take your coat off," I said to Deenie. It was too late for noon dinner and too early for supper. But comfort food on a cold day is always appropriate. "How about bacon and eggs and pancakes?"

Deenie shrugged out of the jacket and draped it across the coatrack by the front door to dry the melted snow. "Don't go to any trouble. I'm not hungry."

Louise still stood by the front door in her stocking feet. "Well? Aren't you going to tell us what happened?"

I started for the kitchen and, over my shoulder, spoke to Louise. "It's none of our business. Do you want to eat pancakes with us?" She'd say no, since she'd need to get home to fix her family's supper.

She stomped past me, snapping on the kitchen light. "You do the bacon. I'll make the pancakes. You've never been able to make them fluffy."

I made excellent pancakes and wanted to say so, but I was too shocked by Louise staying to put up a fight. Deenie must have been as surprised as I was, because she gave me a look that seemed equal parts amazement and discomfort. Deenie hadn't been with Dad for more than a year, but she'd been around our family long enough to figure out the dynamics. I felt like I should apologize to her for inviting Louise.

We trailed Louise into the kitchen, where she bent into my refrigerator, an appliance that stirred happiness in my heart. I'd lived at Frog Creek Ranch with my ex-husband, Ted, for eight years, and dealt with a fridge the size of a ten-year-old child and nearly as old as Dad, with a freezer compartment nestled inside that constantly had more frost than space. I'd never take this beauty—with ice and water *in the door*—for granted.

As with many houses built just after the turn of the last century, my roomy kitchen didn't have much counter space but could accommodate a table that would seat a family and a few ranch hands. I'd opted for a café table and a butcher block.

"You don't have any buttermilk." Louise stated it with the same horror as if she'd found a severed head in the meat drawer.

"Got the powdered." I reached for the cabinet by the stove.

The sigh she let loose could have filled a hot-air balloon to lift her out of my kitchen and float her home. If only. "If that's what you've got."

She swiped it from my hand and found a six-cup glass measuring cup with a spout. Louise knew my kitchen. Before we'd had a falling-out over the silly recall where she'd taken away my livelihood, and then an outburst that I feared would break Dad's heart, she'd regularly stopped out to drop off groceries or baked goods, whether I was here or not.

Louise loved being embedded in all our lives. I'd spent a lot of energy trying to build a fire line between her and my personal business. Obviously, it wasn't one of my best skills.

Deenie leaned against the sink and folded her arms across her chest. She stared out the window above the butcher block, and it looked as if her face melted in sadness. I wanted to offer her a chance to talk about whatever happened between her and Dad. But no way I'd open her up to Louise's judgment.

Louise bustled around, tossing the flour, baking powder, and rest of the ingredients into a bowl without measuring anything. She poured in milk and gently folded everything together while I laid bacon into a cast-iron skillet. No one spoke, and I wondered if I ought to say something to break the silence. I glanced out the window, surprised at the density of the snowflakes catching the light from the window. Dusk hadn't announced itself yet, but thick clouds and snow grayed everything. It was the kind of day made for snuggling in a fluffy blanket with a cup of hot tea and an engrossing mystery novel. "It's really coming down out there."

Deenie stirred and glanced at Louise's operation. Deenie earned her living working in cafés as cook, server, manager, and all three at once. "I like to add a dash or two of cinnamon. Not a lot, or it's overwhelming."

Louise glared at her. "I've been making pancakes since I was eight years old. My family loves my pancakes."

I was certain she chose her words to point out that Deenie wasn't part of our family, as far as she was concerned. She might have thrown it down as an insult about Deenie not having children. Louise held motherhood as the highest accomplishment, which I knew because she never missed an opportunity to point out the tragedy of my not having children. Not that I didn't want them.

Deenie turned her head back to the window without another comment. Whether Louise snapping at her ruffled her or not, I couldn't tell.

"Cinnamon sounds like a good addition. Let's try it." I reached into the cabinet for the spice.

Louise shifted her back to me to prevent me from adding a dash. Not worth a battle, so I set it on the counter and went about my business.

While the bacon sizzled and I set plates on the table, Louise flicked a drop of water onto the hot griddle. She poured the batter in four small rounds and then, like an overfilled teapot, seemed to boil over. She spun to Deenie. "Are you going to tell us what happened or not?"

I stepped between the two of them and faced Louise. "Back off. She doesn't owe you an explanation."

"It's okay, Kate." Deenie sounded worn out. "I'll say that Hank is a good man. He loves his family so much. The rest of it is between your father and me. He can explain anything else he wants."

"He can't tell me anything if he's lying in a snowbank," Louise shot back.

Again with the snowbank warning.

Deenie scoffed. "He's not in a snowbank."

A charred smell rose from the griddle, but Louise didn't seem to notice. "This proves that you're not the person for him if you don't even care that he's out in this storm."

Whoa, whoa, whoa. "Deenie isn't Dad's probation officer," I barked at Louise.

Deenie held up a palm in Louise's direction and walked from the kitchen. "Thanks for letting me stay, Kate, but I'm going to head home."

"Wait." I glared at Louise before I followed Deenie. "Louise is leaving now." I raised my voice. "Aren't you, Louise?"

From the kitchen, Louise said, "Oh, foot!" That was a pretty violent curse for her. "I burned the pancakes. Wait, I'll make more."

Deenie shook her head at the kitchen and then said to me, "I'm going to go."

I wanted to run into the kitchen and drag Louise to the front door and boot her out, then pull Deenie to my couch and sit her down to let her talk. An air of mourning hung heavy, and the corner of Deenie's eyes drooped in a way that reminded me of Boomer, my boxer at Frog Creek.

That's it. This was my home, and Deenie was my friend. Even if I had to claim Louise as a sister, that didn't mean she could run roughshod over me. As I was halfway to the kitchen to give Louise a not-so-nice invitation to exit, my phone rang, and I swiped it off the table.

3

The caller ID showed Zoe Cantrel, Grand County's sheriff, who was appointed after my recall. If I couldn't be sheriff, my next pick would be Zoe. Though in her mid-twenties, Zoe was capable and courageous. She, Carly, and my youngest sister, Susan, had been a powerful threesome growing up. And all were still close. I figured if they formed a triumvirate, they'd rule the world.

Wind popped and whooshed around her words. "Are you at home?"

"Just battening down the hatches here. How's it look at your place?" Because most Sandhills conversations begin with weather updates.

She shouted above the wind. "That's why I'm calling. It's really picking up out here, and we're trying to bring in the heavies."

That meant Zoe and her husband, who ranched with his parents just south of the university research ranch where Douglas lived, were bringing the pregnant cows from the pasture to corrals close to the barn, where they could keep them protected as much as possible.

Even with her yelling, it was hard to make out what she said. "Dispatch called. There's been a wreck about a mile east of Hodgekiss. A tour group of bird watchers. Their van slid off the highway into the ditch and broke an axle."

I whipped my head to the window to monitor the storm. Here, the snow fell harder than earlier, but there wasn't much wind. "Are there any injuries?"

A few of her words were torn away, but she got enough through the speaker. "...okay, just cold...eight people...no rooms at Long Branch...you check it..."

Deenie watched me with concern. Louise stood in the kitchen doorway, realizing something was happening.

I pieced it together. "You want me to go out there and collect the people? Find them someplace to stay until they can get their van on the road again?"

She must have found a bit of shelter, because the wind noise died down a bit. "If you don't want to or can't get out, I'll ride to the house and head in. But even then, it'll be an hour or so before I can get there."

I waved that off. "No. Stay where you are and take care of your herd. I'll give Dean Barkley a call and see if we can put them up at the high school for tonight."

"Thanks, Kate. I owe you."

We signed off with a promise I'd keep her updated.

Louise had retreated to the kitchen and banged a few dishes around, running water. Deenie reached for her shoes.

I headed for my bedroom to change from my sweats into jeans and flannel. "Feel free to stay," I said to Deenie.

She shoved her feet into her tennis shoes. "I'm coming with you. I'll help."

Louise hurried from the kitchen. "You'll need my Suburban to get them to the high school."

Everyone pitching in was the Sandhills way, so it didn't surprise me they jumped in to help. Louise, as a mother of five, and coincidently on the school board, would have Principal Barkley's number, so I turned to her. "Can you call Dean Barkley and see if he'll meet us at the school and let us in?"

Louise pulled her phone from the back pocket of her baggy jeans. "Good thing I'm here to call. Otherwise, he'd put you off. He acts like that building belongs to him."

Though happy I didn't need to look for Barkley's number and I'd rather let Louise make the call, I figured I had enough backbone and legal authority to get the old principal to shelter people in a storm.

Deenie pulled her barn coat on. "Do you know how many people are in the van?"

Since she clearly hadn't heard all the details, I told her what Zoe had said.

Deenie took that in and considered. "Do we have any cots or sleeping bags?"

Louise broke off her phone conversation and said, "We've got enough camping cots and a pile of sleeping bags from Norm being scout master."

It wasn't the official Boy Scouts, just a group of men who liked to relive their youth, so they packed up their kids and headed to a lake and called it scouting.

Deenie nodded. "That ought to work. I hope there aren't any old people."

Birding? Most young people could find something more exciting to do than wander around fields and forests with binoculars and stare into trees for hours. I figured it was mostly old people.

"Can you grab some blankets in the closet?" I pointed to the spare room and slipped into my room to change.

When I was ready, I considered Poupon, who slept contentedly on my couch, despite the rule about no dogs on the furniture. I'd probably be back in a couple of hours. How long would it take to get folks set up in the school, call a few church ladies to organize food, and get back home? But what if something came up and I couldn't get home? He wouldn't care until he got hungry, but I didn't want him to get lonesome.

"Do you mind if Poupon rides in the back?" I asked Deenie.

She gave him an affectionate wink and waved in a "c'mon" way.

As usual, I had to tug him off the couch and coax him outside before we climbed in with Deenie. In her aging Suburban, Louise followed us along the dirt road and over the hill to the highway. The snow was piling up, maybe three inches so far, a wet, heavy, slick mess on the road that caused Deenie's little car to slip around the turn east toward where Zoe had directed us.

I leaned toward the windshield into the swirl of white flakes. "There." I pointed to the taillights of a white van. The nose of the vehicle rested into the borrow ditch. No one milled around in the snow. They must be sheltering inside.

Deenie slowed, and Louise pulled in behind us. As soon as we stopped, I popped out and hurried to the van. *Flock Watch Tours* was painted on the side.

The side door slid open, and a man, maybe mid-thirties, jumped out. Tall and lanky, he wore canvas pants, a fleece pullover, and hiking boots. "They told us the cops are on the way, but thanks for stopping."

Our civilian clothes and "mature" vehicles must have confused him. I thrust out my hand. "We're who they sent." I introduced us as a few heads poked out of the door opening, looking like a family of racoons peeking from a den.

"I'm Ford. We've got some folks who might need extra help."

A compact young woman, maybe in her late twenties, with bright almond-shaped eyes and black hair, shot from the van. She rattled off her demands like an automatic rifle spraying bullets. "We're going to need seven rooms. Only one has to be a double, and that will need to be handicapped accessible because Mr. Levine can't climb stairs. What's the best restaurant in town? I don't know if anyone has food allergies, but it's always best to avoid gluten if possible."

By the time she finished, Louise and Deenie had joined us. Poupon, not surprisingly, opted to stay in the car.

A man, probably early forties, climbed out the passenger door. He had a thick, dark beard and a forest-green beanie stretched across his head, leaving bushy hair escaping underneath. He stuck out his hand to me. He had the look of a small black bear, and I imagined his whole body covered in fur. "Sean Murray. We should get Mr. Levine someplace warm. He looks pale."

I shook his hand. "Let's load up the Suburban. Two people can ride in the back of the car." I paused. "They need to be okay with a dog."

A whip-thin older woman with a smooth silver bob eased herself from the sliding van door. She pulled a long cardigan close and folded her arms. "I'm wondering if we should rent a van and continue to Scottsbluff as planned. If we stay here..." She stopped and scanned the roadside and white landscape stretching into the waning afternoon. "Wherever here is, it could throw us off our schedule, and we're due at a fundraiser in Seattle in two days. We are expected to be there, and it would be a great inconvenience if we don't attend."

Yeah, having just been to a fancy fundraiser in Denver a few weeks ago, I could attest that this woman looked like she'd fit right in with that posh crowd.

A Black man, I guessed in his fifties or early sixties, stepped out, stretched his back, and took a few tentative steps. He was over six feet tall, with an athletic build, and wore casual slacks and trekking shoes. "Mr. Levine really needs to get settled someplace. He's shivering."

Whoever this Mr. Levine was, they all seemed to be concerned about him.

The older lady looked rattled. "Oh, dear. We have to get him warmed up right away. Can you call the restaurant and tell them to prepare chicken soup, but please make sure it's not too salty."

Who were these people? It was as if they'd never ventured into rural Nebraska and had no idea we didn't have twenty-four-seven services.

Louise poked her head into the door of the van. She immediately backed out as if chased by a dragon emerging from a cave.

An overweight man with thinning dark hair and a sour expression grunted as he lowered himself to the ground. He spoke to the tall, athletic guy, who was reaching his hands up in a stretch. "This is unacceptable. Where are we, even? Is the hotel close? I've been rattling around in that van since we left Omaha, and I've had about enough." He searched the group and focused on the older woman. "There must be better ways to *view the birds* than this." The emphasis on those words he'd shot at the woman seemed to have some significance lost on me.

The tall guy winced and slumped his shoulders. "It's the weather. Shouldn't be this cold and snowy this time of year."

Can't imagine where he got that idea. February in the Sandhills was often exactly like it was today. Prone to winter weather. In winter.

I labeled the complaining guy as Mr. Jerk, developing an immediate dislike for him. Even his face had a warped look, though I couldn't put my finger on exactly how.

All of these people needed to get some perspective. I held up my hand. "A snowstorm isn't unusual this time of year. If we can avoid the wind, it shouldn't get too bad. I'll call my cousin Stormy and see if he can tow the van to his shop and get it fixed in the morning, and you'll be on your way."

Mr. Jerk's derisive smile looked a little oily. "Stormy? Ironic name. Is that like your dad-cousin-brother thing?"

I gave him a crusty look at his inbred joke. Not funny.

His scowl showed he was insulted I didn't appreciate his humor. "Can he get us on the road before dark?"

Stormy was Dad's cousin. He worked on cars, tractors, and haying equipment, sharpened ice skates and mower blades, and on slow afternoons, played pitch in his greasy back room with some of the old ranchers who'd retired and moved to town. "Since it's pert near dark now, I'd say there's not much chance. But I can guarantee he'll get on it." I threw in the "pert near" and added a slow accent just to poke at Mr. Jerk.

No cause for him to be surly, but he was anyway. "Tell him we need to get to Scottsbluff tonight. I'm sure we can make it worth his while."

Whatever Mr. Jerk considered Stormy's while was worth probably wouldn't make any difference on a Saturday afternoon. If Stormy had the parts and could fix it, he'd get on it first thing in the morning—on his day off. If he didn't have parts, well, we were a fair piece from anywhere, as I'd love to put it to Mr. Jerk, and it'd take at least an extra day. But I ignored him, because that's what I figured he deserved.

Despite being outside in the vastness of the snowy Sandhills, Mr. Jerk seemed to take up more than his fair share of space. He zeroed in on me. "And you're who? The emergency response people are supposed to be here already. Stick around in case we'll need transport to the hotel."

Louise had apparently had enough of these people and their demands. "There's an old man in that van who needs to get someplace warm and dry." She pointed to the bearded guy and the tall man. "You help him into the rig." To Ford and the younger woman with black hair now dotted with snow, she said, "You two grab the luggage." To the older woman, "Get out of the cold. Sit in the passenger seat."

Ford looked confused and turned to me. "Is there...? Where are we going?"

"We can put you up in the schoolhouse. There are only two rooms in the hotel, and they're above the café in town. So, stairs. Double beds. And drafty windows. Trust me, no one wants to stay there."

"Did you say schoolhouse?" the black-haired bullet of a woman asked. "As in one-room school?"

Sheesh. While we had plenty of those around, Grand County Consolidated could accommodate up to two hundred students. Not that we ever had more than a hundred and fifty at a time, counting the town's grade school. "It has three circular sections with about five or six classrooms in each, a cafeteria, and even a gym with a stage. I think we can house seven people for one night." My polite tone had a bit of an edge.

Mr. Jerk boomed out, "It's a frickin' miracle there's a restaurant in this wilderness. I don't suppose they'll have a decent wine selection, but maybe we can get a steak. I've seen more cows than birds on this trip, so I assume they have beef."

The young woman corrected me. "Eight."

I glanced around the group, and counting the old man, I'd only seen seven.

The black-haired woman pointed at the folks gathering snowflakes on their heads and started to name them.

I concentrated, since most of them hadn't given names yet.

She started with the youngish man. "Ford, the tour guide." He flashed a peace sign my way, his sandy hair wet and straggly. "And I'm Olivia Choy."

Olivia motioned to the classy elderly woman. "Joyce Levine."

Joyce pierced me with a stare, as if acknowledging a servant.

Olivia tilted her head toward the bearded man in the green beanie, and her voice flattened as if she didn't care for him. "Sean Murray."

He reached out again to shake my hand, even though he'd already done it.

The tall man raised a hand in a wave as she introduced him. "Aaron Fields." She indicated the corpulent guy. "Aaron works for Jesse Gold."

Ah, that's why Mr. Jerk—uh, Jesse Gold—had jumped down his throat earlier.

Gold sneered. "Do we really need to go through this right now? I'm cold and hungry and have had it with this whole debacle."

With a nod to everyone in general, I said, "Nice to meet you." I agreed with Gold that we needed to get this show on the road. "The other two?"

Olivia turned to the van, where Deenie and another woman were helping an older man onto the side of the road.

Joyce hurried over to them. "Get him in the car before he gets wet." She bent inside the van and grabbed a fleece throw, tossing it over his head as you might cover an infant in bad weather.

Olivia indicated the group moving steadily toward the Suburban, where Louise stood ready to open the back door. "That's Kenneth Levine, Joyce's husband. We'll be lucky if he survives this trip." There wasn't a whole lot of compassion seasoning her voice. "And Anna Ortiz."

The last person had an unlined face with smooth caramel skin and large dark eyes. She didn't make eye contact with anyone and appeared to be one of those people who tried to take up the least amount of space possible.

Ford had finished transferring the luggage by the time Olivia wrapped up the introductions.

Jesse Gold stomped to the Suburban and lumbered into the passenger side. I figured that would irk Louise, since she'd already assigned that position to Joyce.

Aaron, the tall Black man who looked like he played a lot of tennis, and Sean, the bearded guy in the green beanie, ducked in and crawled to the third seat in back, where Louise's ten-year-old twin boys usually rode. I figured the two men might discover any number of toys, sports equipment, and dropped snacks.

Joyce sat close to Kenneth, fussing over the blanket. Anna took the place next to Joyce and stared ahead, her hands in her lap.

Louise pulled herself into the driver's seat while Olivia, Ford, and I walked to Deenie's car. Olivia pulled open the rear door and jumped back.

I'd forgotten about Poupon. I didn't groom him with the traditional cut, so he looked a little like an eighties rock star with hair fluffed on his head and ears mimicking a wild mullet. I was used to him and had only seen him get aggressive once, when his favorite newborn friend was in danger, but I could understand why he might be off-putting to some. Especially if they didn't like dogs, which was always a litmus test for me.

Olivia studied him for a second.

"I'll ride in back," I said. "Poupon isn't mean, but you don't have to sit next to him if you'd rather not."

It seemed Olivia made her own assessment. "I'm fine. Just didn't expect him."

Ford had opened his door and looked a little less convinced. "Can I ride up front?" Poor guy didn't seem steeped in authority and was a little light on the take-charge spirit. He was clearly out of his depth leading a bunch of people and dealing with a car accident in the most rural of places with a snowstorm coming on.

I swung my arm in invitation, and we all piled in Deenie's warm car and followed Louise the three miles to the other edge of Hodgekiss and the schoolhouse. It used to be the high school, but when asbestos abatement and maintenance on the elementary school that had been built in the early 1900s became too much, they'd co-opted a portion of the newer school, then built a fabulous playground on the north lawn, and after twenty years, everyone seemed to accept the situation.

Poupon sat straight, disdain writ large on his face as he stared out the windshield.

Olivia draped her arm across his back, and her fingers teased his curls. She spoke around his head. "Where is the town? Do we need to make reservations at the restaurant?"

Deenie broke into a grin, the first I'd seen since she showed up at my house. Whatever was going on with her and Dad, I hoped she'd get back to smiling again soon. "We just drove through it."

Olivia twisted to look out the window. "That one street was town?"

It wasn't like Sandhillers didn't know how the rest of the world worked, we simply preferred to do things our own way. Even if there was a better way to do something, change came slowly to our neck of the prairie. "The Long Branch is closed for a couple of days because the owners have gone to visit their son and grandkids in Kansas City. But even if they were open, they've never taken a reservation in their lives."

I punched Stormy's number from my favorites. When I was sheriff, it was good to have the local repairmen at my fingertips. The phone rang once, picked up, then hung up. That's how I knew I had the right number.

"Sorry," he said after he'd connected the second time I called. "This darned phone. I can't figure it out."

He'd been saying that for three years. He'd probably acquired two new upgraded phones in that time. I gave him the rundown on the van and told him that a flock of bird watchers were nesting at the schoolhouse, so we'd appreciate if he could get after it quickly.

He sounded less than thrilled. "It's a bugger out there, Katie. You say they need it tomorrow?"

"There's an older man who probably shouldn't be sleeping on a cot. So, yeah. I can run to Broken Butte or North Platte for parts if you need." I didn't want to do that. Not on a snowy, cold winter night. But my comfort didn't seem the most important thing right then.

My offer probably shamed him, because he came back with, "I'll get out there before dark and see what's up. I seen Newt and Earl at Fredrickson's earlier, so maybe they can help get it loaded on the flatbed."

That arranged, I hung up with thanks. I had a good view of Ford's face as he stared out the window. It had a definite panic patina. "Wha-wha-what are we going to do for food?"

He didn't seem like the kind of guy I'd want in charge of a trip. But thankfully, Olivia, though much younger, seemed ready to take over. "We're going to a school, and Kate said there's a cafeteria. Maybe we can get one of the school cooks to come in. I'm sure the tour company would pay for their time." She emphasized "tour company" in a weird way.

"We'll figure something out," I said. "We wouldn't let you go hungry."

I hadn't been around this band of whiners long, but I was already worried getting them fed would be the least of our troubles.

4

Dean Barkley was at the school when we pulled up, so I left Poupon in the back of Deenie's car. With all his hair, it would take some time before he got chilled, and napping in the back seat of a car was his favorite thing to do. He'd been deprived since I'd been recalled, and I only had an unlicensed pickup for ranch work, and Elvis, with bucket seats.

In his early seventies, Barkley wore the same style of navy blue knit pants he'd worn during the Bush administration—the first one—when he'd taken the job as principal. We'd always called him Principal Barkley, in a slightly mocking way, so it was hard, as an adult, to refer to him as Dean. He'd been at the high school so long no one could imagine the place without his dour presence.

The school had been built in the early seventies, in what was ultra-modern at the time. Three circular classroom sections made the structure look like a clover from the air. A hallway orbited each of the three sections, kind of like a professional sports arena. The sections all converged in the front hallway that led to the office, cafeteria, and access to the gym. Metal gates could be pulled down to lock each section from the others. A round room, called the pod, was located in the center of each classroom cluster with doors that opened to the classrooms. This was a teachers' lounge and planning area, as well as supplies storage. Each contained a bathroom, mini fridge, and coffeemaker.

Dean Barkley huddled in a puffer coat and an HHS knit cap over his nearly bald head. He directed us away from the front doors to a side door in the east classroom section. The door was recessed, making it the perfect place to smoke in a rainstorm. Which plenty of students did, and some teachers as well. Unlike most populated American cities, there was free-range smoking in the Sandhills.

Wisely, Principal Barkley had chosen to give the birders the section that included the library and had a reading area with a couple of comfy chairs and couches.

While Anna and Joyce helped Kenneth up the snowy walkway, followed by Jesse Gold, who scowled at the sky and everything in general, the rest of us gathered the luggage and hauled it in.

The metal door banged closed behind us, and we bunched in the dim hallway lit with security lights recessed under frosted plexiglass every twenty feet along the ceiling. Just enough light to make passage down the hall doable, but dark enough to create scary shadows. This corner of the school was out of the way from the front, where visitors entered to attend ball games, plays, and events in the auditorium, and where parents zipped in to drop off forgotten lunches and homework or to pick up a sick kid. Or, in the case of the Foxes, escorted a student home who'd caused a ruckus of one kind or another.

Principal Barkley, never a spark plug of a guy, looked irritated. "I understand the urgency of the situation here, but I can't let strangers have access to the resources of Grand County."

Louise wasn't having that. "This man needs to sit down. We're taking him to the library."

Deenie took Kenneth's arm. "I've got him."

Louise allowed Deenie to help, then settled her bulk in front of Principal Barkley in a challenging way.

The rest of the bedraggled crew followed Deenie to the library.

Barkley looked like he wanted to protest, but going against Louise's will took the courage of a lion, and he was more like a prairie dog, diving into a hole at the first sign of danger. He muttered a response. "I can give you this classroom section with the library. But I've pulled down the gates to keep you from the office."

"Is there another landline besides the office?" I asked.

Barkley humphed in annoyance. "No. With everyone having their own personal phones, the board decided to save money by eliminating all but the office line." He probably hated change. "But that's not a problem for you. They all have phones, I'm sure."

I couldn't remember the last time I needed a landline, so he was probably right. "So we can't get to the locker rooms for showers? And no cafeteria?"

Principal Barkley looked stern, a face I'd encountered across the desk when I'd argued against suspending my youngest sister, Susan, for releasing a mouse near the cheerleaders during a pep rally. I hadn't saved her, maybe because I'd started laughing when he described Megan Ostrander screaming and fleeing from the gym just ahead of the mouse. "I can't risk people I don't know running willy-nilly around the cafeteria, eating Lord knows what and contaminating foods. And you know the students don't lock their gym lockers. You can contact the UCC and Episcopal ladies to bring sandwiches."

Yeah, I'd already figured on the churches to help out. The women, of course. Men might help dig out the van but would never organize a feed.

Louise's face looked like granite. "The science room is in this section. There are Bunsen burners and workbenches there. I'll gather groceries and feed this crew."

"Oh, now, Louise. That's not a good idea. There's a coffeepot in the teachers' lounge in the pod. You can use that. But it would be best to have food brought in."

Louise narrowed her eyes at him. "We will not give these poor people cold sandwiches. They already think we're a third-world county. We can show them hospitality. They're traumatized as it is."

Dean Barkley looked pained at the idea of cooking in the chemistry lab but then thought better of coming up against Hurricane Louise. "Fine."

Louise literally brushed her hands together as if she'd completed a job well done. "I'll gather the cots and bedding and get food." To me, she said, "You get the people settled."

It seemed like a workable plan. Even though I hated taking orders from the General, as we Fox kids often called her, I saw no reason to push back. Guess Barkley and I both kept our heads down around her.

A wide corridor lined with student lockers circled the section. This one would be the seniors' area. Burnt-orange industrial carpeting covered the cement floor. They'd had to replace it several times since I'd been a student here, but it looked the same. No exterior windows lit this area, and only one door opened to the outside. We were an island, separated from the rest of the school by the locked metal gates.

Deenie appeared around the corner out of the gloom. "I'll go with Louise."

Louise pinched her lips before saying, "I can handle it."

Deenie was already to the door. "You can use another set of hands loading everything."

Maybe Deenie was strategically trying to get in Louise's good graces by being helpful, but if she and Dad were really over, she wouldn't need to curry Louise's favor. I didn't think Deenie operated with ulterior motives, though. She was a generally helpful and kind person.

Without another complaint, Louise thundered toward the door, resigned to accepting Deenie's help.

Dean Barkley zipped up his puffer coat. "Okay. You've got it handled. Don't mess with the supplies. Don't let them disturb anything. Get them out of here as soon as Stormy can get their van repaired. No later than midmorning. Students will be back Monday morning, and I'll want to be sure all is in order by then."

I didn't bother telling him the people would leave as soon as humanly possible because the last place on earth they wanted to be was Grand County, Nebraska, in a schoolhouse, with a meal prepared over Bunsen burners. "Thank you for letting them stay."

I watched the door bang closed and turned to traipse along the corridor toward the library. I'd only gone a quarter of the way around the outside of the section when I heard hushed voices. They came from a dark spot between safety lights, where a nook in the rows of lockers led to a classroom door.

"Not now. Wait until it's over." That was definitely Olivia. She spoke in a low, confident voice, as if trained for public speaking, with each word clear and precise.

A man answered her that sounded like Sean. "Are you sure we can do it now?"

A soft note that I hadn't expected from the hard-nosed Olivia entered her voice. "This actually might work for the best."

Should I interrupt or wait? Obviously, whatever they discussed was private. I edged to the side of the corridor.

"You go back first," she said. A rustle of footsteps walked toward the library.

After a second, I continued down the corridor. Olivia looked surprised when I walked into her view.

"How is Kenneth?" I asked, trying to cover that I'd heard a private conversation.

She looked irritated, as if she had things on her mind and Kenneth wasn't one of them. She didn't bother to smooth her attitude on my account. "Joyce is on top of it. She's got Anna on board. Don't worry about him. Where are we on accommodations and food?"

She could rival Louise for bossy sister energy. "We're gathering what you'll need, and it'll be here soon."

Windows from the library cast light into the corridor. About three times the size of the classrooms, the library wasn't expansive. A desk and two tables were positioned at the front by the door. A gathering of comfortable furniture clustered where the librarian could keep an eye on students from her desk. A few rows of chest-high shelves fanned toward the back wall, where one more table and some tiny chairs were arranged near the picture books in the corner. The wall opposite the windows and the back wall were lined with books. Good thing students could find much of what they needed online, because Grand County Consolidated didn't have a vast collection.

Jesse Gold lounged in a decrepit recliner someone had donated. Kenneth sat on one couch with his head resting on the back cushion, wearing a dazed expression. He had a nice head of light brown hair with only a spackling of gray. His slack face made it appear he wasn't as sharp as he might once have been.

Joyce wrapped her long sweater close around her and rested a hand on Kenneth's thigh.

Anna perched on the edge of the couch on the other side of Kenneth. When I opened the glass-paneled doors, she glanced at me and lowered her eyes.

Aaron stood behind Jesse Gold with his arms folded, showing no emotion.

Sure, their vacation trip had turned south, but there seemed to be a cold current of animosity rattling along the rocks of this creek. I was glad I didn't need to spend the night with them.

"Let me give you a quick tour, and while Louise and Deenie bring supplies, you can pick your classrooms."

5

By the time Deenie texted she and Louise were at the door, the rest had settled on their classrooms. Joyce and Kenneth Levine, who I'd taken to calling Mr. and Mrs. Howell in my head, had chosen the English room. Aaron and Sean picked social studies, with Ford clear he'd be happiest in the hallway.

Imperial Jesse Gold had insisted on his own room. He'd had Aaron drag his bags to a pocket of a room used for small groups or club meetings. It was only big enough for a table and a few chairs but opened to the teachers' pod, as the rest did. I'd rather sleep in a snowbank than room with someone who gave off such bad energy. I immediately backed away from all that aura and woo-woo thinking because those tendencies came from Mom, and I didn't want to admit to any of her influences.

That left the math room for Olivia and Anna.

The science room would be the makeshift kitchen, and the library a lounge of sorts.

When Deenie texted me, I hurried to let her and Louise in. The metal door didn't have a window, just a push bar, and it locked automatically. I couldn't count the times someone wedged the door open while they escaped for a quick smoke, or to drive to Dutch's grocery for snacks. Technically, we didn't have an open campus, but we'd grown up in the wide-open spaces of rural Nebraska, and most of us had a feral streak.

Because the classroom section was circular, there was a dark wedge of empty space where the door opened to the outside. That's where we kept the brick to drop into the doorway so the door wouldn't close and lock us out. The teachers knew about the brick, and plenty of them used this spot for a breath of fresh air.

I clanged the metal bar to thrust the door out, and Deenie burst into the school, face set, arms full of bedding.

I held the door open for her, letting Ford and Sean out to haul in the cots and whatever Louise had gathered for meals. "You don't have to hang around," I said to Deenie, assuming she'd had enough of Louise. "You can take Poupon and go to my house."

She gave me a weary smile. "There's eight people to feed, and your sister can use the help, even if she doesn't think so."

Louise popped in, carrying a roaster pan filled with bags. She seemed cheerful and all business. "I can fix up a mess of sloppy joes. I have enough veggies for a tossed salad. And I made bread yesterday."

Bread yesterday, cinnamon rolls today. Louise's love language was baked goods, but she didn't always opt for yeast concoctions because she had a big family and didn't have time to wait around for dough to rise. But when problems mounted, bread seemed to offer her comfort. Something was up with her. "Thanks for helping," I said, trying to be nice. "But you've got kids at home. I can get these folks fed."

Louise's smile looked as fake as George Washington's teeth. "They're fine. David and Esther can keep an eye on the twins. I'm more useful here."

Huh. Definitely something wrong. "Is Norm at Fredrickson's?"

She seemed offended by the question. "Of course."

Olivia and Anna slipped out of the math room, and Louise spoke to them. "There are a couple of laundry baskets in the back filled with groceries and kitchen things. Bring those into the science room. Tell the guys to distribute the cots and bedding."

Deenie shrugged and headed down the dim corridor.

I grabbed the brick from the nook next to the door, dropped it in the doorway, and trotted out to get Poupon.

About eight inches of snow covered the ground, more than Jerry Delong forecast on Channel Four Weather. My nose stung from cold, and the hint of a breeze tossed snowflakes around. I'd say the temps had dropped to the twenties by now, maybe colder.

It might be a schoolhouse and scout cots, but these birders were lucky not to be on the road. Although, to be honest, those cots weren't anything to brag about. A flimsy folding frame of wood with two two-by-four crossed bars strung with burlap created a sort of sling, but the center had no support and tended to cause backaches. I'd rather sleep on the ground. Still, if that wind Douglas warned about hit us, simply surviving would be a bonus.

With so many people helping, they'd brought in all the supplies in one trip, so I kicked the brick back into its nook after Poupon and I entered the building. Showing no curiosity about this new place, he trailed me to the chemistry lab.

The roaster was already plugged into the worktable at the front of the room. The very spot Mrs. Brown demonstrated dissecting a frog. I could still smell the formaldehyde. The door to the pod at the front of the room stood open. Students were never allowed into the inner sanctum of the pod, which the teachers protected as their private retreat.

Even now, being here felt like trespassing. Not to Poupon, evidently. He crawled under a counter along the wall that the teachers used for a desk. I guessed he wasn't feeling social. Not that I gave the pod much thought when I was a student here, but I'd entertained a vague idea it was nicer, a sort of cozy sanctuary. Instead, it was kind of messy, with a long counter that had one well-worn roller chair with a stained seat, and a couple of those plastic molded chairs that students used. It wouldn't be a place where teachers would kick back and relax.

Louise, as bossy high schooler, mother, and now school board member, didn't exhibit any timidity about where she went in the school. She pulled extension cords from a drawer as if she knew this space as well as she knew her own kitchen, or mine. Louise had resources, man. "There are three packages of hamburger in the roaster. Start browning that and chopping onions. Deenie can make the salad."

Louise often bought beef cows that had died accidentally. A rancher with a downed animal could sell to Louise at super-discounted prices, and since the cows were likely old and tough, she'd have the whole animal butchered into hamburger. With enough added seasonings, she managed to make it edible, and it went a long way to feeding her big family. Not to mention half the county when she donated her cooking to fundraisers. If I had to give Louise credit for anything—and I wasn't sure I did—she was a good cook. But I didn't feel obligated to tell her that.

I wanted to get these folks settled and be home before too long so Poupon and I, and possibly Deenie, would be snug and comfortable. By morning, Zoe could take over. I might need to run for parts, since Stormy's suppliers would be in North Platte or even Kearney, a few hours' drive away. If I got lucky, I'd be able to stay home and check on my small herd, even though they'd be fine in the worst weather.

While I browned the hamburger and Deenie chopped veggies for a salad, Louise hustled around in the teachers' lounge. The others busied themselves in their separate bedrooms/classrooms.

The science room worked well for a kitchen, with three tall workbenches, the one at the front of the room outfitted with a sink and faucet. Two eight-foot standard tables were on one side of the room and a handful of desks on the other, so there were plenty of work and eating surfaces.

Ford shuffled through the door, his shoulders up around his ears. His sandy-colored hair looked soft as satin and tended to drape across his forehead, and he'd periodically snap his neck to flop it back. He watched us with his hands in his pockets. "So, like, do you think we'll be able to leave tomorrow?"

Sean wandered in still wearing his green beanie, scratching his beard and looking nervous. Who wouldn't be, getting stranded and at the mercy of strangers? "Even if we get the van fixed, it'll be a while before we can get out of here. The snow is getting deep."

"If the wind doesn't come up, it shouldn't be a problem," I said. "The county will have snowplows out all night."

Ford and Sean exchanged a worried look. "What happens if the wind comes up?"

Olivia popped in, all brisk energy. "Anything could happen then. In the 1880s, a blizzard hit suddenly. I think this was someplace in North Dakota.

Hundreds of people died. And all these kids were stranded in schools because their parents couldn't reach them."

Ford's eyes widened. "Like now."

Deenie looked up from the red bell pepper she chopped. "That's the Children's Blizzard, or the Schoolhouse Blizzard. Whichever. In January. A really nice day until noon, then the clouds came in, and it got ugly super fast. I think two hundred and thirty-five people died, all across the Great Plains, but they were really hard hit in Nebraska."

I stopped stirring the meat and gave her an impressed stare.

Ford looked even more horrified, and Olivia seemed to enjoy it.

Deenie kept chopping and didn't look up. "Schoolteachers had to try to save their kids, but most didn't have enough wood to burn or food or anything. And they were all really young women. One took her kids to her home, like, a block away, and none of them made it. Another one got a bunch of her kids to her house two and a half miles from school, and they all survived. Some parents died on their way to get their kids. It was tragic."

When no one said anything, she looked up to see us staring at her.

She shrugged. "I heard it on a podcast. I'm a sucker for true crime and disaster."

Ford looked as though he might throw up. Sean sounded slightly breathless and jittery. "That's intense."

Deenie kept her head down, maybe embarrassed. "I have a pretty good memory."

Olivia's face froze, and she developed a sudden interest in the shelves of specimens along the south wall. There were plenty of little jars with dead things floating in formaldehyde.

I'd spent what seemed like a month of Sundays staring at those jars through biology, physics, earth sciences, and finally chemistry classes. Mrs. Brown, our teacher, had an organizational bone bigger than Louise's. Every jar was labeled and alphabetized and sat at an equal distance from every other jar. A burble of laughter hit my chest as a particular memory landed.

Michael and Douglas, the twins, were juniors. They snuck in during a volleyball game one night and stole the nematode jar. They drained the jar and refilled it with water and spaghetti noodles and returned it to the shelf. The jar looked identical to the roundworms in formaldehyde. The next day, while Mrs. Brown went into the teachers' central pod for supplies, the boys opened the jar and ate the spaghetti in front of the whole class. Lots of groans and *ew*s might have been overlooked by Principal Barkley, but when Buster Graham ralphed all over the floor, causing a few sympathy vomits to follow, it led to the twins being suspended for three days. A punishment that didn't bother them much. But Dad made them clean out Aunt Hester and Uncle Chester's chicken house, pigpen, and barn, and that made an impression. At least they hadn't committed another suspension-worthy incident again.

The onions in the hamburger started to send out an inviting aroma. I didn't know about any of the others, but a sudden appetite hit me. The bacon might have gone in the fridge and the pancakes into the trash, but Louise made a mean sloppy joe, so the tradeoff didn't seem so awful.

Anna Ortiz spied us from the open doorway.

Deenie noticed and shot out a hearty welcome. "We'll be ready to eat in a few minutes."

Behind her, Joyce and Kenneth shuffled in. Kenneth leaned heavily on Joyce's arm, a mildly puzzled look on his face.

Anna hurried over and pulled out a chair at one of the lower tables. She helped Joyce settle him.

Deenie acknowledged them with a grin. "How're you holding up there, Kenneth? Is the English room warm enough?"

"J-J-J...S-s-son," Kenneth stuttered at Deenie, then clamped his mouth shut and shifted his eyes to Joyce.

Anna's eyes flicked from Deenie to Kenneth in an anxious way while silence deepened.

Finally, Joyce answered. "Kenneth had a stroke some years ago. He hasn't recovered his ability to speak as yet." She leaned close to Kenneth's face. "But it'll come back, and you'll be as good as new."

Red splotches appeared on Deenie's cheeks. She probably felt bad about peppering him with questions.

For an elderly woman, Joyce seemed to be holding up well. Not a hair in her gray bob ventured out of place, and her makeup looked fresh, even after all of this. Wrinkled hands weighted down with several diamond rings sported long, red fingernails. "Fresh air and exercise will be good for him. Although camping on cots in a drafty school won't help, I'm sure."

Aaron Fields entered, looking over his shoulder, as if checking if he'd been followed. His gaze traveled around the room, seeming to make momentary contact with each person, like a secret agent passing a message.

I glanced at Deenie to see if she'd noticed, but she was tossing the salad in a seafoam-green Tupperware bowl that would be suitable for a baby's bath. Louise had gathered oversized cooking and serving dishes from family members who didn't need them anymore and picked up more at garage sales. She found plenty of places to use them, from funerals and baby showers to school functions and, apparently, rescuing stranded birders.

Speaking of Louise, she bustled in from the teachers' lounge with her arms full of paper plates, plastic silverware, napkins, and cups. She dropped them on the table in front of Mr. and Mrs. Levine.

Ford looked so skittish, I tried to draw him into conversation to distract him. "How did you end up out here? It's pretty early for many of the birds to be back. I haven't seen my first curlew yet."

He cleared his throat. "Oh, well, I was going to show them the Sandhills cranes. You know? And we have hotel and restaurant reservations in Scottsbluff, and we planned on going up the monument to see, the, um, the eagles. But I kinda took a wrong turn. Or not turn, really. I didn't go south when I was supposed to, and then we decided to take the highway west from here. We'd only add an hour by that mistake. But then we slid off the road. And now, I'm not sure what we're going to do, you know?"

Seeing the Sandhills cranes? Interesting. There was abundant birdlife around here. Pelicans, ducks, heron. We were especially known for grouse, or prairie chickens, and their mating ceremony of thumping the ground. Then the usual suspects of curlews, killdeer, meadowlarks, cardinals, and robins, and even then, not enough to warrant a trip out here this time of year. But, despite the name, Sandhills cranes did little more than fly over this area.

Aaron ambled over, close enough to Ford that the young man stepped back. With a pleasant smile, he said, "Admittedly, making this tour so early was risky. I'm afraid that's my fault. I'm a science teacher, and I convinced the company to schedule this extra-early tour because of our spring break."

In February? "I thought you worked for Jesse Gold," Deenie said.

Aaron nodded vigorously. "Yes, yes. Now I do. But when I booked this trip, I was still teaching."

Olivia piped up. "I was hoping to maybe see some eagles. I've heard they gather at Lake McConaughy this time of year as the ice melts and they hunt fish."

At least that bit was true. But the lake was close to Ogallala, seventy miles from here, and that was still a two-hour drive to Scottsbluff, in a totally different direction. This collection of clowns didn't seem very organized.

Jesse Gold exhaled from the doorway, maybe annoyed we hadn't noticed his entrance. "I hope this meal isn't something people like you call goulash. Please God, let it be edible."

Louise paused on her way to the lounge. "I wish you'd said something. I could have made goulash."

With his beanie and beard, Sean looked a little like a garden gnome. "My mom made the best goulash. She used ketchup and tomato soup."

Joyce lifted her eyebrows. "Oh, no. We had a cook when our son was young, and she used crushed tomatoes and tomato paste. The macaroni can't be overcooked and mushy. And plenty of paprika."

Kenneth rallied, and maybe excitement ran under his immobile face. "Jo-Jo-Joel."

Joyce looked away.

Olivia showed some animation. "My mother added a dash of fish sauce and used rice noodles."

"That doesn't sound like goulash," Ford said. "My grandma didn't always have meat, so sometimes we just had macaroni with canned tomatoes."

Anna made a sympathetic little "oh."

Ford looked embarrassed. "It's okay. I love that. Crave it sometimes, you know?"

Joyce stretched her neck. "What I wouldn't give for a glass of wine right now. Did anyone happen to pack any?"

Jesse stopped on his way to the table where the Levines sat. He glared at Aaron.

Aaron faced away from Jesse, so he couldn't have seen the death rays shot at him, but I swear I caught a glimmer of mischief in Aaron's eyes.

Olivia let out a groan of yearning. "Oh my God. After the day we had, wouldn't that be great?"

Sean plopped down at the table across from Kenneth and directed his comment to Jesse Gold. "I'm more of a beer drinker, but tonight, I'd kill for a glass of wine."

Aaron turned slowly and focused a placid expression on Jesse Gold.

The older man looked away and sniffed in that superior way I'd already started to hate.

Ford plodded by Jesse. "My nana always had one glass of wine before supper. She said it made her feel like a queen."

Anna's deep brown eyes filled with compassion. "One glass."

Ford gave her a sad smile. "She never had much extra money, and then after Mom died, she had to take care of me."

Joyce picked up from there. "Sometimes, one glass is all you need to take the edge off the day. It can often make the difference between despair and acceptance."

Aaron tilted his head at Jesse, who still hadn't moved. The big man tightened his lips and curled his nose in a sneer. "It so happens I do have a bottle..."

Aaron coughed into the crook of his arm, a fake cough if I ever heard one.

Jesse Gold corrected himself. "Two bottles. We're traveling in Nebraska. I'm skeptical about the quality of wine here."

Fair. Unless you were friends with Marty Blaire, who owned the feed store and had fine wine frequently delivered by UPS.

Aaron brightened. "I'll get it."

As he passed Jesse Gold, I swore the older man mumbled, "Snitch."

For someone craving wine so much, Joyce didn't seem particularly grateful to Jesse Gold as he sat down at the end of their table. "Anna, would you be so kind as to get Kenneth's sweater from our room? It's the orange one with the label." She made it sound serious and gave Anna an intense gaze, as if speaking words the rest of us couldn't hear.

Anna stood. "Right away." She barely made a sound as she snuck out, passing Aaron on the way in.

Louise hurried out of the pod with a bottle of salad dressing, salt and pepper shakers, and a tub of I Can't Believe It's Not Butter big enough to swim in. "All I've got is Dorothy Lynch dressing. But I promise you'll love it."

Deenie lifted her head. "It's sort of a cross between Russian and French, with its own twist. It's Nebraska tradition."

Poupon chose now to saunter out from the pod and around the table where Deenie and I worked.

"Holy mother of God!" Joyce shrieked.

Jesse Gold jumped from his chair, a too-small plastic contraption meant for teens, not for a man with seventy years of fine dining under his belt and on his belly. He staggered backward, stumbled, and ended up plopping back into his chair, which nearly upended. "What is it?"

I was trying not to laugh, so Deenie fielded the question. "It's a poodle."

"I hate dogs. Cats aren't much better, except they don't bite as hard." Gold eyed Poupon with pure hate.

Sean spoke up, as if trying to irritate Gold. "But a cat will eat you right away if you die. A dog will lie by your corpse and guard you."

Louise hustled back to the center room. "He's harmless. Doesn't even shed much." She eyed the supplies on the counter and spun back to the pod.

Olivia sprang forward. "It's Poupon. Hi, you handsome fellow." She squatted in front of Poupon, and he allowed her to make a fuss over him.

"I'd tell you he's usually more friendly than that, but he's not," I said, getting ready to drain what little fat cooked out of the meat. "He seems nervous. Maybe doesn't like being in the school."

"Or he senses a storm," Deenie said.

"Or he doesn't like the company," Joyce added, her eyes flicking to Jesse Gold.

I didn't much care for him, either, but Joyce made no effort to hide it.

Surprising me, Gold chuckled at Joyce, as if they were buddies and she'd made an inside joke.

Louise appeared and set a variety of bottles and spices on the counter. If I didn't step back, I was sure she'd have stood on top of me. She began pouring and sprinkling ingredients into the meat. "Jesse. That seems like a name that's either way too old or way too young for you. Is there a story behind it?"

Although I'd wondered the same thing—I mean, this guy didn't seem at all like a Jesse—I cringed a little at Louise's nerve.

Gold had been watching Aaron set the wine bottles on another of the workbenches and seemed startled to be addressed. "Oh." It was the first time I'd seen him speak with any enthusiasm. Probably because we were focusing on him. "My father's name was James. He had a fascination with Jesse James, so he named me after him."

"Weird," Louise said.

No weirder than naming babies after the Academy Award best actor or actress winners the year of their birth, as my parents had done.

Deenie raised her head and cast a puzzled look at Jesse, then at Ford. She seemed as if she wanted to say something and thought better of it. "Salad's done."

Louise nudged me. "Get the buns."

Olivia stood from petting Poupon and sauntered toward Aaron, stopping with her back to the room. "How is the wine coming along?"

Aaron looked over his shoulder from where he had the bottles. "I'll need glasses or cups."

Jesse Gold rolled his eyes. "Why didn't you say something? Did you think they'd magically appear?"

Anna quietly slipped into the room and scurried toward Kenneth with a blue fleece blanket.

"You didn't find the orange one?" Joyce said, with an emphasis on *orange*.

"Oh yes," Anna said. "I thought this blanket would be better. Will you help me put it around Mr. Levine?"

"Olivia," Jesse Gold barked. "Get the cook to find glasses for the wine."

Louise's face tightened at that. She drew in a breath, and I wondered if she'd let Jesse have it. "There are Dixie cups in that basket back there. I brought them for you to use with your bathroom stuff. They'll work for wine."

Jesse Gold sniffed. "Paper Dixie cups. Perfect."

"Plastic," Louise corrected with a smug look.

"Even better," he sneered.

This guy. It was hard to offend Deenie, but she frowned at him. "I'll see what Louise brought." She slipped into the pod.

Olivia turned her back and walked away, stopping in front of Anna and Joyce, standing strangely close.

Suddenly, Joyce jumped up and rushed to the workbench where Aaron stood. Her hands clenched, she leaned on the tall table. "This is so nice of you to offer wine," she said to Gold.

He added a lightness to his voice, and I figured he felt that Joyce inhabited the same social stratum. "It's Chateau Margaux Pavillon Rouge '97. French. Three hundred dollars a bottle."

Anna stared at him. "That's a lot for something that is gone so quickly." She looked surprised she'd said it out loud.

Ford looked like he had indigestion, and his bangs flopped into his eyes.

"I'm sure it'll be fine." Joyce's dismissive tone might have been intentionally designed to insult Gold. And from the disappointed look on his face, she'd scored.

Deenie appeared with the Dixie cups, and Aaron worked on uncorking a bottle. As soon as Deenie returned to help Louise, Joyce crowded close to Aaron, maybe to help him serve the wine. These people were all a little off, if you asked me.

Sean stood up and wandered toward Aaron and Joyce. He looked over Joyce's shoulder and then sauntered back to his chair, all of it weird and arbitrary.

Jesse Gold's forehead furrowed, and I figured this guy was always irritated by something or someone. "I need Aaron to open the bottles, anyway. My arthritis is acting up in this weather. I really hate the cold."

Anna, who moved like vapor, rose from her chair and went to help serve the wine. She started with Jesse Gold and set glasses around, waiting for

Aaron to open the second bottle to finish. Even Louise, Deenie, and I were treated.

Ford lifted his cup and in a shaky voice said, "A toast to Kate, Louise, and Deenie for rescuing and feeding us."

Joyce said, "Here, here." And the rest tipped back their cups.

Louise took a sip, then slid her little cup my way. She wasn't much for drinking.

I'd be happy to take her portion. While the wine was smooth and mellow, nothing could rival the wine I'd shared with Baxter in a Wyoming cabin over two years ago. A familiar surge of relief and happiness welled in me. Those months when I'd thought I'd lost Baxter forever had been like the Sahara in a deadly dust storm. Even with Baxter so far away, I felt like I luxuriated in a lush oasis.

Sheesh. Love made me an awful poet.

Jesse Gold frowned when he lowered his cup. He squinted at the bottles on the table across the room, as if reading the labels. He looked at his cup again and sipped, his brow furrowed as if unraveling a mystery.

Louise clapped her hands. "Dinner is ready. Fill your plates. I pulled a chocolate cake from the freezer, so it should be ready by the time you're done."

Everyone must've been as hungry as I was because they lined up quickly. Jesse Gold looked around, maybe wondering who he could order to bring his plate. When he couldn't catch Aaron's eye, he hauled himself up and joined the line. Deenie, Louise, and I stepped back and waited. Poupon wandered over to Kenneth and put his chin in the old man's lap. He gazed up into Kenneth's eyes.

Kenneth rested a hand on Poupon's head and maintained that somewhat amused but blank expression. Except he winked at Poupon, as if sharing a secret.

6

While the others filled their plates and sat down to their wine and sloppy joes, I slipped into the corridor to call Baxter. It seemed odd the difference in time zones was only an hour when he felt so very far away.

He picked up after the first ring. "Please start talking. Say anything," he said. "I miss your voice."

Warmth spread through me like butter melting on hot toast. "That's exactly what I was going to say. But since you got there first, I'll tell you about my afternoon." I filled him in on the snow, the wreck, and getting everyone settled in. "Diane and Carly will probably take off late tonight, after they get to Denver."

"Yeah. I sent my plane and pilot to get them. I'm worried about Aria. I've done some research about the gangs down here. It can be pretty bad."

I barely kept from begging him to come home. "Be careful. We've got a lot of time to make up for, so you need to get back here in one piece."

"Don't worry. Nothing can keep me away from you long." He shifted the conversation. "That storm is turning out worse than they expected. It's gathering steam as it moves your way."

I turned toward the end of the corridor where the outside door was around the corner. I couldn't see the storm from here but would have liked to monitor the situation. "How is it you know more about our weather than I do?"

I actually felt his deep chuckle vibrate in my belly. "I've got resources. I'm wondering if your birders might be stranded more than overnight."

That wouldn't be good. "This is an eccentric group. I can't say I feel warm and tender toward any of them. And some less than others."

"I get it. Everyone around here is suspicious of me."

I should have gone with Diane and Carly. Maybe I didn't have their unique skills with international intrigue, but at least I'd be with Baxter. I didn't suppose he needed me to protect him, but I kind of needed to be with him doing everything I could to help.

Instead of saying all that, I kept to the concrete. "There's something up with Louise. For some reason, she doesn't want to be home, and she's been baking bread."

"You're a regular Hercule Poirot, putting together all those clues." There was a smile in his voice that I wanted to see in real life.

"Not much of an Agatha Christie fan myself. I'm not big on the investigator laying it all out in the end."

"But you're a natural at solving crimes." A wistful sound in his voice sympathized with me for not being sheriff anymore.

"I'd like to solve the mystery of what went on between Dad and Deenie." I glanced across the dark corridor to the light spilling from the science room and the low murmur of conversation. "I thought they really cared about each other."

"Maybe the relationship ran its course." Was he thinking about him and Aria? In my bones, I knew he wasn't thinking about us. I'd allowed myself to doubt him in the past, and I wouldn't let that happen again.

And I had a hard time believing Dad and Deenie had fizzled. They'd been out to my place last week, and the way they laughed and teased made it obvious they were comfortable and secure together. I didn't sense any tension.

Baxter sounded tired, but always determined. "Before we hang up, let me tell you about one last place I'm going to check out. It's down the coast a ways. A bea—"

The light flickered in the classroom across the way, though the security lights in the corridor maintained their gloomy glow.

A shout of alarm rose from the science room just as the lights flared back to life.

"Baxter?" It seemed odd our connection would falter at the same time as the electricity. I wasn't sure how cell signals worked, but I knew it wasn't on the REA lines.

I immediately tried calling back, but got a blinking icon that circled endlessly.

The others were finishing up their dinner when I plopped a mess of sloppy joes onto a bun and piled salad on the side, making it go naked since I wasn't a Dorothy Lynch fan. I tried to hide that tidbit in case I ever wanted to run for sheriff again. Not loving Dorothy Lynch might make people suspect I wasn't a real Sandhiller.

The birders had pushed the two shorter tables end to end to create banquet seating so everyone could be together. Louise was back in the teachers' lounge, leaving the eight birders and Deenie in front of their near-empty plates.

Louise had created some magic with hamburger and her spices. I wasn't a foodie, but I figured this stuff could be served in the kind of trendy restaurants that favored gourmet tater tots, fancy mac and cheese, and fried bologna sandwiches.

While I savored my first bite, Olivia spoke. "Do you suppose that guy made it to civilization ahead of the storm?"

Obviously implying that Hodgekiss didn't fall under the distinction of being civilized.

Joyce smoothed her hair back. "Who would that be, dear?" The endearment sounded almost mocking.

Ford jerked his neck and flipped his hair back, then got up for more food. I didn't blame him.

Sean wiped crumbs from his beard while his eyes flicked from person to person. "Are you talking about the guy in the red hoodie?"

In a voice only slightly louder than a whisper, Anna said, "How do you know it's a guy?"

Aaron pointed at her exactly as a science teacher would to a student who asked a probing question. In his deep voice, he said, "That's right. We never saw them with the hood down."

Jesse Gold shifted in his chair, obviously uncomfortable. He offered his typical frown. "What are you talking about?"

Ford plopped back at the table and spoke around a bite of sloppy joes. "Dude, you had to have seen him." He stopped and tipped his chin at Anna. "Or her."

She looked down at her lap, maybe uncomfortable at being noticed.

Ford continued, "They were at every stop. But not, like, looking at birds. More like looking at us."

Olivia focused on Gold. "Really creepy. In a black SUV. You must have noticed."

Gold looked from one face to another. Color had risen in his face, and he sweated. "I never noticed anyone. Are you sure? No one saw his face?"

Deenie glanced at me with a look that clearly said, "What the heck?"

Poupon, chin still on Kenneth's lap, nudged the old man in a pet-me kind of way. Before I could call Poupon away, Kenneth scratched the fluffy apricot head. I'd never pegged that mutt for a therapy dog. Maybe that was selling him short, I guessed. He was my near constant companion. And though he never had much to say and he kept his emotions stuffed, often, he was exactly what I'd needed.

Joyce tapped her chair away from the table in a refined way. "I don't know about the rest of you, but I'm exhausted. With the time change from the East Coast, this is well beyond my usual bedtime. And Kenneth needs his meds."

Anna rose as if she'd been Kenneth's caretaker for a long time. "Let me help. I'm ready to turn in, too."

Louise appeared in the pod doorway holding a nine-by-thirteen-inch metal pan. "I've cut the cake. You don't want to miss this. It's chocolate with a burnt-sugar frosting."

Ford and Sean both jumped up, eager for the cake. A split-second look passed between Olivia and Sean before they looked away. What did that mean?

7

Sean, Ford, and Aaron each had another piece of cake, talking about baseball, a subject that interested me not at all. Olivia had taken off for her room. Deenie and Louise were cleaning up in the center pod.

I picked up plates and cups the others had simply left, as if we were restaurant staff. Oh well, as soon as we set the science room to rights, Poupon and I would be out of here. Which reminded me I hadn't seen the fluffer in a while.

I wandered back to the pod and found him curled back under the desk. He definitely wasn't having the time of his life. He watched me without lifting his head, and I understood he hated it here and wanted to go home. "Me too, buddy."

Mom believed in auras and vibes and good versus evil. Maybe because of the damage she'd done in her youth—although she might not think of it as damage—she'd developed a pacifist philosophy and spoke of sending positive energy into the universe. But this group here? They put out a noxious riptide, with the worst of them being Jesse Gold, who seemed so offensive no one wanted anything to do with him.

Louise sealed the green Tupperware bowl of salad, with little more than one helping left. The sloppy joes were all but gone, leaving a roaster pan that should soak overnight. I twisted the lid on the Dorothy Lynch, which most of the birders seemed to enjoy.

Jesse Gold, sitting on the opposite end of the table from Aaron, Ford, and Sean, spoke to me. "Did I hear correctly that you are the sheriff?"

Louise ducked her head and spun quickly to retreat to the pod. I could only hope she felt shame for her role in having me recalled.

"I was sheriff. Now I fill in as deputy from time to time."

He struggled out of his chair. "I suppose that's good enough. Come with me."

Excuse me? "We're cleaning up here, and we'd like to get home before it gets late."

Louise stepped out and spoke to Ford. "You're in charge here, right?"

He swung his gaze from Sean to Aaron as if waiting for one of them to step up. Finally, he bobbed his head. "I guess so."

Louise rested her hands on her hips. "I've left my big coffeemaker and set it up for morning. All you have to do is plug it in. There's creamer and sugar and coffee cups on the counter. It takes a minute to heat up and start perking, so don't get worried about the delay. And don't let the wheezing and screeching bother you when it does start up. There's a container of cookies in case anyone gets hungry in the night. And I'll leave the cake."

Ford looked worried he'd forget the details. I could have told him it wasn't DNA sequencing, just food and coffee. Easy enough.

"I should be back in the morning to make bacon and eggs. But if you get hungry before then, I've left the food in the refrigerator back there." The one used to store teachers' lunches as well as science experiments.

"I'm sorry there's no shower, but I brought extra towels and left them in the lavatory." Lavatory? Seriously? Was she channeling a kindergarten teacher since we were in the schoolhouse?

Jesse Gold stood at the door to the corridor. "I need to speak to you in my room." He didn't give me an option.

In my Louise voice, I said, "I'm going home. The sheriff will be here in the morning." Maybe. At any rate, I'd do all I could to make sure I wasn't forced back here with this bunch.

"I insist," he said.

Deenie walked from the pod, wiping her hands on a dish towel. "Go ahead. We're all done. I'll warm up the car, and you can meet me there." Thanks, Deenie.

I supposed Louise wanted to be in charge, or maybe she simply wanted to disagree with Deenie, but she countered with, "I'd like to get that roaster scrubbed before I go home. But you feel free to leave. I can finish up here alone."

Deenie, maybe sensing a game, responded with a hearty, "Let me work on that roaster. You can wipe down the tables."

As opposed to getting nicked in the crossfire between them, suddenly, a talk with Gold didn't sound so bad. "What's on your mind?" I said to him.

He marched out of the room, and I took that to mean I needed to follow him.

I whistled for Poupon. He took his time emerging from the pod, but with his head down, he followed me out of the science room into the dim corridor and around to Gold's compartment.

The table had been pushed to the side and all but one chair stacked against the wall. A cot that would have fit a twelve-year-old perfectly was spread with a faded green sleeping bag. It tickled me to think of Gold trying to make himself comfortable on that tonight.

He sat in the one chair, his bulk slumping off the sides.

Since there wasn't anywhere else to sit, I leaned on the table and folded my arms. Poupon stopped well short of the threshold, plopped his butt in the hallway. A low growl vibrated in the back of his throat. He might be a good judge of character. He loved most tots and had a weird affection for a couple of old ladies, but I'd never seen him preemptively growl at someone. It confirmed my opinion of Gold. I waited, withholding the satisfaction of asking what he wanted.

He fidgeted in the ridiculous chair, and his eyes darted around the confined space as if searching for eavesdroppers. He finally focused on me, a wild glint in his eyes. "Someone is trying to kill me."

That sounded reasonable to me. "Who?"

He curled his nose. "If I knew that, I wouldn't need you, now would I?"

I pushed from the table. "I don't see as you need me now."

He whipped his hand up and shouted, "Stay." With a growl, he said, "If you're law enforcement, you're required to be aware and provide protection for me."

"Look, you're in an isolated part of the country, in a snowstorm, sheltering in a school with seven other people who've been with you on a trip for several days. Doesn't appear as though you're in any grave danger."

Despite the cool temperature of the drafty school, Gold's face was flushed and sweaty. He also sounded winded. "You heard them talking about someone in a red hoodie following us."

"You're locked in here. Safe and sound. They make schools that way these days, you know."

That rubbed him wrong, and he might have had reason to be miffed, since I'd said it in a caustic way. "I've got proof that someone wants me dead."

It wasn't polite that I spouted a skeptical, "Really?"

He didn't react to my attitude but reached for a leather camera case on the floor next to him. He pulled out a tablet and fired it up. After poking and sliding his finger across the surface, he shoved it at me. "Read this. If that's not a threat, I don't know what is."

Was it wrong I noticed he was left-handed and immediately thought about someone telling me more serial killers are left-handed than right-handed. The theory had been disproved, but that didn't stop me from adding it to the list of things that marked Gold as a suspicious person.

I read what looked like a screenshot of a Snapchat post. Which meant the sender had been notified that Gold had saved it. *Watch your back, Jesse James. We haven't forgotten.*

Not Jesse Gold, but James. I handed it back to him. "Forgotten what?"

He threw his head back to look at the ceiling, then at me. "How should I know? But it's a threat, and they mean it."

"Yeah, it seems pretty vague. Who sent it?"

He snarled with disdain. "You're a real Miss Marple, aren't you? I have no idea who sent them. They came from a third-party site."

I gave him a cold stare deep with rigor mortis. "We're done."

He sounded desperate. "There are more."

I held out my hand for the tablet. "Let me see them."

He panted, like maybe he didn't feel good. Louise hadn't added much spice, so indigestion didn't seem like the obvious cause. He slammed the tablet facedown on his thigh. "I don't know how to save them, but they were more of the same. I'm telling you, someone is after me."

If you feel like you're the center of the world, I suppose you might get paranoid. "You're safe tonight."

"I can make it worth your while to stay overnight and protect me."

Wow. Again with the "worth your while" line. Some people thought money could fix everything. "I have no intention of staying overnight. I've got a comfortable home, and that's where I'll be riding out this storm."

"Don't you swear an oath to serve and protect, or something like that? You're obligated to help me. But name your price. I'll pay what it's worth for you to stay here."

I pushed myself upright again. "Not interested."

He sounded confident, like a shrewd negotiator knowing he'd find the price. "Five thousand. That's a lot of money for one night."

I turned to leave. "Have a good night, Mr. Gold." I rarely called anyone *mister*, but it seemed appropriately belittling somehow.

"Ten thousand. Only a fool would walk away from that kind of easy money." Although if he thought a murderer was on the loose, how easy would it be?

I studied him for a second. "Can I ask you a question?"

"No."

I took that as a yes. "Why are you on this tour? It doesn't seem like the kind of thing a man with your resources, who obviously appreciates luxury, would find fun."

His nose wrinkled in distaste. "It's not. And I didn't pick it. But I've got a business deal in the works, and this is what it required."

"Is this deal the reason for the threats?" I wasn't that interested but couldn't help asking.

"How the hell should I know? I'd hire a bodyguard or PI if I wasn't stuck out here at the edge of the world. So you're what I've got. Are you going to help me?"

I tilted my head to the doorway. "You see my partner out there? He doesn't like you. And neither do I. You aren't in any danger, so I'd suggest you try to get some sleep." My snarkiness surprised me. I was generally more polite with people, but the situation, and probably the overall gross vibe Gold gave off, brought me to a lower level of civility.

He pounded a fist on the table. "You're crazy, you know that? For all I know, that person in the red hoodie paid you off. How much did they offer? Whatever it is, I'll pay more."

I shook my head at him but didn't have an answer. Poupon tucked into my leg as I left the room and headed back to see if Deenie was ready. I pulled out my phone, not really intending to call Baxter, but in the obsessive way you do when you've lost signal and want to see if it's back.

It wasn't.

The door behind me slammed closed, and the click told me Gold locked it.

Poupon and I made eye contact, and I was pretty sure he was thinking, "Looney Tunes."

Deenie and Louise both had their coats on when I got back to the science room. The men weren't there, probably in their room or the library. "Let me grab my coat, and we're ready to go," I said.

We circled past the math room, and Deenie knocked, poking her head in when a "Come in" was issued. Olivia sat at a desk, scribbling fiercely in a bound notebook. She glanced up.

Anna was on her side snuggled in a sleeping bag on one of the cots. Her dark hair swirled around her head, and she watched us with wide brown eyes.

Deenie sounded cheery. "Just seeing if you need anything. Or maybe want us to bring you something when we come back tomorrow." I hoped again I wouldn't need to return here.

They both said thanks and no, and we continued on our way.

We passed Gold's door with no inclination to knock, then Louise tapped on the Levines' door.

I whispered to Deenie, "Don't they remind you of Mr. and Mrs. Howell? Stranded on a three-hour cruise?"

She giggled, and Louise sent us a scolding look. It made us laugh.

Joyce cracked open her door, wearing a matching tracksuit of turquoise velour. "Yes?"

Louise acted like an old-timey train conductor checking on travelers. "We're taking off. Is everything okay?"

Joyce appeared mildly annoyed. "Yes, yes. Thank you for dinner and the cots."

Everyone tucked in, Poupon and I were ready to get home.

We made it to the last bend in the corridor and the solid metal door. Deenie banged the metal bar and pushed.

When the door opened, we gasped in unison. Then, as quickly as possible, jumped back into the building. My heart dropped to my boots.

8

Beyond the five-foot covered concrete entryway, an abominable monster of a storm raged. Complete with claws and fangs so horrendous and fierce we were paralyzed for a second while the door banged closed against it, shutting out the chaos.

Snow cones and soy sauce. This was not the escape I'd been dreaming about.

Deenie turned her head slowly to me, the disappointment I felt written clearly on her face. "I don't think we're getting out of here anytime soon."

Louise snuck forward and pushed on the door again. Her jaw dropped.

I looked over her shoulder to see nothing but a solid wall of white. The freight train roar was something the school's thick brick had disguised. I knew there was an expensive piece of climbing equipment that resembled a ship in the playground not twenty feet away—one that had led to a vitriolic school board meeting where I'd had to escort out one enraged senior citizen who objected to her tax money going to something so frivolous—but that whimsical pirate ship might as well have been in Morocco for any sign of it.

Louise let the door close. She reached into her mom jeans and pulled out her phone. "I hope Norm went home before it got bad."

As if she couldn't believe the weather had betrayed us so badly, maybe hoping we'd all misread the scene, Deenie eased open the door again. "It was so nice this morning."

The Children's Blizzard of 1888 all over again. Only, instead of kids in a one-room school with a woodstove and no food, we were adults in a solid structure with heat and, thanks to Louise, plenty of food.

Louise pocketed her phone. "No signal. Maybe it blew a tower down or something."

Deenie's shoulders fell. "I don't suppose you brought extra cots?"

Louise shook her head. "In the Suburban."

Yeah, that's where they'd stay, because I wasn't going into the howling storm now.

"But I did haul in extra sleeping bags. And there's a stack of mats in the library for the little kids to lie down on during story hour." She was already striding away from the door, down the dark corridor.

We retraced our steps around the outside circular hallway to the library in the dim light. I assumed the main switch to the hallway lights was in the office or Louise would have sent them blazing by now. It gave the school a gloomy, cold, abandoned feel. Only adding to the creepy factor Gold gave off.

Halfway around, we came across Ford sitting on his cot. Legs crossed, hands resting on his knees, he opened his eyes when he heard us. He spoke low and slow like a recording at three-quarter time. "Dude. I thought you all took off already."

Deenie pulled an elastic from her wrist and smoothed her hair back into a ponytail. "We're stranded here with you. Blizzard."

Ford blinked slowly, his mouth a little slack. It took him a moment before he spoke. "Blizzard? Like, you can't drive home? Are we, like, going to be stuck here for a long time?"

I tried to reassure him. "Once the wind dies down, it won't take long to dig out. By the time Stormy repairs your van, you should be good to go."

Louise addressed what she probably assumed was his biggest fear. "I've laid in plenty of groceries. Along with breakfast, I grabbed a two-pound bag of pinto beans. If we ration the cookies, they should last through tomorrow. It's okay."

I figured he ought to go back to meditating before he had a heart attack. "This storm probably won't last long."

He didn't look relieved.

Deenie patted his shoulder. "Try to relax. There's not a lot anyone can do. I'm sure your company is used to this kind of thing. They can't blame you. And all your customers are safe."

"Right." He looked like a shocked, skinny Buddha sitting on his cot. Which is to say, not like Buddha at all.

We left him there, far from enlightenment, but at least there were no tears. As we neared the library, lights spilled from the windows into the hallway, giving us a welcome. Aaron and Sean startled when we tromped in.

Before they could ask, Deenie said, "It's a blizzard, and we can't leave."

Aaron jumped up from the overstuffed chair where he'd been sitting. "What are you talking about?"

Sean, still in his green beanie and flannel shirt, lay on a loveseat with his legs draped over an arm. He swung his feet to the orange carpet. "I thought it wasn't supposed to get this bad."

Ford had followed us and stood in the doorway. "It's like that blizzard where all the kids died. This is bad, you guys. Really bad."

Aaron didn't seem ruffled. In his calm baritone, he said, "I've got to see this."

Sean scratched his beard. "Yeah."

All three men filtered out while Louise led us to the mats in the corner with the picture books. We collected them all, hauled them to the science room, and while Deenie and I piled them into three beds, Louise fetched the extra sleeping bags. Also, it turned out, Louise had tossed in a battery-powered camp light about the size of a milk carton. She turned off the overhead lights and placed the light on the floor within easy reach.

There was a bumbling at the doorway to the pod. Someone cleared his throat. I recognized Sean's voice. "Do any of you have aspirin or anything? My head is pounding."

Louise struggled to climb from her sleeping bag and stand up. "I saw some ibuprofen in a drawer back here."

She hustled to the pod and flicked on a light. Sean wandered into the science room, over by the specimens, and peered at them as if reading the labels.

Deenie stayed on her side with her back to him and spoke in a sleepy voice. "Do you need anything?" He must have read the same underlying message that I heard, which was her asking him to leave what was essentially our bedroom.

Louise returned with the pills cupped in her hand. As the ultimate mom, she wouldn't give him the bottle. She'd parse out the recommended dose and no more. He ought to be happy there wasn't children's aspirin around, or she'd no doubt give him that.

I slid one of my mats off my stack for Poupon. He settled himself on my bed while I took my turn in the washroom in the center pod. That was fine with me. I doubted I'd sleep much.

As soon as Louise doused the camp light, and the lone security light in the panel close to the pod kept the room from total darkness, my brain zipped south to Chile.

Where was Aria? Would Carly and Diane be able to find her? What about Baxter? And that's where my thoughts ramped up. He had to be okay. He knew how to get things done, could handle himself in any situation, was smart and resourceful.

But I still worried. And worried. And worried.

At first I wasn't sure I heard anything. Maybe detected a slight stirring in the air. But I grew alert and strained to hear. There, over by the specimens, was a definite scuffing on the floor. Mice?

With slow movement, I reached to the camp light and found the switch. Hitting it and sitting up at the same time, I caught what was making the slight noise.

Olivia stood by the front workbench, her eyes wide and blinking. She gasped.

Deenie and Poupon had the same reaction, which was to open their eyes and give sleepy acknowledgment before closing them again.

Louise sat up. "What's going on? Is everything all right?"

Olivia acted surprised to see us. "Oh. I didn't know anyone was in here."

Maybe I'd turned cynical in the last few years, but something about the lilt in her voice made me think she knew very well we were here. "Why are you sneaking around in here?"

She cast a defensive frown. "I'm not sneaking. I couldn't sleep. Anna is praying. Out loud. The longest prayer list on the planet. I couldn't stand it. So, I thought I'd wander around a little until she finished."

Louise lay down. "If you need to wander, do it in the hall. We're trying to sleep in here."

"Sure." But Olivia exited into the pod, and we heard another door open and close. She must have decided to brave the religious fervor.

I stretched out on Poupon's mat, the sleeping bag under me smelling of campfire and dirt. Poupon lay on his side, legs extended toward me, and I trailed my fingers on his warm side. He let out a sigh of supreme unhappiness before his breathing settled into a steady rhythm.

Deenie must have been exhausted. Maybe she was one of those people blessed with the ability to turn off their thoughts. Or, as Louise accused, she didn't care enough about Dad to worry. But within minutes she began snoring, kind of like the sound Louise's coffeepot would make when it started perking tomorrow.

Louise fought with her sleeping bag, rolling first one way, then another.

Since her bed was on the other side of the dog, I suggested, "You can pet Poupon. It always helps me relax."

To my surprise, her hand landed on his side, not far from where I stroked him. "I miss having a dog around." Her voice didn't have her normal driving edge. Like maybe the dark had smoothed it out.

"Why not get a puppy from Michael and Lauren's next litter?" That was our brother and his wife. They raised Australian shepherds. Just one of their many side hustles.

Instead of biting my head off, as I'd braced for, she sounded sad. "I'd love to, but I can't add one more thing to my plate. And you know, kids promise to take care of a dog, but that never happens. And not because they don't want to. They've got so much to do."

With the lights off and all the bustle of the day over, she sounded more like the sister I used to share a bed with in the upstairs of the house where she now lived.

"How's everything going with you?" I asked quietly, between Deenie's escalating snores.

A bit of that steel came back into her. "Ruthie loves her classes this semester. And she's been chosen as floor rep because the old one quit school. So, she's really thriving. And David decided to go out for track instead of golf, so he's been lifting weights three times a week. I think he's putting on muscle. Esther submitted an essay to the Lions Club contest, and it made the finals. And, you know, the twins are always a handful, but they're both getting straight As for the first time ever, and I'm proud of them."

I let that sit while Deenie kept up her chorus, now adding a squealing noise at the end of every exhale.

"But how are *you*?"

She picked up the pace petting Poupon. "Good. I'm good. Norm is planning a fishing trip to South Dakota with his cousins in June."

Trying to unlock her was a challenge. Not one of us Foxes liked to admit we might need help from time to time. We'd grown up fending for ourselves and were darned proud of our common sense and self-reliance.

Lately I'd been questioning that stoicism. Wondering if maybe the need to constantly keep the herd rounded up and heading for the barn was actually much of an asset. Maybe there was a balance between self-sufficiency and trusting someone else. Perhaps a little messiness in life was acceptable.

In theory, it sounded good. But Foxes were practical and guarded people. And, like most folks in the Sandhills, we didn't change quickly or easily.

How much did Louise depend on Norm? She liked her world in order, everything according to her exacting standards. And I could tell her that never happened. I'd seen firsthand how Louise could break when she didn't let herself bend a little.

Maybe if I showed some vulnerability, she'd let go and talk. "You know how Dad always taught us to be reasonable and logical and not to let emotions get the best of us?"

She sounded more on solid ground. In a loud whisper, she spouted, "And here he goes, getting all twitterpated about *her*."

That wasn't where I wanted to go with this. "And Mom." A dull punch hit my stomach, as always when I thought of her. "She wanted us to constantly put positive energy and love into the universe."

Louise was silent for a moment, then said, "I miss Mom."

I didn't want to go there, either, and, in fact, had decided leaving that bit of my life unresolved might be a good thing for me. If missing Mom was the bee in Louise's bonnet, someone else would have to drag it out of her. "The point I'm making is that I don't think we need to be so concerned with always being rational. And I'm convinced that only allowing ourselves to feel happy emotions is a recipe for a breakdown."

Louise sounded ready to fight. "So, you think I'm heading for a breakdown because I feel proud about my family?"

I sat up, and Poupon stuck a paw out to touch my thigh. This guy was really on edge about being here. He showed me affection or neediness as often as it snows in Death Valley, so reaching out to make sure I stayed close meant something. "That's not what I'm saying. I think something is bothering you, and I'm trying to get you to talk about it."

She tapped Poupon's side, and he raised his head to look back at her. "Nothing is bothering me. I'm busy. I'm always busy, so that's not new."

Okay, this wasn't working. I stuck a toe out of my safety zone. "I'm only saying this because, well, since my divorce, I've tried to hold everything really close. Protecting my heart."

Now she seemed interested. "I told you that. If you stay prickly and bitter at Ted, you're never going to find another husband. And I shouldn't have to tell you, your window for having kids is closing fast."

She really was not making this easy. "On some level, you might have been right."

She sounded excited. "I'm glad you realize your mistake. Honestly, Ted is handsome, and he's got that ranch and a good job and all of that. But I don't think he's that reliable."

I barked out a laugh that disturbed the steady rhythm of Deenie's snores. I waited for her to settle in again, then in a low voice said, "He had an affair. That's the definition of unreliable."

She didn't back down. "I know that. But he married Roxy, and he's made a family and settled down."

As far as she knew. Though I had inside information to refute that. Not that I would mention it. I couldn't care less about protecting Ted, but I didn't want to be any more involved with that rodeo than necessary.

I tried to redirect. "What I'm trying to say is that if you need someone to talk to, I'm here."

Louise kept patting Poupon, and not in a soothing way. "I can see you're reaching out. I'm glad you came to me this time. Diane knows a lot about banking and fashion, but I know more about love and relationships and family. So, let me guess. You've realized you made a mistake letting Josh Stevens go, and now you wonder how to get back with him?"

Sour apples and pickle juice. "That's not...no. Not Josh."

She sounded sage in her reply. "Oh. I see. It's Heath Stratton. I should have known, the way you both keep insisting you're just friends. That's such an obvious trick."

My idea of letting her know about me and Baxter fizzled. It was too new and precious for Louise's critique. At some point I'd need to, but not tonight. I squeezed Poupon's foot, and he shifted. Good boy. "You know, I think Poupon needs to pee. Good talk."

Louise started to protest, but I was already putting on my boots. "Don't wait up." I grabbed my coat and hurried away.

The science room was located to the right of the library. Going toward the outside door on the left was the sliver of the meeting room, where Jesse Gold holed up. Next to him, Anna and Olivia had taken the math room. Aaron and Sean bunked behind the next door, in the social studies room amid the giant maps of the world and the United States and a topographical map of the Sandhills, which labeled all the ranches.

Closest to the outside door and rounding out the section was the English room, occupied by Joyce and Kenneth Levine. That shared a wall with the library, completing the circle for that section. The hallway stopped outside the English room and began again by the library, disrupting what might have made a wonderful inside track. The north wall of the English room was an outside wall, and thus, that classroom had the only window.

Poupon kept close as we exited the science room into the chilly hallway and made our way to the outside door. The air grew colder, and as we rounded the curve, I saw the brick placed in the doorway, allowing the frigid night air to seep in.

Curious who would be out in the blizzard, I poked my head through the doorway to see Aaron and Sean, wearing jackets and hands plunged into pockets. I pushed the door open enough to let Poupon out, and I followed. The roaring wind masked our movements.

Sean jumped when Poupon eased between him and Aaron. He spun to me, slapping a hand on his chest. "What?"

Aaron looked amused as he watched Poupon. "I gotta feel sorry for the guy. Having to expose myself out here would be harsh."

I shrugged. "When you gotta go, you gotta go." We watched Poupon gingerly step to the edge of the protected area. "What are you guys doing out here?"

Sean focused on Aaron, maybe willing him to speak.

Aaron adjusted the collar of his wool overcoat around his neck. It looked more like something a man would wear to work in an office, not exactly the kind of jacket an outdoorsy person would take on an adventure trip. But then, bird-watching might not entail a lot of activity. Except, it might if you wanted to get into the fields or woods. "Got restless. I know Louise was being helpful, but those cots are just below waterboarding on the torture scale."

I commiserated, thinking maybe kindergarteners' mats may not be any better. "It could be a long night."

The storm was still the banshee it had been a couple of hours ago, and I doubted the snowplow crews would risk going out in this. I still couldn't make out the pirate ship climbing structure or the swings. I didn't know if the temperature had dropped to zero, but it was darn-sure cold out here.

Sean raised his arm and pointed away from the playground toward the parking lot. "We've seen a light over there."

I whipped my head that way. "Are you sure? It could be some trick with the snow reflecting off the school's security lights or something."

Aaron, who I assumed as a science teacher wouldn't be prone to wild imaginings, said, "It looked more like headlights."

I stared for a few seconds into the driving snow, seeing nothing but white. "I doubt anyone is out in this."

Aaron clicked his teeth. "You wouldn't think so. But we definitely saw something."

Poupon, deciding he wasn't going to risk life and limb to relieve himself, took care of his needs at the edge of the concrete. I couldn't blame him. "I'll, uh, I'll get that later," I said to the men.

They didn't seem concerned. I held the door open for Poupon to go inside.

Though the area outside the door was protected, a few flurries stuck in Sean's beard. "I'm wondering if maybe that light is coming from that car."

"What car?" I asked.

"The black SUV that's been following us. That person in the red hoodie."

Aaron stared out into the snow. "Maybe. But that would be strange."

I pulled the door open enough to slip inside. "If someone is out there, I hope they're okay. See you in the morning."

9

By the time Poupon and I made it back to the science room, both Louise and Deenie were sawing logs like they were in a contest to see who could stack the most lumber. Since it took me a moment to shed my boots and coat, Poupon commandeered my bed again. This time I shoved him to his mat and stretched out on mine, feeling the uneven seams where I'd pieced two mats together.

To show his resentment of poor treatment, Poupon raked his sleeping bag, spun circles, and dug at it again. He plopped down, wasn't satisfied, and repeated the whole process to the cacophony of Deenie's and Louise's dueling chainsaws.

To add to the hubbub, several knocks sounded on the wall between us and Gold. He probably had his cot too near the wall and banged it with an arm or leg when he rolled over.

Poupon finally dropped down in a tight ball and started his own snoring, much more demure than the others. Deenie and Louise fell into a quieter chorus, as if unconsciously embarrassed by Poupon's subtle wheezing. My shoulders started to ease.

Someone opened a door into the pod. Then clicked it closed. Probably going to the bathroom. As I tried again to relax, more doors opened and closed. Maybe hushed whispers. Something in the hallway. This whole troop seemed to be moving around like mice in a mountain shack.

After a time, the activity dropped off. Probably, like me, everyone was having trouble getting to sleep. Although Deenie and Louise didn't seem to have any problem.

Instead of drifting off, I was disturbed by a pang in my belly. Not emotions this time. I'd taken care to let Poupon relieve himself, but now it seemed like my turn. I listened for a moment to make sure no one else was using the bathroom. It was hard to tell, since our door to the pod was closed, but I'd heard plenty of movement before and didn't now. I assumed I was safe. Using my phone for a light, I made my way around the tall tables.

Uncharacteristically insecure, Poupon didn't want me to leave without him, so he stirred and followed me. I opened the door, and something startled next to me. Or someone.

I swung my phone up to catch a figure slipping through the door to the English room, where the Levines were staying. I caught a flash of red, and the door closed.

Moving quickly, I crossed the pod to their door and eased it open.

Kenneth, in a blue sweater, sat in the teacher's chair. He wore a slightly cheerful but mostly vacant expression. Joyce slept on her side, mouth open. Kenneth raised a finger to his mouth as if it required great effort. He pursed his lips and rolled his eyes toward Joyce, clearly asking me not to wake her.

I whispered, "Did someone come through here?"

His bemused expression didn't change as he gazed at me.

I scanned the room, lifting my phone in a dim spotlight. Joyce gave a quiet moan and rolled over.

I checked their door, opening it into the corridor. Again, the cold draft came from the back door. Leaving Kenneth and Joyce, Poupon and I ventured out to find the outside door closed. I reached down to feel soaked spots just inside the building. It seemed an awful lot like footprints from melted snow.

I eased open the door to the wind noisier than a grade school at recess. When I poked my head out, there was a fresh disturbance in the four-foot snowbank at the edge of the concrete. The snow had collapsed onto the concrete, showing a rapidly filling V that looked like a trail into the dark. Poupon leaned into my leg as I peered into the white wall of snow, searching for headlights or anything else.

Nothing.

With the wind this ferocious, a gust probably shoved the snow around to look like a path. Made sense to me, since no one in their right mind would be messing around outside. Unless they were a dog who needed to pee. But even Poupon wouldn't get into the real snow.

Meaning to pass through the English room to check on Kenneth and ask again if he'd seen someone, I tried their door. It must have locked automatically when I'd let it close. Oh well.

In the gloom from the safety lights, Poupon and I wandered back to the science room, but before going inside, I followed the corridor the short distance to where Ford lay in his cot.

He bolted to sitting when we got close. "What?"

"Whoa," I said, whispering in the quiet hallway. "Sorry to scare you. Were you sleeping?"

He flicked his head, and his hair flopped. "No. Um. Maybe. I might have dozed. But, not for long, you know? It's been bananas out here."

Poupon, now face level with Ford, poked his nose toward him and sniffed. Ford ruffled Poupon's ears, and the dog sat to encourage more of that.

"What do you mean?"

"First Aaron and Sean were in the library forever. I mean, I think they just went to bed. And then Anna came out and asked if I had any Pepto or antacid or something because the sloppy joes upset her stomach. But I left the first aid kit in the van."

I'd been hearing lots of activity as well.

He raked his hair again. "She sounded irritated because Olivia kept the lights on because she was writing." He offered up a chuckle. "And you know, for Anna to show any emotion, it must really have got to her."

"She seems pretty quiet."

Apparently done with Ford's attention, Poupon returned to me, sat, and put his nose on my hand.

Ford adjusted his sleeping bag around his legs. "She's super religious. Reads her Bible all the time and doesn't have a lot to say."

I felt the urgency to continue on the mission that had pulled me out of my own sleeping bag. "Hopefully, it will all settle down now."

Ford plopped on his back. "Probably won't make any difference, since I'm having bad dreams."

I shifted, not wanting to stay and play counselor, but he sounded as if he wanted to talk. "Oh? What about?"

He let out a sigh. "I thought I was still awake, but I must have been in that place between sleep and awake, you know? And I swore I saw a person in a red hoodie sneaking by me and spying on Aaron and Sean. But when I woke up enough to look, there was no one there." He swallowed hard. "I'm freaked, you know, because we're having a thing like the Children's Blizzard. No one could be out in this weather. But they've got me all scared, talking about the person in the black SUV everyone thinks is following us. It's a helluva thing."

Person in a red hoodie. None of this was making sense. As Ford said, this blizzard made it impossible for anyone to get in or out of the school. And until the storm was in full force, the outside door had been locked and the gates to the rest of the building secure. I wanted this whole night to be over, the birders on their way, and me and Poupon settled into our little house on Stryker Lake, mystery novel in hand.

"Hopefully, it'll be better in the morning. And we have Louise's breakfast to look forward to." I said good night, and we hightailed it through the science room and into the pod, where, thankfully, the bathroom was unoccupied.

Poupon waited outside the door for me to finish, even though he clearly thought if I insisted on watching him, he should return the favor.

I snuggled into my sleeping bag, inhaling the scent of scouts past, and closed my eyes. Concentrating on relaxing thoughts, I summoned up sunshine, a prairie of green grass waving along rolling hills, a tall cottonwood by a stream, its branches spreading overhead, leaves rustling in a slight breeze. And Baxter there with me. He smiled with his golden lion eyes, and our lips touched.

My body jerked awake, heart already in my throat. A beeping alarm sent my nerves jangling and my brain scrambling.

Poupon sprang up and started barking, a sure sign of the Apocalypse.

10

Louise jumped to her feet and lunged for the classroom lights. She'd probably trained herself to come to life in the middle of the night for any of her children's emergencies.

Deenie sat up, her mouth open and eyes glazed.

The beeping stopped. It probably hadn't lasted more than ten seconds, just long enough to elevate blood pressure and set hearts racing. Hope it hadn't killed Kenneth Levine.

Louise flipped the lights. Nothing happened.

Deenie patted her chest as if getting air. "What's going on?"

Louise slapped the switch up and down a few times. "I'm guessing the electricity went out."

I reached for the camp light and fumbled to find the toggle before I turned it on, adding to the half-light from the overhead safety light. The workbenches cast shadows into the dark corners.

Poupon's hackles stood up, and he focused on the door to the corridor.

Deenie rolled to her hands and knees and struggled to her feet. She let out a small groan and stretched her back. "This is going to upset all those delicate daisies."

She barely finished her sentence when the door from the pod burst open and Olivia shot in. In black leggings and a sweatshirt that hit mid-thigh, she shouted, "What's going on?"

Anna followed, wearing plaid pajama pants and knitted slippers, a long-sleeved, oversized T-shirt bagging around her. She spoke in a voice barely loud enough to hear. "Is it a fire drill?"

Poupon trotted to the door into the corridor, and I followed him, thinking he might need to go outside again.

Aaron and Sean pushed through the pod door, forcing the two women further into the room. Aaron, still in his khakis with shirt neatly tucked in, said, "I don't think this is a drill of any kind."

Green beanie still on his head—maybe he slept in it—Sean scratched his beard and surveyed the room. "Where are the Levines?"

That was my question.

"Here," came Joyce's voice from the pod.

Anna scurried to the doorway as Joyce appeared with Kenneth leaning on her arm. Anna helped Joyce walk Kenneth toward a chair.

Louise spoke with authority, her hands placed on her plump hips. "The electricity is out." Amid a chorus of gasps and groans, she held up her hand. "Don't worry. There's a generator that supplies the library and office. There will be heat and light. You can bring your cots and we'll gather there."

Sean looked wrung out. The dark circles under his eyes nearly reached his beard. "No offense, Louise. But I'd just as soon not take that cot."

Ford stepped out from the pod. Since he'd been sleeping in the corridor, I thought it was strange he didn't enter from the outside door. "I think the cot is awesome. Reminds me of when I was a kid."

Olivia actually laughed, a sound I wouldn't have expected from someone so serious, and especially as this night had taken a bad turn. "Even as a kid I would've thought they sucked. Who designed those things?"

Joyce nodded. "If I get Kenneth down into it again, I don't think I'll ever get him out."

I put an arm around Louise. "You tried. They're Club Med people in a hostel kind of town."

Louise didn't spare much sympathy for the pampered folks. "Grab whatever you might want to make you comfortable. We can spend the rest of the night in the library."

She flung open the door and stomped out into the corridor.

Everyone started back for the pod, probably to get sleeping bags or sweaters. I decided to give Poupon another shot to relieve himself, and we stepped into the corridor. As I passed the door next to ours, it occurred to me I hadn't seen Gold. Maybe he was a heavy sleeper and hadn't heard the alarm.

I stopped. Poupon glanced at me but kept going. When he realized I wasn't behind him, he turned to me and planted his butt on the carpet. Not willing to go on without me, but not happy about joining me in front of Gold's door.

The hallway seemed to have dropped in temperature already. Always cooler than the classrooms, it seemed unusually chilly now.

I banged on Gold's door and didn't get an answer. If he slept through that, too, he must be really out of it. He hadn't looked all that good when I'd been in his room before going to bed. Maybe he'd taken some medication and was in a deep sleep. Or maybe something had happened to him. Not murder, obviously, but maybe he'd taken cold medicine and it knocked him out. I tried the knob. Not surprisingly, it was locked.

Maybe the pod door was unlocked. Or Louise might have a master key. She seemed to know everything about this place, so I figured she'd be able to get into a locked room.

Just for good measure, I knocked again and yelled, "Mr. Gold."

It surprised me to hear a response. "Go away."

Always the gracious one.

I tried again. "The electricity is out. The library has power, so it'll be warm there."

Through the door, his grouchy response chapped me. "Leave me alone, would you?"

I raised my eyebrows at Poupon. "Guess he made that clear."

A tiny whine escaped from Poupon.

"I get it." Either he needed to get outside ASAP, or he didn't like Gold. I understood both.

We continued around the corridor, and the reason for the unusually cold hallway became clear. Those doofuses had forgotten to kick the brick back inside. Who was wandering around outside since I'd been here earlier? The door remained propped open a few inches. In this weather, that gap made a big difference.

"Morons." I mumbled it to Poupon, who I was sure shared my opinion —of the men and of the lousy weather, since he didn't waste time going to the edge of the protected patio and lifting his leg in the growing bank.

I was about to turn back to the door when something made me pause. Poupon slipped by me into the school, but I focused on the snow where Poupon had left his yellow streak. That snowbank. The one I'd noticed that had collapsed onto the entryway. Earlier, I'd chalked it up to the wind blowing it. But now, it clearly resembled a path. Like maybe someone had gone out into the night. Or come in.

11

Kenneth was allotted the couch. He huddled under a sleeping bag, looking pale and exhausted. Ford brought his cot in and slept flat on his back near the door. Sean and Aaron had dragged two of the comfy chairs close to Kenneth for Joyce and Anna, who dozed fitfully.

Olivia, Sean, and Aaron found a deck of cards and played at a table in front. Deenie curled up in a plush chair in a corner and set up a subdued purring, like an engine on idle. Louise made a nest of the mats and tossed and turned.

I pulled a Sue Grafton book from a rack of tattered paperbacks and settled into a loveseat, allowing Poupon to jump up and, wonder of wonders, plop his head in my lap. It wasn't toasty in the library, but having Poupon's body heat helped.

The next three hours passed like a sloth brushing its teeth in slow motion. Aside from Kenneth, Ford, and Poupon, and possibly Gold, though he slept alone in a cold room, the rest of us struggled, and I, for one, was glad when Louise rose at five and declared she'd get the coffee going and start cooking breakfast.

Deenie uncoiled from her chair and fell into step. Louise didn't complain.

By the time I'd let Poupon out again and returned, everyone had scattered.

The storm was still waging war, piling up the bank outside the door to hip level. It was cold enough to freeze my nose hairs together, so probably below zero. Most ranchers hadn't started calving yet, but this would stress cows in late pregnancy. Last weather report I'd seen predicted warming temperatures by midweek, so hopefully there wouldn't be much loss. But then, the forecasters hadn't called for a storm of this fierceness, so what did they know? It's hard to predict the future.

Aaron and Ford gathered bedding and put the library to rights. I supposed the others were getting dressed and taking turns in the bathroom.

Louise and Deenie clattered back and forth from the science room, bringing in food and supplies. Louise set up a tripod over a Bunsen burner. She'd placed a cast-iron skillet on top, and bacon sizzled.

Deenie had plugged in the roaster pan and was lifting the lid on one of three cartons of a dozen eggs. Louise bought eggs from our sister-in-law Lauren, and I figured at any given time, Louise had six dozen in her basement refrigerator. Eggs kept for a surprisingly long time, and Louise liked to be prepared.

Louise poked at the bacon. "Deenie." She spoke the name sharp enough to be a bullet. "Do not cook those eggs in that roaster pan. I'll finish up the bacon and scramble them in the skillet with the bacon grease."

Deenie kept her face placid, though I thought maybe I detected a touch of tension in her jaw. "If we wait until all the bacon is cooked in that one pan over that tiny flame, before we even start the eggs, which will need to be done in several batches because the pan isn't big enough for this many people, all the timing will be off."

I didn't want any part of this. "I'll slice the bread. We won't have toast, but that chokecherry jelly of yours is good, no one will care." I'd caught sight of a jar of Louise's preserves with the food stash. I figured a compliment on her country fair–winning jelly she was so proud of might make her less likely to fight.

My ploy didn't work, and she ignored me. "We'll feed the crew in shifts so everyone will have a warm breakfast. The eggs will have so much more flavor cooked in bacon grease."

Deenie forced a smile. She adjusted the heat dial and held her hand in the roaster to test it. "Did you notice those people? They aren't the kind who want bacon grease in their eggs. I wouldn't be surprised if half of them are vegetarians."

Louise snapped her head up. "They all ate the sloppy joes."

Deenie raised her hand to stop Louise. "Eggs cooked in the roaster will be fluffier and better than in a cast-iron skillet."

"So. Yeah." I edged toward the library door. "I'm just gonna, you know…" No one paid a lick of attention to me, so I took a few steps back and watched.

"Don't you do it," Louise threatened when Deenie lifted an egg from the carton.

Deenie sounded firm. "Did it ever occur to you that someone else might have an idea different from yours?"

Louise poked at the bacon. "In your case, different doesn't mean better."

Deenie's eyebrows shot up. "So, this is what it's about."

Louise set her fork down and planted her hands on her hips, all business. "What do you mean?"

Still holding the egg, a bit of the easygoing manner slipped from Deenie. "I'm different. I'm not Marguerite."

My stomach rolled and dipped. I never, ever, in a million years, wanted to compare Deenie to the woman who had betrayed us. The liar who had hidden her life for forty years and nearly destroyed Dad. That woman, who I'd loved so deeply, defended so staunchly, and who had upended my very foundation, had no business in my heart, my mind, or my life.

Deenie was everything Mom wasn't. More my generation than Mom's, she was transparent and clear like air after a spring shower. She cared about people, laughed readily, participated in life and community. She was a loyal and honest friend.

Louise drew her head in, as if disbelieving. "Obviously, you're not Mom. And there doesn't seem to be any reason to make a comparison. I mean, Dad and Mom were married forty years and raised nine kids. They made a history together and have a dozen grandchildren. Why would you even imagine there's a comparison to be made?"

For the first time since I'd known her, I saw anger flush Deenie's cheeks. "You're going to defend her? Even after you know she cheated on Hank? After she lied to all of you for so long? After the pain she caused your father? A pain, by the way, that he's come a long way healing because he's had me by his side."

With that, she banged the egg on the side of the roaster and, one-handed, emptied it into the roaster.

"Stop that," Louise said, her voice venomous.

Deenie picked up an egg in each hand and cracked them together, dumping the contents into the pan and flicking the shells into the trash. "You don't have to thank me for helping you cook."

I swallowed a sigh. And that's where I left them and went to slice the bread and set up the table for breakfast.

The others entered by the corridor and helped themselves to the coffee from Louise's giant metal percolator. I always had to ask someone for help or guess every time I was tasked with filling a pot that size, and either made it brackish and weak or hair-growing strong, but Louise had managed to make a decent-tasting brew, even if I settled for Coffee-Mate instead of real cream.

We pushed tables together and took up pretty much the same places as last night's supper in the science room. It's not hard to create a routine. But the head of the table was empty.

Joyce made a noise of appreciation in her throat. "These eggs are perfect. That's not easy to accomplish when you have to cook this many at one time."

Deenie glowed. Louise glowered.

"And this bacon," Ford said. "It's almost worth suffering through last night to get it."

Louise puffed up. "I always get a half a pig and have it butchered and cured at a place in Bryant." As if that meant anything to Ford.

Deenie looked away.

"Anyone see Gold this morning?" I still couldn't bring myself to call him

Jesse. It seemed a silly name for someone so…so…I didn't know. It simply didn't seem right.

Olivia munched on a bite of bread and cast her gaze on Sean. He looked to Anna, who found something interesting on her plate.

Aaron cleared his throat. "I knocked on his door and told him breakfast was ready."

"Did he answer?" I asked.

Aaron raised a forkful of eggs. "No. But he doesn't always eat breakfast. When I started working for him, he warned me he liked to sleep in, and sometimes he doesn't show his face until noon."

Louise tsked. "How can a person get anything done if they sleep half the day away?"

Aaron's voice was cutting. "A man like Gold doesn't need to get anything done. He made his fortune long ago."

Deenie sat up. "I thought he was rich. But not like he was born that way."

Louise challenged her. "As if you can tell."

Deenie didn't back down and took up her defense. "Take the Levines." She smiled and nodded their way.

Kenneth kept that same distant expression, the corners of his mouth turned up slightly. Joyce looked fascinated and raised her eyebrows, inviting Deenie to continue.

"You see, they've probably been born to money. They expect others to do for them, but they aren't pushy about it. And even if you can tell they're judging, they mostly keep it to themselves and are polite."

Joyce took that in as if weighing whether it was an insult or a compliment. Hint, Sandhillers didn't like to rely on someone else if they could do for themselves.

Deenie continued. "But Gold acts like he's owed something and is loud and demanding, mostly by insulting others, like if he lets some slight slide, he'd lose his standing." Maybe from her years working with the public, Deenie seemed to read people pretty well.

The conversation spiked my curiosity. "How did Gold make his money?" Surely not in the service industry.

Olivia grunted. "He cheated people, of course. Probably hurt people. Nothing good, that's for sure."

This made his new deal seem more sinister. I turned my attention to Aaron. "You must know."

A glint of anger shone in his eyes. "All I know is that he got rich about thirty years ago and has been spending every penny on himself since then."

Anna seemed on the verge of tears. "A person with no thought of others has lost his soul. Jesus said, 'But when you give a banquet, invite the poor, the crippled, the lame, the blind, and you will be blessed. Although they cannot repay you, you will be repaid at the resurrection of the righteous.' My father believed that, even though he was cheated by evil men."

Joyce patted Kenneth's hand where it rested on the table next to his plate. "Our son spent several years in Africa working to supply villages with water. Those were years he could have been building a career. But he never regretted it."

Something about the way she said it made me wonder if something tragic had happened to their son. Anna and Joyce made eye contact with what I interpreted as deep empathy.

I pushed back from the table. "Gold didn't look great last night. I think I'll go check on him. If it makes him mad to be disturbed, I guess he can get over it or die."

Seven sets of eyes watched me as I made my way out of the library. Louise and Deenie had both jumped up to bring more food to the table, probably wanting to prove that the birders preferred their offering over the other cook's. They seemed dead set on outdoing each other. If we weren't rescued soon, there would likely be a murder.

Poupon followed me through the murky light of the science room and into the teachers' lounge, head down and something clenched in his teeth.

"What have you got?" I reached down to pry a paperback from his mouth. He must have pulled it off the rack in the library. It was slimy with slobber, and he'd mangled one corner to pulp. Poor guy must be beside himself with worry. I'd never known him to chew anything but steak bones, and then, he abandoned them when the flavor was gone.

I tossed the book on a chair and continued through the gloomy lounge to

Gold's door. I knocked. "Mr. Gold, breakfast is ready." I hardly ever called anyone *mister* or *missus*. Calling this guy Jesse felt icky for some reason, but Mr. Gold? Like he was a teacher, or maybe an old-timey villain. Like Snidely Whiplash. I'd definitely call him Mr. Whiplash and not simply Snidely, because being on a first-name basis with someone so repellent didn't feel good.

He didn't answer.

"Mr. Gold. I'm going to come in your room. I need to check to make sure you're okay."

I figured that would roust him if he was playing possum. When I didn't hear anything, I felt my first real pang of worry. I tried the knob, but it was locked. My next course was to find Louise and possibly a key. I turned to go back to the science room and smacked into someone.

In a shocking synchronicity of thought rare for me and Louise, she stood there with a mess of keys in her fist. "We heard you knocking."

The "we" she referred to must be the everyone who crowded behind her, filling the small pod space.

Since Louise showed no sign of handing over the keys, I moved out of the way for her to open the door. "I don't think we all need to barge in on him," I said.

Olivia planted herself in front of me, at the front of the others. "It's weird no one's seen him."

Behind her, Sean said, "Yeah, and you said it. He didn't look good when he went to bed."

I tried to reassure them. "I knocked on his door when the power went out, and he said he was fine."

Looming right behind Olivia, Aaron said, "He's been having some issues with his heart lately."

That sent a jab of concern into me. "And you're just now mentioning it? Like maybe you could have brought it up when he didn't show up for breakfast, or maybe last night when he didn't go to the library with the rest of us?"

Sean poked his head around Aaron and Olivia. "That's not fair. Just because Aaron is Gold's assistant, it doesn't mean he's responsible for the jerk."

Louise pulled the key free and turned the knob, stepping back and swinging open the door into the narrow, dark room.

A gush of smells, none of them good, billowed out. Feces, vomit, faint chemical, all making me want to gag and telling me what I'd see wouldn't be pretty.

"Ugh." Olivia ducked her head and spun away.

Aaron and Sean didn't back up, but they didn't advance, either. Rustling and murmurs meant the others bunched in the room behind me.

Deenie was suddenly walking past me to the doorway of Gold's room. There was no safety light in this cubby-sized room, and she held Louise's camp light up. She hesitated and caught my eye, clearly telling me she didn't want to go any further.

I reached up for the light and brushed past Louise, who had frozen. Probably like Deenie, dreading going further.

It wasn't my job anymore, but who else was going to take the lead on this grisly task? I stepped into the room, held the light up high, at the same time calling out, "Mr. Gold."

It was even worse than I'd expected.

12

Gold lay on his back in the middle of the room. The cot balanced at a wacky angle against the wall, with the sleeping bag in a heap, partway tangled in Gold's legs. His head was thrown back, eyes bugged out and unseeing, maybe with red veins, though it was hard to see in the murky light. One arm was flopped to the side, fingers curled as if a clenched fist released in death. The other arm rested across his chest, fingers entwined with his shirt collar, like maybe he'd been pawing at it. It gave me the feeling he'd been clutching at his throat, and I felt strangled.

It was his mouth that made me stifle a cry. His lips peeled back and his teeth clamped in what looked like absolute agony. Along with his arms and tangled legs, it gave a horrifying impression of someone who'd died writhing in pain.

"Is he...?" Louise stopped and swallowed before saying, "Dead?"

Deenie squeezed past her. "Obviously. Make sure the others don't see this. It'll upset them." Maybe wanting to be more composed than Louise strengthened Deenie's resolve.

For once, Louise didn't balk at taking orders. She turned around, probably glad for something to do. "Everyone back to the library. No need to see this."

Joyce's voice rose above Louise's, repeating the question Louise had asked, but in a much more solid voice. "Is he dead?"

Louise replied, her voice practical, as if someone hadn't suffered horribly in the next room, "Yes, he's dead. Kate is trained in dealing with this kind of thing, so we'll let her do what's necessary. We're going to get out of her way." Oh, now she respected my sheriff training. Thanks.

There was a mix of hushed voices and sounds of them shuffling back into the science room and likely the warmth of the library.

I took a second to detach from being a regular human witnessing a person who had been alive not long ago and now was a pile of bones and flesh. A soul who had once animated the body, making it a person with thoughts and feelings—and let's be honest, a real pain-in-the-butt kind of guy—was no longer here. It was an awesome and terrifying mystery I'd never get used to. But I compartmentalized all of that enigmatic hoo-ha and shoved it out of the way, as we Foxes were adept at doing, and pulled on my professional law enforcement persona. I needed to perform all the functions an unattended death required in Nebraska. That meant an investigation into cause of death.

Deenie sniffed and wiped her eyes. With Louise gone, she didn't have to be so self-controlled. "I've never seen a person dead, like in real life. I mean, I've been to open-casket funerals and wakes and stuff. But this isn't like that. This is ugly."

I set the lamp on the table. "I don't think he had a gentle time of it."

In a hushed tone, she said, "What do you think happened?"

I pulled out my phone and started to take photos of everything, hoping I'd have enough battery life to record the whole scene. I focused on a clump of semisolid matter not far from Gold. "I don't see any blood, but he vomited what looks like sloppy joes. He's clutching his throat. Some kind of stomach thing? Or a heart attack or something."

"Oh." The word sounded small and scared.

Louise appeared in the doorway again. She seemed to have scraped herself up and was ready to take care of business. "I soaked the beans overnight, so I'll get them cooking as soon as I clean the eggs out of the roaster."

After what I was looking at, I couldn't imagine eating anytime soon. But, thanks to Louise, the others hadn't seen this. "Okay. Good. Thank you." A thought occurred to me. "Hey, do you know if there are any disposable gloves in the chem lab? Like if they do experiments or something?"

"Be right back," she said and disappeared.

I knelt and snapped images from different angles.

Louise returned to the doorway and thrust her arm out toward Deenie. "Here. Two pairs."

Deenie lunged forward to accept them. "Thanks."

Louise brushed her hands together. "Okay, then. I'll be cleaning up breakfast if you need anything."

When Deenie handed me the gloves, I set my phone down and snapped them on. I muttered as I continued to take pictures. "I heard a bunch of banging on the wall, that would have been around eleven. I wonder if that's when he died."

Deenie backed toward the door, maybe wanting to leave. "Didn't you say he talked to you when the lights went out around two o'clock?"

"Through the door. I didn't actually see him." Something under the tipped cot caught the light from my phone. I focused on it and stepped over Gold's body to bend down and inspect it.

"What is it?" Deenie asked, not making a move closer from where she'd popped back after handing me the gloves.

Glad for the gloves, I reached down and plucked it from the ground. "A syringe." Not a big one. An ordinary six-inch plastic, common for anyone brave enough to give themselves injections. I set it back down. Hating to touch the body and compromise anything, I felt compelled to check for an injection site.

The cuff of Gold's left shirtsleeve wasn't buttoned, the arm that was thrown out. But the right cuff, the arm on his chest, was snug on his wrist. I shoved the left sleeve up to the crook of his elbow. "Huh."

Deenie couldn't help herself, apparently. She snuck behind me and leaned over my shoulder. "Oh. Wow. He's a junkie."

It might look that way. In the crease of his elbow, several tiny blue dots showed where he'd injected himself several times. "Curious."

"It explains a lot." Deenie sounded relieved.

I wasn't so sure it didn't raise more questions, but an overdose did supply one possible cause of death. Finished with photographing the body, I started around the small room. A bottle of wine sat on a table next to a Dixie cup with a red stain in the bottom. A corkscrew with the cork still skewered rested next to it. "Hmm."

I turned to take pictures of Gold's suitcase that lay open on the floor. Folded clothes were neatly stacked under a strap. I glanced at Gold. He wore the clothes he'd had on yesterday. So, he hadn't changed into pajamas, or stripped down to his skivvies, if that's how he slept.

Another bottle of wine rested on the other side of the suitcase next to a leather toiletry bag. Guess he really had been worried about drinking box wine out here. A file folder lay under the toiletry bag, and I pulled it out and flipped it open.

The eighth-inch stack of papers appeared to be information on Medicare. Clinics, doctors, procedures and their costs. A whole sheaf of facts and figures. "Wouldn't you say Gold was well past sixty-five?"

Deenie looked puzzled. "I'd say seventies, maybe even early eighties. Why?"

I held up the folder. "He's been digging into Medicare pretty deep for someone who should have been on it for years."

Deenie zeroed in on me with a bright expression. "Or he was planning to defraud Medicare. I mean, it's all over the true crime shows now. It's big business."

"Uh-huh." I slid the folder back under the toiletry bag. "Those shows will make you see crime everywhere." Although, Gold had mentioned a deal he was working on. But why it would require him to join a birding tour in Nebraska made no sense.

The toiletry bag was unzipped, as if he'd used it last night. Inside, there was toothpaste and an electric toothbrush in a case, a metal razor, and shaving cream with a label that looked fancy. A wood-handled brush, dental floss, and antiperspirant, again not any of the brands you'd find at Walmart. The toothbrush was dry. "Huh."

Deenie couldn't contain herself. "What?"

"Looks like he planned on getting ready for bed but didn't even brush his teeth."

She hesitated. "Well, it could be that he wasn't feeling up to it."

Louise appeared in the doorway. "Obviously, he wasn't feeling up to it. The man is dead. I doubt he felt like a shave and nose-hair trim hours before he succumbed."

"Louise." I said it in such a way she'd understand my telling her to knock it off. This sniping was getting on my nerves. "Did you need something?"

"I was only going to ask if you want a cup of coffee before I drain it and start another pot."

Deenie huffed out an irritated breath.

I grumbled at Louise. "If I did want coffee, which I don't, I'd want the fresh stuff, not something scorched and bitter."

"Well, excuse me if I hate to waste food."

Ignoring that, I asked Deenie, "Did you see Gold after I left his room last night?"

Her gaze shifted to Louise, then back to me. "He was using the restroom before I did. And I waited for him. When he came out, he looked super pasty. And sweaty. I mean, like sick sweat. I asked him if he was okay, and he snapped at me. I wasn't sure I heard him right."

"And what did he say?" Louise shot the question as if ready to doubt anything Deenie said.

Deenie ignored her and looked at me. "I thought he said, 'All right, for someone being murdered tonight.' And when I asked him to repeat it, he told me to go to hell."

"Murdered tonight? Maybe it was a metaphor since he was sick." Except he'd tried to hire me to protect him. I hadn't killed him and didn't know if he really was murdered, but, dang, I sure had a stab of guilt I hadn't taken him seriously. "But he was worried about someone being after him. He got spooked when the others mentioned the black SUV and the person in the red hoodie."

Deenie nodded, her eyes bright with obvious intrigue.

"And that's it?" Louise said.

Deenie looked away from her. "Yeah. Except, when I went into the bathroom, I could tell he'd been throwing up. He wasn't too neat about it and didn't bother to wipe up. I cleaned it up, then washed my face. That's about it."

"Why didn't you say anything?" I asked.

She hesitated and glanced at Louise. "I thought maybe the sloppy joes upset his stomach, and I didn't want Louise to feel bad if that was the case."

"What?" Louise's mouth dropped open, and her fists slammed onto her hips, making her appear ready for battle. "Why would that even occur to you? Every kid in this county has eaten my sloppy joes for the last twenty years, and not one of them has ever gotten sick. What's the matter with you?"

"Whoa." I hurried to step between them. "I think the question is what's the matter with you? Deenie was only trying to be nice." Plus, it seemed a stretch to say no kid had ever puked her sloppy joes. Kids are always barfing. It's the way of the world.

Louise let her gaze go from me to Deenie, a series of emotions chasing themselves across her face. Anger, resentment, puzzlement, defensiveness. I waited for her to explode in Louise fashion, telling me why I was wrong and schooling me on the correct way to feel.

Instead, she dropped her arms, unclenched her fists, and let out a pent-up breath. She addressed Deenie. "Thank you for trying to spare my feelings." She raised her chin, turned, and walked out the open door toward the science room.

That was a response I never would've expected from Louise. Maybe the raging blizzard was actually hell freezing over.

I carefully pulled out the contents of Gold's suitcase and displayed them on the floor. Nothing unusual. Everything was folded, but points for neatness didn't matter now.

"Thanks, Deenie. I'm not sure what it means that he was sick. But it's important."

It sounded like Deenie wanted to defend Louise, even if she wasn't here. "Well, maybe he doesn't digest tomato sauce well. Or onions don't agree with him. And we don't have any idea what he ate earlier in the day. And the wine. That might have bothered him."

I picked up the Dixie cup. Along with the stain, a few miniscule grains, purpled from the wine, clung to the side. "There's a syringe and maybe a little residual powder in the cup. But there aren't any pill bottles or drugs in Gold's belongings."

"What's this?" Deenie pointed at a spot slightly darker than the dirty orange carpet of the room.

We inched toward it, and Deenie lowered the lamp. "Oh," she breathed.

"It looks like a shoe print in wine."

She squinted at it. "A very small shoe print."

"And who spilled the wine?"

"Maybe it just looks like a shoe. Or maybe Gold spilled a tiny bit of wine, and when he stepped in it, only a portion of his shoe pressed in the stain."

"After having some at dinner, seems weird he'd opened another bottle here." I snapped pictures of the stain, posing my finger beside it for perspective.

"And he said he couldn't open a bottle himself because of arthritis. So, someone else had to open it."

I nodded. "Which means someone else was in here with him after I left," I said.

I tried to capture everything on my phone, knowing the investigators would want photos of the scene immediately after we found the body. Every unattended death had to be investigated, whether someone suspected foul play or not. And I wasn't sure I could come down on either side of that equation with Gold. "I think we're about done here," I said.

Deenie let out a relieved sigh and lifted the camp light.

I gave the room and body a final inspection to make sure I hadn't forgotten anything. Deenie swung the light, and something glinted under the table.

"Wait." I lifted my phone and pointed the flashlight under the table, aiming toward the darkest corner. But after all the work it had done, the poor bit of technology gave up the ghost and died. "Drat."

"What's wrong?" Deenie asked, a note of trepidation in her voice.

"Battery's gone. Can you bring the light over? I want to see what's under here."

Clearly not wanting to get closer to Gold's body, she scuffed over and held the lamp lower.

"It's his tablet. Maybe he'd been holding it when he died." A sudden thought popped into my head. I stood up and spun around the room. "His camera bag."

"What camera bag?" Deenie asked.

"He pulled the tablet from his camera bag to show me a threatening message." I checked the corners of the tiny room. Lifted the cot, ruffled the sleeping bag. It was gone. "It's not here. It doesn't make sense that he would have taken it anywhere last night. Especially as sick as he was."

Deenie lowered her voice as a kid might when telling a ghost story. "This is all suspicious." She swallowed. "He got super sick and threw up. I don't know what that means. And the syringe. And now the missing camera bag."

"Let's not jump to conclusions." But I was thinking the same thing.

Deenie shook her head in disbelief. "I listen to all these podcasts and watch true crime shows. I never thought I'd be in the middle of a real-life murder."

On my hands and knees, I scooted under the table and reached for the tablet. I backed out and sat, pressing the power button to fire it up. "Maybe there's something on here that might give us a clue."

"Like a suicide note? Because suicide would be a lot better than murder. If he's been killed, it has to be someone locked in here with us. And that's too terrifying to think about."

13

The tablet didn't come to life. Dead, like my phone. Like Jesse Gold.

I cast about the room and in Gold's bag for a power cable and came up empty. Maybe he stored it in the missing camera case. The tablet was the same brand as my phone, though, and would probably use the same charger cord.

I tugged Deenie's arm and headed out of the room. "Come on. Let's see if anyone has a battery charger. We need to make sure we document everything for the crime scene investigators. If this storm doesn't break, we'll probably have to move the body outside so it doesn't decompose."

She made an odd clicking in the back of her throat, and I hoped she wasn't going to be sick.

After we left the room, I locked the door, certain Louise had the keys in her pockets. The camp light made little progress against the pitch dark, but I rummaged in one of the laundry baskets of supplies and found a package of zippered plastic bags. After sealing the tablet inside one, I peeled off my gloves and tucked the tablet in my waistband, draping my flannel shirt over it.

Louise bustled into the pod lugging the roasting pan. She set it on the counter. "I'm going to get the beans started in here over two Bunsen burners."

A braver woman than I, Deenie questioned her. "Wouldn't it be easier to cook them in the library where you can plug in the roaster pan?"

I looked around for cover to protect me when Louise exploded all over Deenie.

But she didn't. She emptied ingredients, including seasonings, from a heavy pot she'd brought. "It would be easier, but I don't want to be around those people any more than I have to."

That made me feel bad that she should be home with her family and instead had to put up with this group—and a dead body to boot. "I'm sorry you're stuck here with all of this. Are you okay?"

She lifted her chin. I recognized the Fox tough hide that masked any sign of weakness. "I don't know what I was thinking. I completely forgot about lunch. I planned dinner last night and breakfast today. But the beans won't be done until supper. At least there's enough bread left, I think, to make peanut butter and jelly sandwiches."

Deenie seemed taken aback. "You have peanut butter?"

Louise, obviously bouncing back to her old self, gave Deenie a derisive look. "Of course I have peanut butter. It's in my go-box of groceries. A lot of times there's a picky eater. Or, like now, an emergency."

I couldn't let that go and said to Deenie, "Louise is more prepared than any Marine."

Louise accepted that as truth. "But we'd better hope we get out of here tonight. I have coffee for tomorrow, and there are enough eggs to go around, but there's no breakfast meat, and I'd have to serve saltines and the rest of the peanut butter for lunch."

Right now, Louise and I had different priorities. I tilted my head to the door. "Come on. We need to talk to the bird brains."

She dumped her trash in a can. "I'll stay here. You don't need me there, and I have things to do."

Fight with her or give up? I shrugged, and Deenie and I made our way to the library, where I found Poupon stretched out on Ford's cot, chewing on the same paperback.

I grabbed the book from his jaws, even more slimy and gnarled than before, and set it on a table. I thought about nudging him off the cot and repeating the phrase he always ignored about no dogs on the furniture, but, like arguing that Louise should attend this meeting, I didn't see the point.

The group, now only seven, had pulled a loveseat and stuffed chairs around the couch. They all huddled there, with Ford opting to plop in a beanbag chair.

Olivia stood as soon as we walked in. "What's happened? How did he die?"

Aaron, always calm, slid close to one side of the loveseat as if offering us a place to sit. "I'm sure it was a heart attack or something."

Deenie saw the opportunity and lowered herself on the other end, placing her elbow on the armrest.

I looked at Aaron. "You said he had diagnosed heart issues. But I didn't see any medications in his things."

For the first time, Aaron seemed a little unsure. "Oh. He was supposed to take something. Maybe that was what got him. He should have taken medication but he'd forgotten to bring it."

I perched on the edge of a library table. "You're how many days into this trip? Three? Wouldn't he have called in a prescription at a stop along the way?"

Aaron shrugged. "I wouldn't know."

Except, he was Gold's assistant. Which might mean taking care of things like prescriptions, reservations, dry cleaning, and...I didn't know what assistants did, actually.

Anna perched on the couch with the Levines. She looked nervous and rubbed her hands in her lap. She spoke with a stony edge, barely above a whisper. "'When an evil man dies, his hope dies with him. Everything he expected to gain from his power will be lost. Those who do right are saved from trouble.' Proverbs, chapter eleven, verse seven."

Deenie's eyes sharpened, and her piercing focus clearly told me to note Anna's quote.

Kenneth's gaze slowly turned to me but appeared vacant. He mumbled, "James. Jimmy. Jessa. Jesse James."

Joyce squeezed his leg and looked annoyed with the whole situation. "Do you have any update on the storm or the progress of the van? We have a very important event to attend in Seattle."

Ford shifted in his beanbag chair. "I checked outside. The wind might have gone down a little. But probably not enough to get plows out and stuff."

Deenie agreed. "I'd say maybe tonight or, by the earliest, late afternoon."

As if she'd been holding back, Olivia burst out, "This is bullshit. I cannot believe we can be stranded in this place. There must be something we can do."

Sean frowned at her. "It's not like she can control the weather."

Olivia lasered him with her eyes. "Like you know anything."

He pursed his lips and lowered his voice into a growl. "I at least know all your fit-throwing and demands aren't getting us out of here any sooner."

"It's better than sitting around and accepting everything that happens without a peep," she snapped back.

The two of them were spatting worse than my ten-year-old nephews. We didn't need this. "Okay. Let's all take a breath. First, I need to ask if anyone has a cord for my phone."

No one volunteered. I didn't think it likely that out of this group of seven travelers, no one would have a charging cord to fit my phone. "Come on. I need my phone to document Gold's death. If I can do the preliminary investigation, you'll be released from the scene much sooner than if we have to wait for the sheriff and state patrol." That might or might not be true, but I tried to make it sound convincing.

Joyce sounded even angrier than before. "Didn't you already do all that? Process the death scene?"

Should I correct that to *murder scene*? I didn't care much for these folks before, but they were really starting to pop my birthday balloons. I spoke through my teeth. "I'll ask again. Does anyone have a cord?"

Joyce lifted her chin and looked down her nose in an expression exactly like that of my ex-mother-in-law, Dahlia. We'd never seen eye to eye, and it wasn't only because she towered over me. It might have been because I wasn't at all interested in fashion and makeup. But I think the real reason is because Dahlia's fondest desire was to have Roxy, Ted's lifelong on-again-off-again girlfriend, as her daughter-in-law. Good news for them all, that's exactly what happened. But, I'm not bitter.

Still, Joyce's attitude was triggering, but if Joyce knew how close she came to getting clocked, she didn't show it. "We left our cords in the van. So, you can forget about us."

Olivia regarded my phone. "I have one, but it won't work with your phone."

Sean piped up. "Same."

No one else spoke, and Deenie gave me an incredulous look.

Why they seemed set on standing in my way, I couldn't guess. Unless one of them really had killed Gold. But why would the rest cover up for a murderer? I wasn't in the mood for their games and strode over to where Poupon sprawled on Ford's cot. His head was up, and he panted even though it was far from hot in there, clearly not enjoying himself.

"We'll get out of here eventually." I scratched behind his ears, something he tried hard not to show he enjoyed, though his half-closed eyes gave him away. With one hand still in his fur, I reached the other over and clasped the strap of Ford's backpack.

The side pocket was unzipped, and a few cords dangled free. I yanked them out. One cord had the connection I needed. "This is perfect."

Ford half rose, as if wanting to snatch the cord from me. Then he sat back. "Oh, hey. I forgot I had that. Cool. Yeah. You can use it for your phone."

Deenie was watching the group, her focus going from Aaron next to her, to Olivia, around the circle to Anna and the Levines, and ending on Sean, before giving me her attention. The glint in her eye looked like a countdown.

She was ready for the reveal, letting me know she knew the assignment. I couldn't wait to find out what she was picking up in their expressions and body language.

"I think it'll work with this." I reached under my shirt and pulled out the tablet. "This is Gold's tablet. Maybe it'll give us a clue what happened."

Sharp-eyed, Olivia rose to her feet and advanced to me. "What do you mean by clue? Obviously, he had some medical emergency. You don't think it could have been anything else, do you?"

Deenie watched Joyce, leaving me to Olivia.

Interesting that Olivia had jumped to my suspicion of foul play. I stayed matter-of-fact. "Sure. It's possible he had a heart attack or aneurism burst, stroke, or any number of things."

"Or a brain tumor," Ford said. "Wasn't he complaining about headaches over the last few days?" He looked around the circle for confirmation.

Sean tucked his lower lip into his mouth, massaging his beard with his top teeth, something I always found nasty. "That's right."

Aaron frowned at Ford before talking to me. "Do you suspect it might not be natural causes?"

I tried for casual. "No. Nothing points in that direction." While I was known for keeping my thoughts to myself, and growing up in the middle of nine kids taught me to master a poker face, I'd never been a convincing liar. And I doubted I carried it off then. "There needs to be an investigation with any unattended death. We're stuck here, and I'm a sworn deputy of Grand County. I might as well do what I can now so you won't be delayed when the weather clears."

I found an outlet and plugged the tablet in, setting it on the table.

Olivia folded her arms across her chest. She sounded skeptical. "How do we know you're a deputy?"

"Yeah," Sean said, eliciting an annoyed scowl from Olivia.

Deenie bolted to attention and stared at Olivia. Something lit a fire in her, and I was curious to find out what.

I lifted my eyebrows and took in the group. "I don't have my credentials with me. And if you don't want to cooperate, that's fine. We can all wait until they dig us out and we notify the state patrol. They'll send someone up to interview you and get statements. With this weather, they might be busy, though, and their nearest office is in Ogallala, more than an hour's drive away. It shouldn't delay you more than two days, I wouldn't think."

Aaron had his focus on the tablet I'd placed on the table with the cord stretched to an outlet.

I held the power tab and waited. Nothing. "This is going to take a minute before I can open it." I switched the charger to my phone, and the battery icon lit up. "I'll get this charged first."

Olivia returned to her chair and threw herself into it. She wasn't much bigger than me, so she had plenty of room to stretch out.

"Deenie and I will talk to you individually in the science room." I rummaged around in the librarian's desk and scrounged up a warped spiral notebook with enough blank pages to take the interviews. The only thing to write with was a Bic pen with a cap so chewed I wished I still wore my gloves to remove it.

Joyce frowned at me. "I'm sure you don't need to talk to us all. What could we possibly have to say about Jesse Gold? I think it's obvious he was a despicable man, and none of us wanted anything to do with him. Frankly, he made this trip a misery for everyone."

Aaron's deep voice took over. "You don't need to interrogate us. We're strangers who came together on a bird-watching trip. Some of us have become friends as such, but we share nothing except a love of birds, and three days traveling in a noisy van."

Olivia dangled her legs over the side of the chair like a sullen teen. "We didn't even talk that much. Birds and stuff. And then this mess. None of us know a damned thing about Gold and, like Joyce said, none of us wanted to."

Deenie squinted hard at Olivia. She reminded me of a bird dog spotting quail.

They were all working pretty hard to avoid talking to us. That was interesting.

I gathered up my used notebook and pen and reached for the tablet. But as I lifted it and set it on top of the notebook, something caught my eye.

I stretched my neck and pulled the tablet closer, wrinkling my brow and squinting, as if that would enhance my sight.

The longer I stared, the clearer it came. It might not make sense. But it was a clue.

14

The library, with its bright lights and at least some heat, seemed like the best place for the rest of them to stay.

I hugged the notebook and tablet to my chest like a schoolgirl carrying her books. With a flick of my head toward the hallway, I indicated for Deenie to join me. "Give us a minute to set up in the science room. Then we'll call you in one at a time."

No one responded to me, and I took that to mean they weren't happy about it. That bothered me not one bit. There wasn't one of them I wanted to be my buddy.

Deenie left the library ahead of me, but my excitement made me zip by her and into the science room. Louise must have been in the center pod, because a weak light filtered out from the camp light.

The air in the science room was chilly, but an early smell of onions from the beans simmering made it seem warmer. The one safety light in the ceiling gave the whole place a creepy feel. It would have to do.

Deenie rushed behind me as I set the tablet down on one of the high tables.

She sounded as breathless as I felt. "What is it?"

I pointed to the tablet. "Look."

She bent down, then picked up the tablet and held it close to her face. "It's words. Something. I can't make it out."

Louise barreled into the room. "Did you remind them I've made coffee? I suppose we can pass around the cookies if they're hungry, but I'd rather hold those back in case we're stranded here longer. We can ration them so no one starves."

"I don't think we'll need to start eating each other," I said. "I didn't tell them specifically about the coffee. They're all in the library, so it might be obvious when they smell it."

She stomped toward the door. Not because she seemed angry or anything, but because stomping was Louise's normal gait. Even as a kid, we always knew it was her walking around the bedrooms upstairs because all the downstairs light fixtures rattled.

Deenie placed the tablet back on the table. "Can you read it?" she said to me.

Louise stopped. "What is that?"

I pointed to the table. "It's Gold's tablet. I can almost make something out on the screen."

Louise walked over and gave a rueful chuckle. "Screen burn-in."

Deenie and I both sent her a questioning look.

"It happens when you leave your computer on with the same screen. The companies all say they've fixed it and it won't happen. But I've got kids. And believe you me, the companies haven't found a way to make them remember to shut their programs down. The twins have Sonic the Hedgehog burned into theirs, and they'll just have to live with it because I'm not getting them a new one until they get to junior high. And I told them that."

Deenie nodded. "The ghost image. That's why all the screen savers change pictures."

"So, Gold had something pulled up when he died, and it's burned into the screen," I said to their nods. "What does it say?"

Louise grabbed it from the table and stuck it close to her nose. "Archer. This last line is Archer something."

Deenie leaned next to her, head close. "I think this first word is 'remember.'"

Louise nodded. "Yes. I think that's right."

"Remember Archer?" I repeated. "Who's Archer?"

Louise wrinkled her nose as if that'd help her. "I think it's an *H* and the word."

Deenie squinted. "Yep. An *H*."

I figured the two of them would be able to see as much as I could. "Is there a time marker on it?"

They each held the tablet with one hand and together, they tipped it closer to the light and both leaned in. They looked so cute together, though I'd never tell them that.

Louise straightened. "I saw a magnifying glass in the science supplies back there. Just a second." She bustled to the pod, leaving Deenie and me in the twilight of the overhead bulb.

While we waited, I remembered something. "When Olivia was talking, it looked like you had an idea. What was it?"

Deenie's eyes lit up. "I don't know. But something about her voice or inflection or the way she said certain words really sounded familiar. I know I've heard her before."

If she knew the answer, she would have said, but that didn't stop me from asking. "Where?"

She shook her head. "I can't place it. This whole thing, from the minute we met these people, it feels like I know something but it's just out of reach. It's there, and I can't see it."

Boy, did I know that feeling. "Like the pirate ship in the playground."

She gave me a puzzled look, but I didn't have time to explain about the blizzard and staring into the snow because Louise tromped back to us. She held the magnifying glass in one hand and carried the camp light with her other.

Louise set the lamp on the table. "Here." She reached for Deenie to hand her the tablet. "Go remind them about the coffee, and let me look at this."

Deenie started to argue but must have decided against it. She dutifully trod out of the room. Given enough time, it was possible Louise could wear all of us down. Or chase us all away, which seemed like the more likely, and sadder, possibility.

"Can you read it?" I asked.

"Looks like yesterday's date. And..."

I waited.

"Yeah. I'm pretty sure it's 11:25 p.m."

Behind me, Deenie said, "Are you sure?" Her footsteps must have been masked by the carpet when she returned. Or maybe she'd never left.

Louise popped her head up from scrutinizing. "As sure as anyone can be with this ghost image," she snapped at Deenie. "But that's what I'm seeing."

Deenie nodded and concentrated on me. "If that's right, and he was looking at it when he died, that would mean when you knocked on the door when the lights went out, he was already dead."

Louise set the tablet down. "I think you need to charge this up and see if it shows up better."

I frowned at the tablet. "I don't think that will work. We don't know Gold's password, so all we'd see is the screen saver, and we might lose the ghost image."

Deenie rolled her eyes. "Won't matter anyway. The cord you were using for your phone somehow broke." She said it with a sneer on the last two words.

Criminy. "It what?"

A hard note entered her voice. "I don't know what it was like when you plugged it in, but the connector part of the cord is pulled loose from the wires, and they're unraveled."

She handed me the phone. Maybe the thirty percent charge would last until we got out of here. These people. What were they hiding? A murderer? "I'm sure it was fine before."

Deenie flopped in a high stool at the workbench. "I'm frustrated. Because I think maybe Olivia's voice reminds me of a podcaster. And I can't remember which one. I'm sure if I pulled up my podcast library I'd figure it out. But I can't look at my phone because it's dead."

Louise collected the lamp and headed back to the pod. "It wouldn't work anyway because you can't get online to listen to your programs."

Deenie sighed. "I'm pretty sure I had some of them downloaded. Whether it's the one I need, I don't know."

I wanted to kick something. Or someone. "There's not one of them who will admit to having another cord."

Louise set the lamp down with all the gentleness of a grizzly bear swiping a salmon from an Alaskan river. "If all you need is a cord, why didn't you say so?" She stomped toward the door. "Binda keeps a basket of them in the card catalog." Binda was the school librarian, who had retired two decades ago but volunteered on a full-time basis.

"There's a card catalog?" I asked.

Louise was already out the door. "Binda likes to have a backup."

Deenie tapped the table with the tip of her index finger in an agitated way. "I'm all in knots about this. We've got a group of people who don't seem to have anything in common. None of them are upbeat and happy, and they don't act as if they even like each other. But they all seem to be keeping a secret."

That's how I felt.

"And then, Jesse Gold dies." She stopped tapping and crinkled her brow. "And what's with that name? Jesse Gold. It sounds made-up."

"He did say his father was a Jesse James fan," I offered.

"Yeah, but I'm not buying that. I think it's a fake name. I mean, if you were an arrogant dick who wanted to sound important, Gold would be just the name. It's like a rich guy's stripper name."

Louise trudged into the room. She held her hand up draped in cords. "Take your pick."

Deenie met her halfway and surveyed the offering.

"There is something off with those people," Louise said. "And not just because they spend money to chase birds. I mean, they don't even shoot them for food."

We both gave her expectant looks, inviting her to elaborate.

It took a second for her to read our expressions, and then she explained, "They were obviously talking about something when I went in. They weren't expecting me, and they all shut up."

I shrugged. "They were probably carping about having to talk to us. Or having us interrogate them, as Aaron said."

Louise agreed. "Probably. But then Ford sounded exaggerated, like acting in a play."

"What did he say?" Deenie asked, a hint of impatience in her voice.

Louise opened her eyes wide and overacted. "Had to be a drug overdose. He kept acting like a junkie looking for a fix."

Deenie and I frowned at each other.

Lousie continued. "And Aaron said, 'It sure could be. He was acting weird. And he must have flushed the drug container down the toilet.'"

"Sounds like a setup to me," I said.

"Obviously," Louise shot back. "But then they started talking about this person in the red hoodie, and I got the distinct impression that was all for my benefit, too."

Deenie picked a cord. "Sorry, Kate. None for your phone." She drilled Louise. "What did they say?"

Louise waved her hand. "Oh, I don't know. I wasn't listening to what they said so much as how they said it. I have kids, and I can recognize when they want you to hear things and when they don't. Say, their brother is dating someone and they don't want to tell on him, but they think you should know, they'll walk by the open kitchen window and mutter, as if to themselves, 'I wonder if David will ask Ashley to homecoming?' Or if they think you don't know they want a new computer for Christmas, they'll sigh while they're doing homework and tell their sister, 'Brandan gets all As because he's got a new Toshiba and it's so fast.'"

Deenie's jaw clenched for a second before she let her frustration go. She wasn't as used to wandering around Louise's pastures of thought before she got to the gate. "You didn't hear them say anything important?"

Louise thought for a second. "They said Jesse Gold got really nervous every time he spotted the person in the red hoodie. He told Ford to try to get the license plate of the SUV."

Except Gold acted as if the first mention of the SUV and red hoodie was at the sloppy joe feed.

That seemed like a lot of detailed information from someone who swore she wasn't interested. Louise could be more useful in the investigation than I'd thought. "Would you sit in on the interviews? You might catch something Deenie and I miss."

Louise dropped the cords on a table. "I have no interest in this. I'm freaked out that a man is dead in the next room. I know you all have this morbid fixation with murder and clues and figuring out the puzzle. But I'm simply not interested in death."

Deenie came back at her. "It's not morbid to want justice when someone has been wronged."

Louise seemed ready to fight. "How do you know he was wronged? What if he simply died? And what if it was awful and painful and he was terrified and alone? What if there's nothing after this and he's ceased to exist? And all you want to do is gawk and paw through his private things. Where's his right to dignity? Where's your humanity?" She broke off, near tears, and rushed to the center pod.

Deenie and I shared a shocked stare. Then I went after her.

Louise rifled through one of the laundry baskets, slamming down a stack of paper plates, then accidentally crushing a Styrofoam cup with the creamer container.

I put a hand on her arm. "Hey. What's going on with you?"

She shrugged me off. "Nothing. I think it's gruesome the way you all act like this man's death is some riddle that needs to be solved. He was alive yesterday, and now he's not."

What she said made me wonder if she was thinking of our sister. Her death had rocked our family.

Mom was an artist and would fall into manic phases where it seemed she'd forget about her nine children, sometimes for days at a time, while she sculpted clay in her studio downstairs. Dad worked on the railroad and was gone for thirty-six to forty-eight-hour stretches. But Glenda held us all together. She made sure we had something to eat, even if it meant assigning Louise to cook oatmeal for our crew. She divvied up the chores to keep the house neat and the laundry done.

Losing her was a blow to our stability, and testament to how much we'd all loved her. Because the family worked to stay together after her death. We'd always been close, but after Glenda was gone, we struggled to fill in the gaps she left in each others' lives. Louise, as second oldest, maybe assumed her duty was to be the leader. Except where Glenda had a magical way about her that made us fall in line, Louise used brute bossiness to try to bend us to her vision of the world. Even if I believed she wanted what she thought was best for us, she was very often wrong.

At any rate, you couldn't force a Fox to do what a Fox didn't want to do. I wasn't the only stubborn one among us. (Or even the most stubborn of us. Thank heaven for Diane's and Carly's doggedness. They'd help Baxter find Aria. I knew they would.)

Slowly, as the years passed, we'd all grown into our adult lives. The younger siblings left for school or moved out on their own. Several of us married, most started having kids. And finally, Mom's secret life had thrown a grenade into everything we'd known.

It was possible that Louise couldn't accept the cycle of life, the way families grew apart as they started the process all over again with their own kids. And maybe she blamed the drift on Glenda's death.

Or maybe not. Who knew what went on in Louise's head? All I understood was that something was hurting Louise, and I doubted Gold's death was the reason. But thinking of Glenda guilted me into reaching out to Louise again. "Whatever is upsetting you, I'd be happy to listen."

Louise lifted the lid from the pot of beans and stirred. "Can you get me another canister of fuel? I think this tank is getting low."

Guess Louise wasn't ready to open up. I couldn't say I was disappointed. Unlike Louise, who poked and pressured me to unburden myself and let her advise me, I was plumb fine not digging into her problems. I found another fuel canister on the supply shelf, handed it over, and left.

Deenie waited for me in the science room, her face tense with concentration. "I'm going to plug my phone in the library. Maybe I'll figure out who Olivia reminds me of."

"Can you bring Aaron back with you?" I had to start somewhere, and he seemed the most rational of the bunch.

Louise banged around in the pod, maybe making more noise than necessary. But if that's what it took to work off her anxiety, it wasn't hurting anyone, except maybe a pot or two.

It didn't take Aaron long to get to the science room. While he crossed to the table where I sat, his gaze traveled to the specimen shelf, then back to the pod. Was he like Louise, squeamish about a dead body lying around?

I knew I was.

Louise appeared in the doorway and held up two candles that looked like they'd been in a drawer for a while collecting dirt, pencil shavings, and the grunge that accumulated in a desk. "I found these and a few matches. They won't last long, but we can put them on the table while you talk. I've got my camping light, but I'll need that while I cook."

Aaron lifted his head. "If the science lab is stocked at all, I think I can do better than that."

He followed Louise back to the pod.

I borrowed Louise's phone for the flashlight and took a moment to look in Gold's room again. She'd been reluctant to hand it over, admonishing me not to drain her battery, too. So I didn't stay long. I didn't get any fresh insights.

When I rejoined them in the pod, Poupon was sitting in the middle of the room, staring at Gold's door. As soon as I was safe in the pod, he slipped back into his hiding place.

Aaron rummaged around in drawers and the science supply shelf. He'd arranged six D batteries, duct tape, a roll of wire, a bag of alligator clips, and a retractable pencil on the desk. He turned to Louise. "Do you happen to have a jar?"

She was busy chopping more vegetables. I swore she hadn't brought in the volume of food and supplies she used. The food had to be miraculously multiplying, even though the thought of loaves and fishes and all things holy was too lofty for my opinion of Louise. "I don't think so."

Aaron snatched a pint-sized Mason jar from her basket. "Can I empty this into something?"

Louise snapped her head around. "That's chokecherry preserves. I put it up myself."

He didn't look all that impressed and instead poked his hand into her basket again to pull out a mixing bowl. "I'll spoon them out into this. You'll thank me."

Intrigued, I watched Aaron attach the alligator clips to the wires, tape them to a cutting board I noticed he never asked Louise's permission to use, and insert the pencil lead into them. Using an abundance of tape, he strung the batteries together and slid the cleaned Mason jar over the clips and lead.

He looked over his shoulder at me and grinned. In the shady light of the camp lamp, I saw the delight on his face and thought he'd probably made a good science teacher. "Ready?"

I nodded.

With one wire already attached at one end of the giant sausage of batteries, he touched the other wire to the opposite end. There was a sizzle and flash of the pencil lead, and then the whole thing exploded with a brilliant light. "Voilà! Homemade light bulb."

Behind me, Deenie gave a standing ovation. I hadn't heard her arrive. "This is great! Now we can light the science room and back here."

Even Louise seemed appreciative. "It's almost like magic."

And then the light popped out, making the room seem darker than before he'd started.

"Well." Louise could make that word hold her weight in *I told you so*. "That's worse than using candles."

15

Aaron laughed. "That was only to impress you with science. I'll make another one. But I only found one light bulb, so that's all we've got."

While Louise went about chopping and stirring and rearranging her provisions and adjusting the flames on the two Bunsen burners attached to small green fuel canisters she used for the beans, Deenie and I watched as Aaron connected wires to a twelve-volt battery and the light bulb. He arranged the Mason jar over the top for another lamp.

Aaron brought his contraption to the science room and set it on the table. Deenie and I sat, and I opened the notebook.

"Okay," I said. "Let's get started."

He glanced at us, the excitement of demonstrating science gone, replaced with a guarded expression. "I'm not sure I can help you out much. I haven't worked for Mr. Gold for very long."

"First of all, your address."

He rattled off the number and street of a house in Ohio.

"Any medications you're taking?" I poised my chewed-up pen on the page.

He gave me a puzzled expression. "Medications? Why do you need that?"

I shrugged in a dismissive way. "Standard questions."

He looked unsure but answered. "Nothing. Some Tylenol. That's about it."

"You were a science teacher? High school?" Deenie had been fascinated by his tinkering.

His low voice sounded like a lullaby. "For almost forty years. Retired a year ago." He reached into the pocket of his pressed button-down shirt and pulled out a paper clip. He held it in both hands resting on the table and fiddled with it.

"What made you want to work with Jesse Gold?" Deenie asked.

He chuckled, with separate *ha, ha, ha*s. "I'm not sure I ever wanted to work for that man."

Deenie kept on. "Then how did you end up doing that?"

His hands kept busy, and his story filtered out. "My wife and I met at our first teaching job, way back in 1978. A small high school. Maybe not any bigger than this one here."

I'd guess there weren't too many high schools with a student body of about one hundred and fifty in all twelve grades, but that didn't seem pertinent to the conversation.

He glanced up at Deenie, a gleam to his eye. "My wife, wow, what a looker. And smart. That woman knew everything. And you better believe, she wasn't shy about telling you. She was an English teacher."

I couldn't help but smile along with him. He seemed to genuinely enjoy the memory and invited us to join him.

"She was almost as tall as me. These legs that never quit. Was a debater in college and coached the high school teams. They won championships left and right. Not that most people noticed, because they were always cheering on football or basketball."

Deenie gave a *hmm* in agreement. "And what skills will that get you in life?"

Again, he gave that short *ha, ha, ha*. "I'm not one to bad-mouth sports for kids. Teaches teamwork and dealing with challenges. But, debate, you're right. It sets people up for life. And my wife, my Sarah, she gave every one of those kids the gift of a lifetime."

A drop of affection for him and his wife hit me. "My best friend is named Sarah. She's a gift, for sure."

Deenie laughed. "And then some."

I wanted to get back to Aaron's relationship with his employer. "You were telling us how you hooked up with Jesse Gold."

He twisted the clip in his hands and began to work the curves out. "I was getting there. I like to start at the beginning, and that was with Sarah."

Aaron might be more frustrating to follow through a tale than Louise. I drew on patience, not my strongest suit.

"Sarah wasn't one to settle for the first Tom, Dick, or Harry to come along. She made me pursue her for two years before she finally said yes. And that woman, she challenged me every single day, the same as her students. She expected the best out of me, and, because she was who she was, that's the version of me that showed up for her."

I'd bet it made him a better teacher, too. This whole story was probably designed as some lesson for Deenie and me.

He bent the wire of the clip. "I wanted babies, and my Sarah, she had to debate with me about that. Back and forth. I had to bring evidence that we'd be better off as three or four than we were as two. But eventually I convinced her."

He'd drawn in Deenie. She propped her elbow on the workbench and rested her cheek on her palm. "I never had kids. Just didn't seem like the right time, and then time runs out."

I was glad Louise wasn't here. She'd be sure to point out to me that I didn't want to make the same mistake as Deenie.

In other circumstances, I might have loved Aaron's *ha, ha, ha*. But here, I questioned the authenticity of even that. He winked at Deenie. "It wasn't easy raising those two babies on teachers' salaries. But I wouldn't give them back for any money. Course, they're all grown up now. Even have a grandbaby out in Ohio." *Ha, ha, ha.* "He looks like his mama, but you should hear how he argues. That baby is his grandmama through and through."

His affection for his family felt authentic, and yet, I sensed he wanted to make us believe in his simple life.

He kept toying with the paper clip. "Our babies were little bitty beans still. My, we were a happy unit. Sarah and I loved our work, and we adored those babies."

I felt the gray clouds looming. It would be great to stop him now and leave the image of this happy family in my mind. But I assumed it was turning dark.

His hands tightened on the clip. "Sarah started feeling tired. I pitched in with grading papers and reading essays so she could nap after work. It happened quicker than I could have imagined."

Deenie's face fell. "Oh no."

Aaron glanced up at her. "Yes. 'Oh no' is right. It was kidney failure. We went through all her family, trying to find a match. And that didn't work. She was failing fast, and I couldn't do anything to help her."

My chest tightened. This beautiful story was turning ugly.

"But a friend of her cousin's knew a guy, who knew a guy. And he said he could get Sarah into a trial. Kidney transplant."

Deenie and I didn't say anything while he bent the clip into right angles.

"I wasn't any bigger fool then than I am now. Which is a big fool, no doubt." *Ha, ha, ha.* "I figured there was something shady about the supposed trial. And I knew if Sarah was in her right mind, she would have made me research and debate about the procedure. She'd have insisted I find out where the kidneys came from and who was doing the surgery."

His hands quit moving, and he sighed. "But she was so far gone by then. And I was desperate. I took our savings, the kids' college funds, too, but they weren't much, since they hadn't even started kindergarten yet. And I gave it all to those people."

"And there was no kidney?" Deenie squeaked.

"Oh, there was a kidney," he said.

"But it wasn't a match?" I asked.

His shoulders slumped. "Blood type was right. But turns out the kidney had been harvested too long before they'd used it. And it hadn't been prepared properly."

Deenie reached out and squeezed his shoulder. "I'm so sorry."

He inhaled and sat up. "Thank you. I should have known something wasn't right when they did the procedure in a strip mall. At a place they called a clinic, but it only had one operating room, and it wasn't all that well appointed. Later, I found out there was a whole organ-harvesting ring and some of the surgeries were successful, but some, like Sarah's, were botched."

We fell silent until Aaron closed his eyes and lifted his face to the ceiling. "More than thirty years later, it hasn't gotten easier."

After Glenda's death, they'd told me time would heal the pain. It hadn't. And I thought Aaron probably had it right.

"I'll never stop missing my Sarah. And her children, not only our son and daughter and grandbaby, but all the kids she would have taught over her career, have missed out on so much." He set the clip down on the table. "But what kills me is that charges were never filed. After her death, I contacted the police. They tracked down the kidney to an organ-stealing scam. That kidney had been stolen from a person. All for a profit."

Deenie clamped a hand over her mouth, stifling a gasp.

My stomach flipped. "Were they able to shut down the group who did it?"

Aaron picked up the clip and twisted it until it broke. "Oh yes. They knew who did it. Problem was, the devil had disappeared. Probably new identity. New name. Untraceable."

We didn't say anything while he lined the two bits of clip next to each other on the table.

He glanced at me with a tired nod. "And you're still wondering how I came to work for Mr. Gold."

Well, yes. I nodded back.

"I finally got my kids through school, paid back all my debts, and got to retire. Thought it was my time to see the world. I took off on a bucket list trip. But, and I'm not proud of this, I didn't protect my nest egg as I should have. And I ended up being one of those stupid, naïve fellows who get hacked and robbed."

"Oh no!" Deenie looked on the verge of tears.

"I was in Vietnam and found myself broke. I met Mr. Gold in a restaurant. His assistant had recently quit. And between you and me, I'm not surprised. Anyway, he needed someone who spoke English, and when I say that, I mean he wanted an American. And since there aren't many American job seekers in Vietnam, I was hired."

Too bad I couldn't get online and do a little backup on the stories we were hearing. This one seemed legit, but who could tell? Not everyone was as bad a liar as I was.

Deenie maintained her usual accepting expression, but her question surprised me. "Did anyone on the trip have a reason to kill Jesse Gold?"

Oh. Wow. We were going to jump in with both feet, not even holding our noses.

A hint of alarm hit his dark eyes. "You think someone killed him?"

Deenie waved that away with a chuckle. "Oh, no. But the investigators, they're going to want us to cover the bases."

He seemed to consider the question. "No one on this trip is a murderer, obviously. But I suspected maybe Gold wasn't as much of a birder as he pretended to be."

This was interesting. "Oh? What makes you say that?"

He glanced around, as if thinking to keep a secret. "I heard him talking to someone about windfall profits. To be honest, the way he said it, well, it sent chills up my spine. I was sure whatever he planned wasn't legit."

Deenie leaned in, seeming thrilled by a mystery. "What do you think it was?"

He hesitated and looked almost afraid to say. "I couldn't be sure. Obviously. But he argued with someone named Black before we left Vietnam. Gold didn't want to leave the country. But apparently, whoever he was dealing with insisted they meet in person, and they said they'd arranged for it all to look completely legit and innocent."

This tracked with what Gold had said to me, about a deal and people wanting him to join the tour.

Aaron kept on. "I heard him talk about Medicare, and government workers being idiots. I admit to doing a bit of online research and was shocked by how many scams are out there. We're talking millions and millions of dollars."

Deenie looked down at her hands on the table, and I could almost feel her struggle not to look at me or say anything about the papers we'd found in Gold's bag. She lost and glanced up at me, eyes dancing with the new information. She got control of her enthusiasm and in a serious voice asked him, "You're sure no one on the tour had anything against Gold?"

Aaron shook his head, then added a humorous lilt to his voice. "You know what they say, always suspect the least suspicious."

"And who would that be?" Deenie asked.

I saw no reason to interrupt her interrogation.

"Anna," he popped off quickly, and his jovial expression grew serious. "She never says much, keeps her Bible close, but I don't think that girl misses a thing."

16

We watched Aaron ramble out, looking heavier than when he'd entered. I did feel bad for dredging up bad memories.

Deenie rose. "Who's next on the agenda?"

"Let's go with the Levines." It was an arbitrary choice.

Aaron's lamp had lost some luster, and I figured we'd lose those batteries soon. There seemed to be quite a supply of them on the science shelf, so if we had the right sizes, maybe we'd be able to keep the light going. With my pre-chewed pen and wrinkled notebook, I didn't have to wait long for the Levines.

Deenie and Joyce helped Kenneth to the table and settled him before Joyce lowered herself in the chair next to him.

Deenie sat at the other end of the table as if she expected to observe, not participate.

"Did you get a chance to look at your phone?" I asked Deenie.

She frowned. "It somehow got unplugged. I taped it into the outlet this time so it can't accidentally get yanked out. I'm so close to figuring out who she sounds like. It's driving me crazy."

Joyce glared at Deenie. "Who are you talking about? What's driving you crazy?"

"Never mind." Deenie clamped her mouth shut.

Joyce assessed her. "Deenie. That's an unusual name." It sounded snotty and judgmental.

Deenie wasn't liking Joyce any more than I was. She sat up straighter and in a stony voice answered, "Short for Gardenia."

I interrupted. "Maybe let us ask the questions for a bit."

Kenneth stared vacantly at the light. Joyce, her spine like a fresh piece of rebar stuck in concrete, turned cool eyes my way, her face expressionless. She didn't bother to reply.

I gripped my pen. "Okay, Kenneth and Joyce Levine. Your address?"

Joyce slowly closed her eyes and even more slowly opened them. Utter disdain personified. She rattled off something on 57th Street in "NYC," not New York City. "It's the Upper East Side."

If she expected a response from me or Deenie, we disappointed her. I rolled on. "Any medications with you?"

To my surprise, Joyce didn't balk. "Ambien for Kenneth. He doesn't always sleep well. And digoxin for his heart."

Keeping my manner official, I asked, "Why are you on this bird-watching tour?"

Maybe Deenie had expected to stay silent but couldn't help herself. "You don't really seem like the outdoorsy type who would like traipsing around in the country. Especially when you risk bad weather."

Joyce patted Kenneth's hand where it rested, slightly curled, on the table. "I'm not much for this kind of thing, but Kenneth loves birds."

Deenie and I both gave Kenneth a skeptical glance. His expression remained the same, as if something in the hand-rigged light fascinated him.

I tried to sound gentle. "Kenneth doesn't seem very interested in anything, to be honest."

To my surprise, Joyce's voice cracked. "You didn't know him before. Vital, strong, always on the go."

"Before?" Deenie asked.

Joyce readjusted herself, and her voice strengthened. "Before his stroke. He commanded a room. So powerful." Her gaze rested on him in an almost worshipful way. "He founded one of the most prestigious law firms in the country. You wouldn't know the name. Living out here."

Sure. For all she probably assumed, we commuted by covered wagon and still warred with the Injuns.

Deenie sounded way more sympathetic than I felt. "How long ago was his stroke?"

Joyce's hand continued patting Kenneth's in a way I'd find as annoying as when my brother Robert used to hold me down and tap on my chest, something he called water torture. "Years. But he's been making progress."

I struggled to find a way to ask what Joyce could possibly have been thinking to drag this man, who didn't seem to be aware of much and had little stamina, on a trip like this. "Why would you want to bring him on a tour that requires walking and long stints sitting in a van, when he doesn't seem to be very fit?"

Joyce sucked in her lips as if to keep from breaking down. She exhaled. "Bird-watching is a passion my husband shared with our son, Joel. Oh, the hours they spent hiking the woods with their binoculars and their little notebooks. It was the happiest time of Kenneth's—our—lives."

Deenie's voice was low and sad. "You're not close with your son anymore?"

Joyce lost her imperial manner and became a mere mortal mother. "We lost our chance. Our son grew up, and suddenly, everything we did or said was wrong. According to him, we didn't understand the world, had no empathy, were only interested in wealth. All the things a rebellious young man will say when he's breaking away and finding himself."

Deenie and I stayed silent, and I hoped it would create space for Joyce to go on.

She did, now an edge to her voice. "He joined the Peace Corps, and we supported him in that endeavor. He taught school in the ghettos of Los Angeles. And we stuck with him in that as well. Always believing he'd eventually make the right choice and return to us, get his law degree, and join Kenneth. At that time, the firm represented a good deal of civil rights pro bono cases. And I was certain that would appeal to him."

She broke off, and when she didn't resume, I prompted her. "But he didn't come back?"

Joyce twitched her neck to the side and sucked in a breath. "He would have. I'm sure of it. But he fell under an evil influence. And then, it was too late."

Deenie couldn't wait for Joyce to finish. "Oh no. He died?"

Joyce kept patting Kenneth's hand, and she inhaled and exhaled twice before she could continue. "Drug overdose. We didn't find out for weeks afterward. It nearly destroyed Kenneth."

Deenie and I both shifted our attention to Kenneth. He stared at the bulb under the Mason jar. Perhaps he looked a little less cheerful, but it was hard to tell.

Joyce plumped herself up again. This was a woman who knew how to take a punch from Fortune and come back with a sharp uppercut. "He kept working, no matter how difficult it was for him. Always had the respect of his colleagues and rivals. But he lost his spark. Then the stroke sidelined him."

Deenie clucked in a perplexed way. "But why this trip? Now?"

Joyce again rested an adoring look on Kenneth's face. It reminded me a little of the way Nancy Reagan doted on Ronnie. "He's been showing signs he's fighting to come back. I thought if he watched for the birds, got to be with others who shared his passion, it might inspire him to recover more quickly. I'm desperate to try anything. Including a five-day van ride with strangers to the West's wild reaches."

Before we could reply, she drew herself even more erect. "And see what that's got us? Trapped in an ancient school with no electricity, being fed prison rations, sleeping on cots designed to kill us. And the crème de la crème, being interrogated by two hillbillies who have no clue who we are and what resources we bring to bear."

Stunned, Deenie and I both sank back in our chairs.

Deenie started talking while I was still struggling for a response. "If you have an abundance of resources, I'd invite you to bear them now, because I, for one, would like a long, hot shower, a toasty fireplace, and a glass of whiskey before falling into my cozy bed. All of which I'd be doing this very minute if I hadn't thought a group of birders stupid enough to not check the weather, miss their turn on a wide, open highway, slide into a ditch when the roads weren't even bad, and end up without emergency provisions might appreciate a little help getting by while they wait for someone to save their elite asses."

Before I could applaud, Louise shot from the pod. "I may not be serving you Chateaubriand with Bananas Foster for dessert, but you're getting healthy, filling meals."

Joyce didn't seem at all put out with her dressing down. "Be that as it may, I believe I've answered your questions. I assume we're free to return to the library before Kenneth freezes to death."

"Just one more question," Deenie said, for all the world sounding like Columbo. "Do any of the other travelers have a reason to want Jesse Gold dead?"

Joyce gave a disdainful scoff. "I wondered when you'd get around to accusing one of us. And I've given this some thought. No one on this trip would kill so much as a spider. We're environmentally conscious, and that makes us keenly appreciative of life. However, if you dig deeply enough, I suppose motivations could surface. If I were you, I'd look to someone who has the knowledge of poisons and how they work."

"And who would that be?" Deenie asked.

Joyce's sour expression showed her shock at Deenie's ignorance. "Why, Aaron Fields. He's a science teacher. And he'd been working for that horrid man. I'd say those two facts would give you pause."

Since Deenie had taken care of the questioning, I kept writing notes. "Thank you. We'll be in to get someone else in a few minutes."

Before they got to the door, Louise added, "We'll have lunch in a half hour. It won't be a salmon salad with homemade croutons and a light vinaigrette, my apologies."

With Kenneth leaning heavily on her arm, Joyce ignored Louise.

When they'd staggered out the door, I grinned at Louise. "Chateaubriand?"

Her returning smile looked shy and kind of cute. "I read about it in a novel, and I've always wanted to go to a restaurant fancy enough to serve it. Norm would hate it, though. Can you picture him in a suit and tie? Getting dressed up just to eat."

Something about that broke my heart a little. "As soon as the weather breaks and you can get away, let's go to Denver and make Diane take us for Chateaubriand." Because, I made myself believe, she and Carly would be back from Chile, and Baxter would be home safe.

Louise headed back to the pod. "Don't be silly. I can't run around the country for something so frivolous."

17

"Did you notice?" Deenie sounded like an excited kid at a birthday party.

I glanced from my notes. "Notice what?"

Her eyes danced. "Joyce's feet. They're tiny. Like maybe a size six or even five."

Oh. I hadn't looked. "The wine stain."

"Exactly." She fidgeted. "That means it had to be Joyce."

I thought about the details. "From the grains in the Dixie cup, I'd bet he was drugged. But then, he threw that up. So, probably not enough left in his system to kill him. The murderer would have discovered Gold was still alive and would have had to wrestle him, subdue him, and get a syringe into his arm."

Deenie's excitement faded. "And Joyce isn't strong enough to do that."

I pictured the crime scene. "And Kenneth wouldn't be able to help. That would leave getting the others involved. And since they're practically strangers, I can't see them helping out with murder."

Louise rustled around in the pod, making peanut butter and jelly sandwiches, no doubt.

I turned the mystery around and around. "Even if she somehow managed to do all that, what would be her motive?"

Deenie's lips bunched, and she moved them side to side. It was kind of a cute concentration face. I could almost see her knitting theories and pulling out the stitching. "It's got something to do with their son. She didn't tell us the whole story."

It seemed complete to me. "Doesn't get any more final than a drug overdose."

Deenie unclenched her mouth and blew out in frustration. "We're missing some connecting tissue. It's so much easier listening to podcasts than it is to figure it out on our own. If we don't solve this soon, I'll go insane."

I stood. "I'll go get Ford. See what he's got to say."

Deenie jumped up. "I'll go. I want to see if my phone is charging."

In a few minutes, Deenie stomped in. "Not enough charge. I think maybe they unplugged it, and Joyce alerted them that we'd be back in so they could plug it in at the last minute."

"Why would they unplug your phone? You didn't tell them you wanted to find a podcast, did you?"

Deenie hesitated. "Not exactly."

I gave her a stern look.

She looked guilty. "Olivia wanted to use the plug-in, and I told her I needed my phone for the investigation."

That wasn't good. "Anything else?"

She looked away. "I might have mentioned that I had information in a podcast on my phone."

Not that I would have chastised her, because we all step in it from time to time, but I didn't get a chance because Ford stood in the hallway behind her, looking sheepish. "It's probably just slow to charge because, like, the generator doesn't put out that much electricity."

I didn't think that was how it worked, but I'd have to ask Aaron for the details. And something told me he would back up Ford.

"Come on in and have a seat," I said to Ford.

He dragged his feet, like a ten-year-old instead of a thirty-something. He seemed untethered and drifty. I couldn't feature the tour company hiring someone so timid to lead a group on an outdoor trip where so many things could go wrong. He dropped into a chair and leaned back as if trying to get as far from me as possible.

I flipped to a blank page in my ratty notebook. After getting his Southern California address, I asked about medication.

His face lost all expression, and he grew suspicious. When no one said anything for a stretch of time, he ventured, "It's medical. I know it's not technically legal in Nebraska, but I've got my medical card for California. And I swear I don't use it when I'm driving. Just, you know, at the end of the day. You can relate, right? I mean, you've seen these people."

It took me a second to catch up. "Oh, you mean…"

He still seemed cautious. "Weed. Yeah."

I gave him a scolding expression. "It's not legal, you're right. You need to get rid of it."

"Sure, sure. I totally will." He wouldn't, but I didn't care.

On to more pertinent information. "How long have you been working for Flock Watch Tours?" Still thought it was a stupid name.

He crinkled his forehead in thought. "Oh. N-n-not long."

Deenie gave him the same smile she probably used with her breakfast customers. Relaxed and happy to see them. "You don't need to be nervous. We don't think you murdered Jesse Gold."

He forced a laugh that sounded an awful lot like a strangled cat. "What? Dude. I mean, obviously I didn't kill anyone. But you think, like, someone did? Kill him, I mean?"

I put on my most authoritarian manner. "Not at all. We're required to ask questions."

His Adam's apple bounced down his skinny throat. "W-w-well, I didn't."

Deenie interrupted with a voice like velvet. "What made you take a job with Flock Watch Tours?"

He glanced at her and then me.

If she ever wanted to give up waitressing and go into counseling or law enforcement, I figured Deenie would be a natural. For the same reason she probably raked in tips. When she turned it on, she could make people feel safe and welcome and important. "It's okay, hon. We're getting the facts down so the official investigators can release you all and get you back to your birds."

He gulped, and his shoulders lowered an inch or two from his ears. "I see. So, yeah. Flock Watch Tours. This is my first trip with them. Thought it might be fun, you know. I like birds and stuff."

"What were you doing before you started with them?" Deenie asked.

Since she appeared to be establishing a connection with him, I took notes and let Deenie do the talking.

"I've been out of the country."

She brightened up, and I didn't know if it was an act or if she was truly interested. "Really? Where?"

He responded to her enthusiasm by showing a bit of excitement himself, like most people did around her. How could Louise be so down on Deenie? The world loved her.

"Vietnam," Ford said.

That made her pause. "Really? There are so many places I've dreamed about going, but never Vietnam."

His smile looked genuine. Bless Deenie for getting him to open up. "Me neither. It's not like I ever had the money to travel, but if I did, I think I'd want to go to Rome or Paris or Ireland or something. But, you know, I loved Vietnam. It was so green, and the people were great."

Deenie allowed a touch of sadness into her voice. "Lucky you, getting to travel. I wish I could afford to go any place farther away than Rapid City."

He warmed to her. Who wouldn't? "I hear you. I never expected this to happen."

It was as if I had disappeared and the two of them were getting to know each other. "My family never had much, so I've never seen travel as a possibility," she said.

"Yeah. If it wasn't for SNAP, I might have starved growing up. My nana was a hell of a cook. She could really stretch that stuff. And make it taste good."

Deenie had him unguarded, and she leaned in. "You were raised by your grandmother?"

That lost-kid aura was back. "Mostly. I mean, my mom was around some when I was little. But then she died when I was eight, and it was just me and Nana."

"No father?" Deenie's voice carried sympathy.

A spark of anger lit deep in Ford's eyes. "I had a sperm donor. A cheat and liar. The worst guy ever. Nana told me Mom was super pretty when she was young. And real gullible. And she fell for this guy. He got her pregnant and married her and then hauled her up to Oregon. And when she finally came to her senses and grabbed me and came home to Nana, the guy refused to give her a cent. I mean, talk about rich. He was so damned rich he could have bought and sold Fort Knox." He gave Deenie a wistful smile. "Fort Knox. That's what Nana always said. I don't even know what Fort Knox is."

Deenie let out a small chuckle. "Grandmas." She waited. "Did your mother or grandmother ever think to go after your rich dad? Maybe do a paternity test and sue for child support?"

Ford raised the side of his mouth like a dog snarling. "He got in trouble with the law, and he skipped out. No one knew where he went. Like, vanished. Probably changed identity and moved to a different country."

"That's rough," Deenie said. "But look at you. All grown up and traveling internationally. That showed him."

His face lost the fight. "Yeah. Showed him. Except Mom and Nana didn't get to see it. If we'd have had even a little of that bastard's money, Mom could have gotten the treatment she needed, and she might be alive today. I hope he rots in hell."

There was silence in the room. Ford's last words settled around us, disturbing in their passion.

Deenie cleared her throat. "Just asking, because the investigators will want this in their report, but can you think if anyone on the tour made threats to Jesse Gold? Or would have a reason to want him dead?"

Ford stared at Deenie in surprise, and then I could almost see the wheels turning in his head. "That Joyce, man, she's a mean old lady. I mean, I wanted to like her because, well, you know how much I loved Nana and that. But she's a tough one. And she didn't like Gold. Not at all. I never heard her threaten him, but the way she looked at him, it gave me the willies."

Another suspect questioned, another accusation. And not two of them the same. "Thanks for that. Now, what about the others? Can you remember seeing them around midnight last night?"

Ford frowned at me. "I saw you. And Sean and Aaron. But after I thought I saw that red hoodie person, I took another dose and passed out."

"Dose? As in—"

He nodded. "Weed. Yeah."

Deenie inhaled with finality. "Okay, Kate? Got what you need?"

I tipped my hand at Ford. "Yeah. Thanks. We'll break for lunch. Deenie will let you know when it's time."

"Sure," he said, getting to his feet. He stopped and put a hand on Deenie's shoulder. "Th-th-thanks for, you know, being so nice and stuff."

She patted his hand before he withdrew it.

We watched as he left the room, and Deenie whipped around to me. "Oh my God! He did it!"

"How are you coming up with that?"

Deenie jumped up, as if she couldn't contain herself. "He was in Vietnam! Did you see the hatred in his face when he talked about his father?"

"His father, sure. But Jesse Gold isn't his father. He didn't even know him until three days ago."

"That's what he wants us to think. But there's something he's holding back. As soon as we understand what that is, we'll have him."

"I do know he's no birder."

She nodded as if it confirmed her suspicions. "How do you know?"

I gave her an insider's grin. "That first day, he said he'd brought them out here to see the Sandhills cranes."

Her eyes fluttered wider. "See? Anyone who knows anything about birds knows the Sandhills cranes only fly over the Sandhills. They stop in the eastern part of the state. Not here. Sheesh."

Louise poked her head out of the back. "What about his name?"

Deenie and I both swung around, surprised to hear from her. "Whose name?" I asked.

Louise lifted her arms, palms out as if we were not catching the obvious. "Jesse Gold. He said he was named after Jesse James. You know who killed Jesse James, don't you?"

Deenie hesitated, and then it looked like a spotlight snapped on inside her head.

I also remembered. Our youngest brother, Jeremy, had gone through a whole outlaw stage, and his favorites had been Frank and Jesse James. He dressed up in cowboy clothes, with a holster strapped to his waist, wooden spoons instead of guns, since Mom and Dad were pacifists. He pestered us with details about the outlaws' lives, including the murder of Jesse James. "Robert Ford."

Deenie snapped her fingers. "When Gold explained about how he got his name, something tickled my brain, but I couldn't place it. This was it."

Louise disappeared into the pod and returned carrying a platter of sandwiches. She announced, "I think it's still warm enough to eat in here. Go tell everyone that lunch is ready."

18

Deenie went to alert the troops to the mess hall, and I fell to helping Louise. We brought out paper plates and a giant beaker of lemonade she'd stirred up from powder. Her go-basket of supplies seemed like Mary Poppins's carpetbag. I was doubly impressed to see a jar of her famous dill pickles, as well as pickled beets and bread-and-butter pickles. She'd also sliced up a plate of carrot sticks, cucumber discs, and celery Deenie hadn't chopped for last night's salad.

All in all, it was a better meal than I often made for myself.

Deenie thundered into the room ahead of the others. She grabbed a plate and slammed a sandwich and sides onto it. "You're not going to believe this. But my phone was unplugged. Unplugged! I'm going back to the library to babysit my phone while you keep an eye on them in here."

Anna and Joyce escorted Kenneth into the room, edging around Deenie without saying anything. Sean and Aaron followed, talking about the third game in some World Series played in the last decade. Olivia brought up the rear, a thick hardcover book clamped under her arm.

Deenie glared at them as they filed past her. "I don't know who's behind my phone being unplugged. And I don't know why, but I can tell you, I *will* get to the bottom of this."

Olivia made a comical face intimating that Deenie was ridiculous. "I think this isolation and Gold's accidental death is getting to you. Someone tripped over the cord. Stop being paranoid."

Louise clapped her hands the way Mrs. Wilder, our kindergarten teacher, used to do when our class of ten five-year-olds was running amok. "I understand this might not be the sophisticated meal you're used to, but it's what we've got. There's cake for dessert, though."

Olivia left off insulting Deenie and was surprisingly kind to Louise. "This is amazing. Thank you for being here and doing this." Could she have an ounce of humanity after all?

Louise puffed up with pride, and I wanted to hug Olivia for that boost. It softened something on Louise's edges, and she relaxed the tiniest bit. "What are you reading?" She indicated Olivia's book.

Deenie spun around and left in a huff, presumably to guard her phone.

Olivia pulled the book from under her arm and held it up. "I found it in the library. It's probably thirty years old."

Louise broke into a grin. "I can't believe they still have those. We used to spend study hall in the library going through those *Time-Life* books. My favorites were the series on the Civil War. All those dresses with the big hoops. I used to imagine wearing them."

Olivia slid the book back under her arm. "I'm a sucker for true crime. There are a bunch of those old *Time-Life* books in the library about that. I'm reading about Bonnie and Clyde."

Ah, yes, those books in the back, where we could page through the pictures while we gossiped and giggled. Until Binda got after us. This school contained so much of my childhood. Like Louise, I'd spend my share of hours killing time in the library. Sarah and I used to pore through those well-worn books that weren't shy about printing gruesome pictures of crime scenes, along with executed criminals.

Poupon poked his head from the pod, looking groggy. The soggy paperback clamped in his teeth, he plodded his way past the bunch of folks filling their plates and sidled up to me. I pulled the book from his jaws. "You picked a fine time to learn how to read. Come on."

It wasn't hard to understand that, much as he didn't want to go outside, he had business to attend to. We made our way around the corridor, the air getting chillier as we approached the outside door.

Toad turds and gooseberry pie. The door was propped open again. When had that happened? As far as I knew, everyone had been in the library all morning.

I left the brick in the door and let Poupon out ahead of me. Again, the snow at the edge of the concrete looked disturbed. There were tufts of snow in what could possibly be footsteps to the door.

I squinted into the wind, searching for a black SUV, a person in a red hoodie, or some other sign of life. Nothing. The wind roared, sweeping the snow to create a three-foot wall at the edge of the concrete. The snow hadn't fallen in a consistent blanket of the same depth. The wind would pile it here, scoop a shallow spot there. With the naked eye, there was no telling how much we'd accumulated. I estimated the temperatures were hovering around zero, but again, my perception didn't guarantee accuracy.

However, turning the other way, I made out the gray outline of what I was sure was the pirate ship. If I used my imagination.

Poupon didn't venture past the berm at the edge of the concrete. He hated cold and snow, and the frigid air quickly seeped through my flannel shirt, but we both dallied about going back inside.

I felt certain whoever murdered Jesse Gold was in that schoolhouse. With only half of the suspects interviewed, I wasn't thrilled to resume. There was no clear killer. Clues scattered like leaves in October. Everyone had an alibi, no one's motive seemed strong.

"I need to look at the body again," I told Poupon.

Usually close-lipped and prone to keep his opinions to himself, this time was no different. He didn't protest when I directed him inside and kicked the brick back to its place in the corner. He shook the snow from his curls and let me lead the way back to the science room. Never a ball of fury, Poupon seemed unusually depressed. I didn't blame him. We hadn't been locked in here even twenty-four hours, but it already felt like an eon. And with the storm still blowing, we'd be here a while yet.

Olivia and Sean were the only people at the table when Poupon and I entered the science room. Either we'd been outside longer than I thought, the rest had eaten quickly, or maybe they'd taken their food to the library, where it was warmer.

They stopped talking, and Sean rose.

Olivia pushed back from the table. "You ought to get your facts straight if you're going to argue with me about anything."

Sean rubbed his beard and fired back. "I know what I'm talking about. If Lincoln would have replaced McClellan with Grant right away, the Civil War would have been over in a year."

Olivia folded her arms and watched Sean amble toward the door. "You're armchair quarterbacking the best president this country has ever had."

From the depths of the inner pod, Louise raised her voice. "He's right. McClellan's incompetence cost thousands of lives."

Olivia drew her head back in shock. "I didn't know she could hear us." She muttered that, as if talking to herself, not to me.

I wondered why Sean and Olivia hung out here together. They acted like they couldn't stand each other. Except, there was that weird exchange I'd overheard in the hallway. What did they mean when she'd said, 'Not now, wait until it's over'?

Maybe they did like each other in the romance-y meet-cute kind of adversarial way. But why wouldn't they want us to know?

Olivia started for the doorway to the hall.

"Can you tell Deenie I'm going to help Louise clean up, and then we'll start talking to Anna?"

Olivia rolled her eyes. I didn't know if that meant, "Sure, I'll be happy to pass along your message," or "Go to hell."

19

I slipped into the pod, thinking I'd check up on Louise and maybe grab a sandwich or snacks.

She had her back to the door and was hunched over the teacher's desk where she'd placed Aaron's light bulb lantern.

"Did everyone get enough to eat?"

She gasped and spun around, slapping a palm on her chest. "Don't sneak up on people!"

Surprised I'd caused that reaction, I quickly apologized. "Is there anything left of lunch?"

She tilted her head back and spied out the doorway. "I don't know. I left the food out and came back here. There's something about those people that makes me squeamish."

I didn't point out that even though the birders might not be a barrel full of monkeys, not fifty feet away from where she sat right now, a dead man was slowly decomposing. Thank goodness the school was so cold. "Yeah, I get it." I looked over her shoulder. "What are you...? Is that a *People* magazine?" I laughed. Not that there's anything wrong with celebrity gossip, but it didn't seem like the kind of reading Louise would be interested in.

She slammed her hand over the pages, though it was too late to hide it. "I found it in the library. I don't read it regularly, not at all unless it's in the doctor's office or something. I mean, I wouldn't spend a cent for this. But here, in this place, with these people, oh, I don't know. I just want to forget things for a while. Maybe fantasize about a different kind of life in a different place. Is that so wrong?"

So many things about that made me pause. She regularly watched daytime TV talk shows while she kept house and cooked for her crew, and they featured lots of celebrities, so maybe it wasn't as out of character as I'd thought at first. And Louise had looked almost wistful when she'd mentioned the hoopskirts of the Civil War to Olivia.

That she sounded so lost and afraid seeped under my skin. It also seemed out of character for her that she took the time to defend herself instead of changing the subject to something she needed to fix in me. I didn't want her to be embarrassed. "Nothing wrong with some brain candy. I know you'd rather be at home with your family."

She looked away from me. "You don't know anything."

Whoa. That felt like an undeserved snark out of left field. "You don't want to be with your family?"

She still didn't look at me. "They depend on me too much. It's time they learn to do things for themselves. Look at us. By the time we were their ages, we were doing our own laundry, cooking for ourselves, and looking after the younger kids. Mose and Zeke can't even scramble an egg."

I folded my arms and studied her. "That's true. But you've always tried to give your kids the kind of home we didn't have."

"And you all have made fun of me for that. Don't think I didn't know. So now, maybe I'm admitting you're right. I've coddled them too much."

I probably ought to feel guilty for all the fun we had at Louise's expense. Mostly behind her back. But she'd wreaked havoc in my life, and I figured that made us about even. "You always did what you thought was right. And your kids can't doubt you love them. What's burrowing in your den now?"

She peered up at me, her eyes miserable. "You spend your life sure of your path. You see the tragedies of others, and you think you'll be spared. And then you find out that no matter what you do, how hard you try to do the right thing, you can't escape fate. It comes crashing down on you."

What the hell was she trying to tell me? "Is everything okay with Ruthie?"

As Louise's oldest child, Ruthie had grown up nervous and shy, clinging to all the dos and don'ts she'd had drilled into her. In uncharitable moments, I thought of her as a goody-goody, and I often encouraged her to break a rule or four. Now a sophomore at the University of Nebraska (Go Big Red), she was bound to have her beliefs tested.

Louise sniffed and smiled, despite whatever despair she struggled with. "Ruth, as she'd like to be called now, is doing so well. She's thriving in a way I'd always hoped. And, between you and me, kind of envy. I didn't want to go to college at the time. I wanted to marry Norm and start our family. But there's always a piece of me that wishes I'd struck out on my own. Just once. And now it's too late."

This was a side of Louise I'd never seen. "Come on, now. It's never too late. What is it you want to do? Go to school? Why not take some online classes while the twins are still young, then do some summer school at the university to get a taste of campus life."

She stared at me as if I'd grown a big purple head. "Your life is so simple. You only have yourself to think about. And that's the problem with you."

Okay, this sounded more like the Louise I knew. Dang me if I didn't encourage her, because this felt more familiar. And if there was one thing most of us Foxes were not, it was emotionally healthy. "I don't feel like I have a problem."

She scoffed. "Maybe not now. But you won't listen to me when I tell you that some day, and maybe sooner than you think, you're going to wake up and you'll be all alone. And you're going to need someone to stand by you, and there won't be anyone because you've been too busy having a career and being selfish to have bothered finding a husband and having a family."

I let her words drop to the ground. Then turned them around on her. "You're the one advocating for our family to stay together. I guess I assumed you'd always be there for me."

Now she really scared me with a total departure from her normal. "There's where you're wrong. Who knows how long I'll be here for you."

20

The bathroom door swung open, and Ford walked out, cutting short our conversation. I hadn't known he was in there. Keeping track of these people shouldn't be this hard, but it seemed they slunk around without me knowing where they'd pop out.

Before I turned to him, I said quietly to Louise, "Thanks for the warning."

Ford stopped short and glanced from me to Louise, a worried tinge to his eyes, his hair flopped on his forehead and needing a wash. "Is everything okay? Like, are we out of food and the storm is going to last a few more days?" His eyes shifted to the closed door behind which Jesse Gold's body lay.

Louise narrowed her eyes at him. "You, too? As I told Kenneth and Joyce, this may not be gourmet cuisine, but you're not going to starve." Although she'd mentioned worrying about rationing the cookies for the same reason.

"Oh, sure. I mean, thank you for doing all of this. It's just, man, I'm from California, and you know, all that talk about the Children's Blizzard has me spooked."

Poor guy. He could use someone to take care of him, but it wasn't going to be me. "It's not so bad that I couldn't make it to the nearest house if I had to. And I'd send someone back on a snowmobile. It wouldn't be fun, and I'd get danged cold, maybe frostbite on a finger or toe, but no one is going to die."

He looked hopeful. "C-c-can we do that now?"

I raised my eyebrows at him. "Did you not hear the part about frostbite? In this case, I'm going to opt for caution being the better part of valor and wait it out."

His face fell. "Oh, yeah. Sure. That's probably okay." His gaze was again drawn to Gold's door.

"Thanks." He didn't seem to get my sarcasm, so I followed up with, "Can you tell Sean I'd like to talk to him, please?"

"Sean? You don't think he's got anything to do with Gold's death, do you? Because I can tell you he's a good guy. Wouldn't hurt anyone."

Louise rolled her chair back and squeezed around me to the pot simmering on the Bunsen burners. We were lucky that if we had to be stranded, at least we had Louise. She knew what she was doing, and if her ever-expanding provisions baskets held out, we'd keep eating until someone saved us.

Maybe they'd be digging us out now. It couldn't happen fast enough.

I guess I needed to remind Ford of our mission. "I'm going to take a statement from everyone to get a head start for the death investigators."

He nodded as if it were the first time he'd heard that. "Sure. I get it. I'll tell Sean." He wandered out.

Louise shook her head at me and gave proof she heard our interviews. "That one needs to lay off his 'dosing.'"

Or something. It still seemed odd a tour company would hire someone like Ford.

I leaned under the counter and gave Poupon a scratch behind his ears. He didn't lift his head, just watched me. That soggy paperback rested under his chest, and I left it there. "I'm going to have to replace that or Principal Barkley will throw you in jail. You owe me, fella."

He didn't act the least bit grateful.

21

Back in the cold science room, I pulled the cuffs of my shirt over my fingers and waited.

Deenie came back in first. "I opened my phone but didn't find what I was looking for before it died again. Hopefully, it'll stay plugged in while we talk to Anna, and I can do more after."

A slight movement at the doorway drew my attention to Anna, who hesitated outside the door.

"I thought Ford was going to tell Sean he was up next," I said.

Anna seemed embarrassed and looked at the floor. "Oh. Olivia told me I was next. But I can go get Sean."

Too many suspects and witnesses had me confused.

Deenie shrugged. "Doesn't matter who's next. We have to talk to everyone."

"Come on in," I said. "This won't take long."

With slow steps, she made her way to me, every few seconds her eyes shifting to the dark doorway of the pod, maybe uncomfortable with Gold's body not far away. She sat straight several inches from the table, her hands in her lap. In a whispery voice, she said, "I don't know what I can tell you. I hardly spoke to Mr. Gold the whole trip."

I nodded and flipped to a fresh page. "Let's start easy. Your address."

She gave me a location in California with an apartment number.

"I don't know California very well. Where is this?" I asked.

Her full lips turned up in a ghost of a smile. "It's in the redwood forest. Really beautiful."

"I've always wanted to see the redwoods." It wasn't a lie, but I thought it might relax her a little to talk about it.

She nodded, and though she looked solemn, I wondered if this passed for excitement for her. "I never want to live anywhere else. I was born and raised among the trees. My parents are buried there."

I guess we've all lost loved ones, but it seemed for this bunch of tourists, the losses were right on the surface. We Foxes tended to ignore and bury trauma. Maybe we figured if we acted like things didn't hurt, they'd stop causing pain. I would be the first to admit it doesn't work that way. We weren't the most emotionally brilliant clan.

Moving on. "What medications do you have along with you?"

She seemed to expect the question. It'd be stupid to think they weren't talking among themselves when we weren't there. "I'm a diabetic. I take insulin."

Deenie kept her head down, but I was sure she wanted to give me a meaningful glance about the syringe.

I didn't comment and acted like we were having an ordinary conversation. "I imagine there are plenty of birds in the redwood forest. Why did you decide to take a birding tour in Nebraska? I can't imagine we can outdo the California coast."

She looked me in the eye, and without hesitating, like an actor reciting lines she'd memorized, she started in. "I don't know a lot about birds. But I love nature and being outdoors. My father instilled in me a deep appreciation for the land. And I wanted to see another part of the country. Something very different from where I love."

That last word jarred me a bit. I'd expected her to say *live*.

"You got that, for sure. The high plains have to be a one-eighty from the coast and the redwoods. What do you think of the Sandhills?" Deenie asked.

She remained dour. "It's not to my taste. I belong in the woods. It's a mystical place. Gets into your soul and holds you there."

I knew how the place you were raised could burrow deeply into you and became part of your blood, your breath. That's how I felt about the Sandhills. A sharp prick in my brain reminded me that Baxter and I had some negotiating to do.

That was followed by a stab of fear for him. And Aria. And the hope that Carly and Diane could do what they did and get everyone home safely.

"Were you able to spend a lot of time outdoors when you were growing up?" I asked, trying to bring my attention back to the job at hand.

Her face opened up as if the sun broke through clouds. Her eyes lit with affection, and the word that popped into my head was *lovely*. She looked lovely. "Oh, yes. We had a farm. Didn't have a lot of money, but we made or grew almost everything we needed. We processed goat cheese and supplied area restaurants. Sold eggs and produce at farmers' markets. It was the best childhood a person could want."

It did sound idyllic. "Do you have brothers or sisters?"

"Oh, no. Just me and Mama and Papa. And then Mama crossed over when I was young, so that left the two of us." She looked at her hands. "But Papa and I were close. I thought he'd grow old on the homeplace. And I'd stay there forever."

I pressed my chewed-up pen on the address I'd scribbled down. "Your address has an apartment number. I take it you don't live on the farm anymore."

She shifted her focus beyond me to the dark pod entrance. Her voice dropped even quieter. "No. I had to move to the city to make a living."

Getting her to talk was like prying open a curled-up armadillo. "What do you do?"

Her glance flicked to me, then down to her hands. "I'm a CN at a nursing home."

"A certified nurse? Do you like it?"

Her mouth twitched. A smile? Irritation? "I wanted to be an RN. But I couldn't afford all the schooling, so I opted for my CN. But my patients need me, and that feels good to help them."

Maybe I could get her to relate to me and, hopefully, get her to loosen up. "I used to manage a ranch and loved it. But I ended up having to leave it. I still miss that place. The trees especially. They aren't redwoods, but out here, each tree is special because you really have to take care of them."

"Why did you have to leave?"

I hadn't expected it to still hurt. Especially now that Baxter and I were together. Somewhere inside me, I remembered the innocent hope I'd started that first marriage with. "Divorce. He had an affair, and that was that. But my life is really great now."

She considered that. "I always marvel at how people can move on from tragedy."

Maybe we'd get someplace now. "How long have you been away from your farm?"

Sadness crept back into her soft brown eyes. "Over twenty years."

I wanted to ask what happened, but something told me to wait.

Tears accumulated in her eyes, and she went on. "I should never have left."

If I stayed still enough, maybe she'd feel secure and tell her story.

She looked outside the gray circle of light cast from the camp lantern. "Papa thought I should explore more of the world before I settled down with him at the farm. He always worried I didn't have enough friends or do the things that other teenagers did. Like parties and makeup and who knows? We agreed I'd go to nursing school. For him, it was a backup career that would sustain me. For me, it seemed practical because I assumed I'd take care of him in his old age.

"School was fun. And living in the city was exciting. I took up with a wild crowd, and I drifted away from Papa."

She gulped and took a deep breath.

"I visited him every once in a while. But not enough. I think he got lonely. And he trusted the wrong people."

She closed her eyes. "They ruined him. He thought he was responsible for so much tragedy. He wasn't. And instead of going home and making him understand what a wonderful person he was, I was partying and living a life of selfishness."

She brought her gaze back to me. Her eyes looked bleak, raw with long-held grief. "He killed himself. Couldn't take the guilt. And I wasn't there to help him."

This poor woman needed a hug. Or someone to squeeze her hand, give her some comfort. But she held herself rigid, outside of my reach.

"I'm so sorry."

She nodded, her face stony. "He was a good man. He gave so generously, loved so freely. And he never lived to age fifty." She glared at the opening to the pod. "And someone like Jesse Gold, who held his riches only for himself, got to live to be old. I understand God has his own plan, but in this case, it wasn't fair."

I watched her closely. "It's frustrating. I believe in justice, and when we can't get it, well, sometimes it makes you mad."

Her gaze whipped to me. Her shoulders slumped, and she folded her hands in her lap. "Is that all you need?"

Deenie jumped in, maybe influenced by Aaron's assessment that someone like Anna could be a quiet killer. "Can you account for where you were around midnight?"

Anna's eyes rounded, and she seemed to shrink, maybe thrown off by Deenie's tone. "I, well, Olivia and I were asleep. I read for a while and started my prayers, and she was polite enough to give me privacy for that. But then we both dropped off."

I said, "You're sure Olivia went to sleep as well?"

She offered a shy smile. "Oh yes. I'm a very light sleeper. If she'd opened our door, I'd have woken up. And I didn't."

"Thanks," I said and watched her rise from the table.

"Just one more question," Deenie said, as I counted on her doing.

Anna paused and turned.

Deenie kept to the point, I'd give her that. "Do you have any reason to suspect any of the others of killing Gold?"

Anna drew in a quick breath, as if affronted. "Oh, no. Absolutely not."

Deenie tilted her head and invited more. "Are you sure? No one? Are you telling me everyone loved that man?"

Anna blinked a few times, then sighed. "Jesse Gold wasn't a nice man. He was hard on everyone, but especially Ford."

Huh. I thought she was heading for Aaron.

Deenie nodded for her to continue.

Anna shifted her focus to the floor. "I heard Jesse Gold tell Ford he was going to tell Flock Watch Tours what a disaster this trip was and get Ford fired. And I know that upset Ford. He said he'd have to stop Jesse Gold."

Here we go again. Another accusation.

"Thank you," I said, making her dismissal clear.

We watched her silently leave.

Louise poked her head out of the pod and drew in a breath as if ready to pontificate.

I held up my hand. "Don't say it. You're sure Anna killed Gold."

Telling Louise to not say it was like telling the wind not to blow. "You heard her say it wasn't fair that he got to live and her father didn't."

"But she's got all that religion, and there's the whole 'thou shalt not kill' thing," Deenie said.

Louise lifted an eyebrow. "Maybe she's an Old Testament kind of gal."

22

Deenie rose and stretched. "I'm going to check on my phone."

Louise darted back to the pod.

I got up to check on Poupon and use the restroom. When I finished and opened the bathroom door into the pod, Louise was standing above the beans, lid in one hand, spoon in the other, eyes dead ahead, studying a dark wall, which I was sure she wasn't seeing.

She jumped and clanged the lid down. "Quit sneaking up on me."

I hadn't been sneaking. She'd been in the pod when I entered the restroom. Her thoughts had her so far down a hole she'd forgotten her surroundings. And that far into her own head couldn't be a good thing.

"You've been acting strange." Staring into space, not taking every opportunity to push her agenda, even showing signs of forgiveness and frivolity, those weren't typical Louise behaviors.

She lifted the lid and stirred before turning to me. "Do you remember how lost Carly was after Glenda passed? She hardly said a word for two years."

Remember? I'd tried my hardest to be there for that girl. The sadness in her eyes had diced my heart into tiny bits. She'd barely recovered when her father's small plane crashed into a hillside only a couple years later. That she'd eventually regained her spark was nothing short of a miracle. Her early tragedies probably played a major role in spurring her into the life of adventure and intrigue she lived today.

Those thoughts spiraled into my worry about what was happening in Chile. All I had was my wild imagination, and it was placing Baxter, Diane, and Carly in the jungle, hacking their way through vines and brush to a remote camp of huts with people in aboriginal dress surrounding a bonfire and Aria tied to a stake.

Even for me that was demonstrating a wild and dreadful imagination. They were probably fine. All four of them—Aria, Diane, Carly, and Baxter—were brilliant and brave. I had to trust them and shove the worry to the back of my brain.

I brought my focus back to Louise and what she'd said about Carly. I leaned my butt against the counter, where Poupon rested below. "Why are you thinking about that?"

She scrunched up her face as if fighting tears. "I think the most horrible thing in the world is for a parent to lose a child. Like, Mom lost Glenda."

I didn't want to feel compassion for Mom. But there it was, right alongside my still-sharp grief. I kept quiet.

"And the second worse thing is for a child to lose a mother."

I couldn't let that go. "Come on. We were all grown before Mom left. And besides, she wasn't much of a mother. You're so much better with your kids."

Louise's throat hitched. "It was always you defending her to me. Now you act like you don't remember how many times you told me that she loved us in her own way and we should accept it and appreciate the unique person she was. And then you'd go on about how she taught us all to think logically and to love unconditionally."

I laughed. "I gotta be honest with you. That doesn't sound like me. I don't remember ever saying so much about it to you."

Louise seemed annoyed. "Maybe not all at one time. And not in those words. But you felt it. And you can't deny that."

I held up my hand. "Fine. But what has that got to do with what's happening with you?"

She winced, like maybe a sharp pain flashed through her. She considered me for a second. Then exhaled. "Nothing. I'm fine."

I'd let her off the hook earlier. Dad's voice echoed in my head. He drilled into us the idea of responsibility for each other. Always being there, ready to help. Something deep and hard festered inside Louise. I couldn't look away just because she was making it hard to help her. "You're not fine. You've said all the kids are great. Norm is regular Norm. So what's that leave?"

She parried. "You've never appreciated Norm. He's a good man."

"Hang on, there. Norm is a great guy. I've always liked him. We all have." That said, I nosed in again. "Whatever it is, I know it's big. Maybe I can't help, but I can share it with you."

Her voice sounded tight. "You think I tried to wreck your life. Which I didn't, and I never would. So why would you want to help me now?"

I didn't relish rehashing our old grievances. Maybe I did harbor resentment for her filing the recall. I hadn't quite forgiven her for hurting Dad so much, though he insisted she hadn't done any damage. But I'd eventually get over it all. Right now, Louise was sinking, and I could throw her a life jacket, even if I might not give her a whole rescue boat. "You're always telling me about how important family is. I agree. So, come on, Louise, I'm here. Talk to me."

She hesitated and turned back to stir the beans that didn't need tinkering with. "You're right. But this is hard."

I placed my palms on the edge of the counter and braced my arms, waiting her out. With a glance down to make sure the fluffer was still hanging in there, I let my eyes wander around the desktop to the *People* magazine while Louise took her time gearing up to speak.

Something caught my eye. Oh, man.

Louise started in slowly. "I just found out about this, and I'm processing it."

I heard her, but it hit the back of my brain because right in front of me, the magazine suddenly seemed like a billboard. "What the...?" I leaned forward to get a better look.

Louise stopped abruptly, and I spun around to give her my full attention, but I was too late.

She glanced at me, then to the magazine, then back at me. With a clang, she slammed the lid down on the beans. "Sorry to distract you."

She took off on a run out into the science room. Without slowing, she grabbed her coat. Great. Now she was going to walk to town? In a fricking blizzard?

Drat. "Louise, wait." I leaned closer to the magazine to make sure I'd actually seen it right. Then I snatched my own coat and took off after Louise, the sister who had shredded my life, the one who made my jaw clench so tight I worried I'd shatter my teeth, the woman I had fantasies of shoving off the Grand Canyon.

My sister.

Who needed me.

23

I ran down the corridor after Louise. "Hey. Stop. We can talk about this."

Poupon scrambled from his hideout and came after me.

"You've already made it clear you aren't interested," she hollered back.

She hit the door and was outside in a flash, not bothering to grab the brick. Maybe she did intend to walk to town, though I doubted it. She either forgot the door would automatically lock her out, or she assumed I'd be there to let her in. Since Louise knew all things about the school, that meant she wanted me to make the big gesture of following her out.

I picked up the brick and wedged it into the threshold. "You stay inside," I said to Poupon, who probably had no intention of going into the cold.

He dropped to his butt but kept his eyes on me.

I stepped out. "Dang." I thrust my hands through my coat sleeves and zipped up. My breath fogged in front of me, and my ears stung almost immediately. "You couldn't run off to a room inside?"

Louise hunched her shoulders against the wind and stared into the blizzard.

The wind howled and kicked up so much snow it was like looking through a cotton ball. I couldn't tell if snow still fell or if the wind was whipping it around. The only certain thing was that the air around us swirled in a frozen curtain of white.

"Go back inside and chase after whatever distracted you from my little problem." Louise kept her eyes on the nothing beyond the covered doorway. "I need some air. Then I'll finish making dinner."

I bumped bundled-up shoulders with her. I figured she'd talk better if she didn't need to look at me. "I'll go inside when you do. You might as well get those lips flapping so we don't end up human popsicles."

She pouted two more seconds longer. "I have cancer."

It hit like a cannon ball shot into my gut. I bent over, hands on knees, my heart thundering around in my chest.

This couldn't happen.

Not again.

Not to another sister. The universe, God, the odds, whatever or whoever ran the world couldn't be so cruel to inflict this onto us. We'd already tendered our sacrifice with Glenda's death. They couldn't take another. Whoever *they* were, better get ready for me, because I wouldn't allow it.

I jerked upright and sucked in a breath. "No. This isn't going to happen."

Louise hadn't moved, her gaze straight ahead. "Oh, it's happening. A lump in my left breast. Doc Kennedy says it's malignant and my prognosis is about fifty-fifty."

Scream. Cry. Shake my fist at the heavens. I wanted to do all of that. And yet, none of it would help Louise. I'd save my hysterics for later. Definitely after I had more information, because what she'd said sounded like doom info as opposed to real facts. Louise needed me to be right here, right now, giving her support. "Fifty-fifty they'll cure you."

"Fifty-fifty I'll die."

I threw an arm around her shoulder, only getting it three-quarters of the way to her far side, leaving my fingers exposed to frostbite. "Foxes are good at beating the odds. So, we'll fight this, and we'll win. Medicine is amazing these days." Not like when Glenda grew sicker and sicker and finally slipped away.

Louise wasn't having any of my nonsense. "Foxes are definitely not good at beating odds. You lost a recall. Mom, well, I don't even know what to call that whole episode, but the odds were miniscule we'd have to deal with anything like that. And I don't have to tell you about Glenda."

"That just means we're due for a win now. And we're going to win. How is Norm taking it?"

She gave a sad *ha*. "I haven't told him."

I hugged her. "He needs to know so he can help you."

No tears spouted, but her voice cracked. "Do you know how this is going to kill him?" She let out a laugh. "Wrong choice of words. But Norm relies on me. We've been together since we were sixteen and..." She lifted her chin and inhaled. "I know you all think Norm is this strong, capable man. The steady hand raising children, guiding them and disciplining them."

Actually, no one thought of Norm that way. He was genial. Would give you his last Milk Dud, or help you change your oil. But he wasn't a fireball. And I was probably not the only one who believed he was henpecked. Not that it seemed to bother him.

Louise continued. "But Norm needs someone to inspire him. He doesn't always think ahead, and he's not very organized. He'll do whatever I ask, but generally, I have to ask."

My toes were turning into ice plugs. We should continue this inside. "You'll need to give him the chance to take care of you and the kids. He's an adult. He can do it." I applied pressure on her shoulders to move her toward the door.

She shuffled a little and leaned into me. "The reason I haven't told him is because I needed to gather my strength. When I tell him, he's going to fall apart. And I'm going to have to help him to accept it and grow into it. And, honestly, Kate, I don't feel up to it right now."

I wished I was like that huge blue plushy monster in the kids' movie so I could pull Louise into a warm hug. I wanted to make the world a safe place for her, where she could believe she'd be taken care of. All I could do right now was get her out of the storm. The literal blizzard, not the cancer hurricane overtaking her.

I pulled her closer to the building. "I understand. But we'll be there for both of you. He loves you. And he'll get there. In the meantime, you've got all of us. And we're a formidable team when we have a mind to be."

She finally quit resisting me and yanked open the door. "What in heaven's name?"

At the sound of her shock and outrage, I glanced around her into the building.

Deenie stood just inside. She huddled into the old barn coat with a scared look on her face, like she considered running away.

Poupon stood next to her, anxious eyes on me. Could he actually need me by his side?

Louise burst inside. "Were you eavesdropping?"

I shoved in behind Louise and kicked the brick to the side. It was only slightly warmer by the door, but at least the wind wasn't blowing here. If you didn't count the heat billowing off Louise.

Deenie backed up several steps. She shoved her hands into her coat pockets. "I didn't mean to. I went to the pod to get coffee because they finished the pot. And you guys weren't there. I got worried and went looking for you."

Those fists found their spots on Louise's hips. "You need me to make coffee? You can't figure out how to do it?"

Deenie bit back. "I know how to make coffee. I was concerned something happened to you."

"And just what could happen to us locked in the school during a blizzard?"

I could think of at least one thing…murder.

Louise was itching for a fight.

Deenie was ready to give it to her. "Wouldn't be impossible to get locked outside, would it? Why can't you ever forgive people for not being you?"

"What is that supposed to mean?" Louise said.

I got it right away. What a succinct way to say that everyone has their own way of doing things, their point of view, their unique experience and understanding of the world. "She means that just because people don't think and act the way you would, it doesn't mean they're always wrong."

Louise zeroed in on me, and I braced for the tsunami.

Instead, she slumped against the wall and covered her face with her palm.

That sent the sirens and lights spinning inside me. "Louise? Are you okay?" I reached for her.

Deenie's look of shock mirrored how I felt. "I'm sorry. Honey, let's get you someplace warm."

Louise dropped her hand and looked from one of us to the other with an expression of true puzzlement. "What's wrong with asking people to do the right thing? To want those you love to be moral and ethical, to be helpful and kind? What's wrong with teaching your children to work hard? Trying to be good and do your best leads to satisfaction and happiness. I'm trying to help people. Why can't anyone understand that?"

Oh boy.

That was a whole basket of twisted logic to unpack all at once. It had taken Louise forty years of digging into that mountain, and I doubted I could extract her in one afternoon of being stranded in a blizzard together. "Deenie's right. Let's go back to the pod. At least with the beans cooking, it's a little warmer."

We traipsed down the corridor. I was so weary of the twilight gloom.

We'd get some unsettling weather in the Sandhills. Thunderstorms, blizzards, the incessant wind, but gray days never lingered for long. It wasn't like Omaha, which had the Midwest steel skies for weeks. Or like the northwest where Anna Ortiz lived, with rain, fog, and damp. We had an abundance of sunshine, and that was something I counted on.

With a murder investigation, a sister hovering on the edge of sanity, the horror of finding out she had cancer, Baxter and others off in a foreign country facing any manner of danger, and Deenie and Dad in some kind of situation, opening the door and wandering into the snow didn't sound like a bad way out. They always say that in the end, freezing to death isn't such a bad way to go.

For crying out loud.

I pulled myself up. I absolutely didn't feel that way. Baxter and I had a promising future to start living. Louise was going to beat this disease, for sure. I didn't need to solve the murder since I wasn't sheriff anymore, and this storm was going to break at some point and Poupon and I would go home to our Highland cattle. As for Deenie and Dad, much as I'd like them to stay together, that problem wasn't mine to fix.

We made it back to the science room. Deenie picked up the camp light, and we filed into the pod. This time, she shut the door. It almost seemed cozy with the three of us, the two dim lights, and the simmering beans with their earthy smell.

Louise plopped down in the swivel office chair. I jumped up to dangle my feet off the counter, and Deenie pulled up one of the uncomfortable plastic chairs with a metal frame and a molded seat. We formed a triangle with Poupon back in his spot under the counter.

Deenie spoke first. "I'm sorry I heard what you didn't want me to hear. But I did, so let me start with saying I'm so sorry about your breast cancer."

Louise kept a stoic face. "Thank you. But I really don't want to talk about it."

That was such a Fox thing to say, but also fair. She got to decide about that topic. I went next. "I love you, Louise."

She scoffed.

I held my hand up. "No. Let me go. We all love you. No question." Now I had to pick my way across a minefield. "I've always believed you mean well and have my best interests at heart."

"Of course I do."

I fired off a firm look to shut her up. "There's a 'but' here, so hang on. As much as I love you, I often don't want to be around you. Because you insist that I live according to your rules. Here's what I'd like you to understand. You aren't in charge. And the good news is that you don't have to be."

She bristled up. "I only want what's best for you."

"How about you let *me* decide what's best for me. And let Susan decide what's best for Susan. And let Carly and Michael and Jeremy all make their own choices. Think how letting go of those reins would feel? You aren't responsible for us."

"But..."

Deenie said, "Let her finish."

To my shock, Louise shut her mouth.

I softened my voice. "And think about giving Ruthie more room to make her own mistakes."

That was too much for her to keep quiet. "She's my daughter. You don't understand that when you're a parent, you need to teach your children. You—"

I interrupted. "I'm a daughter, and I understand that if you don't give your kids reasonable autonomy, they're going to revolt and you might lose them forever."

She looked dubious.

"Or they could end up treating you like your brothers and sisters do," I added.

She smacked her mouth closed on her retort. I figured she'd put it together. She knew we avoided her. Laughed about her behind her back. Tolerated her but didn't always want to include her.

I clapped my hands to the counter by my thighs. "That's enough. If you want to relieve some pressure, I'm giving you a free pass to rail on any of my many shortcomings." It was only fair, since I'd taken her role by assuming I knew how to fix her problems. I already felt guilty for supposing I knew best. The hypocrisy of me delivering that speech to her didn't escape me.

Louise looked shell-shocked. Maybe she'd absorb a little of what I said. She wouldn't change overnight. Right now, when she faced this cancer battle, she didn't need to do anything other than survive.

Louise focused in on Deenie. "Since we're all here in an executive session, I'd like to hit the next agenda item."

Deenie squirmed in her hard chair, and the plastic squeaked.

I shared her trepidation and wondered if I ought to intervene.

Too late. "What's going on between you and Dad? If you've hurt him, I can guarantee there'll be consequences."

I almost laughed at Louise's threat. Deenie was an independent woman who lived her life on her own terms. She didn't have a job contingent on popular vote. She made her own living and had the kind of easy relationship with herself I envied.

Deenie gave a wry chuckle. "What makes you think it was me who's in the heart-breaking business?"

She got me there. I assumed whatever their rift, it wasn't on Dad. He always seemed like a mellow creek, meandering wherever the terrain took him. Sometimes having to tumble over rocks. But eventually hitting smooth water again.

Those rocks, in my poetic metaphor, since Mom left might mean a bender that could last a few days and lead to a bar fight if we weren't vigilant. But that had been an isolated incident. Still, he had that in him, so maybe Deenie knew what she was talking about.

Louise folded her arms across her round chest, squeezing her boobs close to her heart. "I'd like to hear it."

"It's not our business," I said.

Deenie smiled at me, but her voice carried some heat. "It's okay. Louise isn't going to rest until she knows the details, whether she's entitled to them or not."

Louise sat up straighter. "He's our father, and he's been through a lot. He's vulnerable, and we need to protect him."

That was too much for me. "Deenie isn't a predator. And Dad is an adult. Remember what we just talked about? You trying to run people's lives according to your standards?"

She looked chastised.

Deenie inhaled and looked from Louise to me, as if fortifying herself for a race. "Here's the truth. I don't necessarily disagree with Louise that I'm too young for Hank. He came into the café, and at first, he was like any other customer. You know, I flirt and tease everyone. I love my job and have fun with all the folks. But Hank started coming in when it was slow. He'd order coffee, and we'd talk. And we hit it off."

She stopped and blinked back tears. "I wasn't looking for a relationship. And I don't think he was, either. We liked hanging out together. So, we took some walks after work. Then dinner. Watching movies. Friends. I thought Hank liked being with me because I was like another daughter, one who wasn't busy with her own life."

Louise drew in a breath as if slapped.

Deenie was quick to explain. "Oh, not that he resents you having jobs and families. He loves that you're all adults. Sincerely delights in watching you and your kids grow. But, you know, he was hurting and lonely after your mother left."

That familiar stab of anger and betrayal made me grit my teeth.

Louise glared at me, I guess still blaming me for Mom fleeing to Canada. That was an issue between us we might never resolve.

Deenie's voice was soft. "But Hank eventually wore me down. He seemed ready to move on. And I finally gave in. I let down my guard, and that was stupid of me." She clamped her lips together.

When neither of us said anything, she continued. "So, the last few months, I thought we really had something meaningful. We laughed. We talked about everything under the sun. We didn't always agree on everything, but debating our differences was always respectful and fun. I mean, try getting your dad to listen to Beyoncé. That was a challenge. But he eventually came around. Not before I listened to *a lot* of Sinatra."

I burst out laughing at that. "Dad does love Sinatra."

Louise at least found an indulgent smile.

Deenie chuckled, then sobered. "So two days ago, we're making the bed..."

Not sure I wanted to hear *Dad* and *Deenie* and *bed* all in one sentence, but we were adults here.

"He lifted his pillow, and there was this hawk feather underneath."

Louise gasped.

My stomach lurched. I started speaking right away, not letting any scary thoughts take anchor. "It's weird but not a big deal. I mean, it could have blown in the window."

Louise looked at me like I spoke Mandarin. "Really? That's what you think?"

Deenie tilted her head at Louise. "That was your dad's reaction. He was paralyzed. I thought maybe he'd had a stroke or something. I reached for the feather to get it out of the bed, and he freaked out."

"Freaked out?" I hated to think of Dad doing that.

Her brow wrinkled, maybe irritated I questioned her, or with her own bafflement at his actions. "He shouted at me not to touch it."

Dad shouting was certainly out of character, and more than a little concerning.

"I didn't understand. I thought maybe he was teasing me. But then he picked it up like it was a newborn kitten and marveled at it."

Louise's breathing came hot and fast, but she didn't say anything.

Deenie kept going. "I asked him what was going on, and he explained to me that Marguerite believed feathers were a sign from the universe. He said she collected them when she found them because she thought they confirmed her intuition."

Blood pounded through my ears, and my stomach felt full of rocks.

Louise said, "She used to hide them for us to find. She said she was regifting them to us."

I croaked, almost against my will, "She told us it was a sign of love." But that was a lie. Everything she did was a lie.

Deenie stood up, as if she couldn't contain her emotions in that stupid plastic chair. "After all this time and what she'd done to him, I couldn't believe a simple feather could throw him into a tailspin like that."

Louise snapped back, "They were married for over forty years. Of course it would affect him."

Deenie bit at her. "But she betrayed him. Lied to him. Ripped his heart out. How could he still think she loved him?"

Louise hugged her arms closer and glared at Deenie.

Deenie ignored her and spoke to me. "That's when I made the big mistake. I told him I loved him. Flat out. In the middle of a huge fight, the only one we've ever had, I shouted it out loud."

"What did he do?" My voice still sounded croaky.

A dry cough of a laugh. "He did nothing. Held that damned feather like it was gold and said not a goddamned word to me."

Louise adopted that sanctimonious attitude of hers. "What did you expect? You said yourself that you'd only been going out for a short time. And he had a lifetime with Mom. It wasn't fair to tell him you love him."

"Whoa there, sister." I could see Deenie was hurting, and Louise wasn't helping. "You have no idea what's going on between them. Mom's been gone a long time, and she didn't exactly leave under the best circumstances. Have you forgotten she abandoned Dad to be with the father of three of her kids? Two of them conceived while she was married to him." My voice rose louder and louder as I got to the end.

Louise stood up, probably so I wouldn't be towering above her. "Don't treat me like I'm ignorant. I lived through it the same as you. But people make mistakes."

I snorted. "Mistakes? If Mom considered she'd made a mistake in her life, I'm sure she thought it was the years she spent here, the nine kids she had, the time she wasted pretending to love Dad."

Deenie had stopped being the subject of our conversation. I wanted to give her support and understanding, but Louise had hijacked the conversation.

Louise stomped her foot. "How can you say that? She had some emotional problems, I'll give you that. But anyone would after the life she lived. You can't doubt she loved us. What about the kindnesses, the advice, the gifts that were somehow always exactly right for each of us. If she didn't pay attention and love us, we would have known that. And you have to admit, until the day she left, we felt loved."

Deenie's face showed disbelief and betrayal. "I can't believe you defend a woman who caused your father so much pain."

Since we were adults, Louise had always sniped about Mom's shortcomings as a mother. It had been me who defended Mom, always believing exactly what Louise had just said in Mom's defense. "We've all excused her behavior too long," I said. "She's gone now. And we need to accept it and move on."

Louise gave me a gape-jawed look. "Gone? How do you suppose a hawk feather got into Dad's bed?"

"Well, it's for darned sure Mom didn't put it there. She's cozied up to someone named Marty in Canada." My biological father, though I couldn't say that out loud without throwing up. "Maybe they're planning their next domestic terrorism caper."

Louise gasped.

Deenie snickered.

I turned to Deenie. "And that's how you left Dad? Holding the feather?"

She nodded. "Pretty much. I asked him if Marguerite walked in the door right then, would he take her back. When he didn't answer, I left."

I couldn't blame her. "Can you do me a favor? Just don't make it final until I talk to him. Maybe he was shocked. When he has time to think about it, he'll come around."

Deenie's voice sounded tight, as if she held back tears. "I told him I loved him. If he couldn't react then, I don't think I want him to weigh whether he'd trade me for a liar and cheat."

I couldn't help a guffaw. "Do you know a man anywhere who has good immediate emotional responses?"

Deenie swiped at her eyes. "I'm done making excuses for men and making everything okay for them. If he wants me, he'll need to win me back. And it better be good, because what he did? That's not okay."

She was right.

Louise lasered her. "If you left, then where did he go? I couldn't find him anywhere."

Deenie waved her off. "Maybe he rode off into the sunset with your mother."

"Mom is gone. Good riddance," I shouted, surprising myself.

Very quietly, Louise said, "Then who do you think left the feather?"

24

The last thing I wanted to think about was Mom leaving feathers around. She had fled to Canada to be with her true love, and there was no way she was back in the Sandhills harassing Dad.

Deenie picked up the can of coffee. "Guess I'd better get this back to the zoo and feed the monkeys. Hopefully my phone will be charged."

I grabbed her arm before she could get far. "Not until you see this."

"What? Wait." She jerked back. "I need to get my phone."

"In a minute." I felt relieved getting back to the business of sleuthing murder and away from the messy business of life. "This is going to blow your mind."

I ushered Deenie to the desk where Louise still had the *People* magazine open. I snatched it up and started flipping through pages. "Look at this. You're not going to believe it."

Louise hurried over. She tried to wrest the magazine from me, and we ended up losing my place. "Would you stop it? So I snuck a gossip magazine back here. It's not grand theft, and lots of people read it. Or it wouldn't be so popular."

I fought her off. "Knock it off. I want to show Deenie this."

"You want to show her but not me?" Louise sounded mad and hurt at the same time.

I turned my back and hunched over for protection while I searched for the picture. She slapped my shoulders, but not hard enough to show she meant it.

I finally found it, rolled up the magazine, and whirled. Holding it over my head out of Louise's reach, I waved it at Deenie. "Here. Look at this."

While Louise tried to intercept the pass-off, Deenie reached behind Louise's back, and I whipped my arm around and slapped it in her hand like a relay baton.

Deenie stepped closer to Aaron's homemade lamp and held the picture close. No longer trying to snatch it back, Louise leaned next to Deenie and stared at the photo.

Deenie inhaled. "No way."

Louise sounded every bit as stunned. "What are the odds of us seeing this? I think it's fate."

Not masking my irritation, I said, "It's coincidence, Louise." Up until Mom left and Louise suddenly became her defender, Louise would never ascribe mystical aspects to anything. Now she was all about the woo-woo.

"But that's some coincidence," Deenie said, nose still close to the magazine. "Kenneth and Joyce sure clean up good."

"Depends on which couple you're talking about," I said.

Louise let out a whoosh of air, close to a whistle of appreciation. "I'd say both couples are pretty fancy."

I peered over their shoulders at the small picture among a collage of images from a major social event in Hollywood. It was some kind of charity fundraiser with the A-ones of the A-list. I recognized the big celebrities and actors, but the money folks and influence wielders, both social and political, I'd never have recognized.

Except this time, one picture showing two older couples caught my eye. A heavyset woman, dripping in diamonds and wearing a shimmery silver dress that draped across her, stood next to a short, bald tuxedoed man. She held a glistening gold trophy.

They presented the trophy to another couple, who had their hands out to accept it. That other couple we knew as Joyce and Kenneth Levine. The woman wore a sapphire-blue dance dress that clung to her body and flared around her knees. The man we called Kenneth had on black slacks and a shirt to match her dress. They both grinned.

The caption read, *Kenneth and Joyce Levine award the tango prize to Benjamin and Eliana Klein.*

Louise stepped back and glanced from Deenie to me. "Does this mean that those people in the library are not Kenneth and Joyce Levine but are really..." She looked at the magazine. "Benjamin and Eliana Klein?"

"That's my take," I said.

Deenie's forehead wrinkled, and she sucked her front teeth. "But why would they pretend to be someone they aren't?"

Louise started toward the door. "Let's go ask them."

"Wait," I said. "Let's hold on to this for now. Maybe we can use it."

Deenie frowned at me. "I think we ought to get them and lock them in one of the rooms until they dig us out. Obviously, they're the murderers."

Louise agreed. "Or at least he is. He's faking being disabled. So, he's a liar. Joyce—uh, Eliana—may not even know. Let's lock them up."

I held firm. "Obviously she knows. She's using a fake name. They're pretty old. And there's no heat in any of the other rooms. What if Ken... Benjamin had a stroke between now and..." I flipped to the cover to see the date. "Six months ago. And he's really sick? We can't put them at risk. And if they know we know and he really is fit as a fiddle and Eliana is in on it with him, we all might be in danger."

Louise said, "Joyce told us he'd had his stroke years ago."

"Sure. That proves she's a liar. But what if he's really sick? Do you want to play fast and loose with his condition?"

They both hesitated. Deenie exhaled. "Okay. You're right. But we need to keep an eye on them."

I pulled my phone from my pocket and checked it. "Still no signal."

"I'll go check on mine." Deenie walked out of the pod into the science room and toward the corridor.

I wasn't liking any of this. All I could do was hope Zoe would dig us out of here soon. "We might as well keep doing the interviews. Let's talk to Sean next."

Deenie gave me an okay as she walked out.

Louise narrowed her eyes at me. "I still think we should lock them up in their classrooms until the real cops get here. We've got plenty of blankets."

25

I took the nearly dead camp light to the science room and flipped through my notebook. Aaron, who worked for Gold and was a science teacher, lost a wife to kidney disease. He tried to dodge suspicion and accused Anna of the murder.

Joyce and Kenneth Levine, who were really Benjamin and Eliana Klein, were on the birding trip to jumpstart Benjamin after his stroke. Their son died of an overdose. They'd accused Aaron, because he was a science teacher.

Ford, the bumbling and timid young pothead, was trying to hang onto a job he was totally unsuited for. He pointed at Joyce, because she was a mean old lady who didn't like Gold.

Anna, who mourned her father who had committed suicide, thought maybe Ford could have lashed out and killed Gold to keep from getting fired.

Everyone had an alibi and someone to vouch for them. Aaron was with Sean, so unless they teamed up to kill Gold, they were in the clear. Anna and Olivia were tucked into the math room. I'd seen Benjamin and Eliana, as well as Ford, all around the time stamp shown on Jesse's tablet, which is when we assumed Gold had died. All of them or none of them could have slipped around the school, skulking, hiding, and avoiding.

What new information would Sean add?

He walked into the science room—it hadn't warmed up any—and still hunkered in the gloom from the one overhead light and Aaron's fading science experiment. I envied Sean's warm beanie, and even if I wasn't a fan of facial hair, his beard looked kind of cozy.

I invited him to sit at the table. "Deenie's not joining us?"

His hand slipped on the back of his chair as he pulled it out. "Uh. No. I guess not. She was looking at her phone."

I settled in. "Okay. Let's get after this, then." I asked about his address and meds.

He lived in Silver City, New Mexico, and he had no prescriptions with him.

He leaned his elbows on the table and jiggled his leg. "This whole thing is starting to get to me."

Me, too, buddy. But I acted surprised to hear it. "Really? How so?"

He scratched his beard. "Riding in a van and then the storm. But being stuck in here. Dark and cold. And not knowing when we'll get out."

"Not being in here with a dead man? And maybe locked in with a killer?" I watched him closely.

His hand rested on the table, but his fingers twitched, like maybe he wanted to scratch that bushy beard some more. "You think that someone killed him, then? I thought it was an overdose."

I tightened my lips in skepticism. "I'm not willing to say it's murder, but definitely not an intentional overdose. I talked to him after supper. He didn't seem to be in any frame of mind to kill himself."

Sean blinked rapidly. I hadn't been through FBI profiling, but everyone knows that's a sign of lying. Or hiding something. Or maybe nerves. Actually, I didn't know.

He seemed to reach for something to say. "What about that person who's been following us? The one in the black SUV."

I chuckled as if he'd told an amusing story. "The mystical person in a red hoodie? In a storm like this, how would that even be possible?"

His cheeks colored above his dark whiskers. "Ford told us you said you could leave the building and get out if you wanted. Doesn't that mean someone could also get in?"

"But the doors are locked from the inside."

He blinked again. "But what if someone left it propped open and that person snuck in?"

That's exactly what I'd wondered. "Or maybe someone here left the door propped open to make it look as though they forgot to close it. And then after they killed Gold, blamed his death on the person in the black SUV."

He laughed, but it didn't sound lighthearted. "That sounds pretty farfetched."

I nodded and wrote nonsense in the notebook to make Sean wonder if I'd noticed some 'tell.' I hadn't but wasn't above provoking him. "Tell me, why did you come on this tour?"

He quit fidgeting, and his eyes filled with such sadness it struck me in the gut. I hadn't noticed before how deep and warm his eyes were. "My sister. She loved birds. She wanted to be an ornithologist. When we were young, she talked about birds all the time. Read books about them. It drove us all crazy."

I really didn't want to ask this, knowing how much losing a sister can hurt. "I take it she's not an ornithologist."

He closed his eyes briefly. "No. She didn't get to see that dream come true. That's why I'm here. Doing it for her."

I hoped it made him feel better to see the birds his sister never would. Though forcing himself to follow her passion seemed a strange way to honor her. "Is the trip making you feel closer to her?"

He focused above my head, gazing into the far reaches of the dark room. "Man, she had big dreams. She really loved people. Everyone. Like, even people who didn't deserve it. That's what got her in the end."

End. I hated hearing that. "Do you mind me asking how she passed?"

Those expressive eyes landed on me. "She trusted someone. Tried to help him with his dream. And it killed her."

That was pretty vague, but I thought it might be all I was going to get, and it didn't have anything to do with Jesse Gold, so I reached for a cliché. "They say only the good die young."

Sean's voice cut like a razor. "Jesse Gold wasn't so young. And I don't think he was so good, either."

Sean had been with Gold for three days, I'd only been with him a few hours, and I had the same impression. Still, I pressed him. "Why would you say that?"

His leg started jiggling again. "He never had a nice word to say to anyone. Especially Aaron. Jesse Gold acted like the world owed him every comfort and advantage. Like his money entitled him to love."

"It seems like maybe the rest of you have bonded on this trip. Did anyone get along with Gold?"

Sean gave me a surprised look and took to scratching his beard again. "Bonded? No. I don't think so. We didn't know each other before this trip, and I don't think we'll ever see each other again."

That seemed like a quick reaction. Not like something he had to think about.

I probed a bit more, maybe I could coax something from him to help pin down the killer. "Sometimes going through a bad experience together, like getting stranded in a snowstorm and dealing with a death, can bring people close."

He shifted and jiggled his legs. Maybe he was going to cough up some information. "I know you're trying to figure out if one of us killed Gold. None of us did. But, if you want to dig into someone with motive, maybe look at Olivia. She's always scribbling and talking about writing a book. Like a murder-mystery thing. So maybe she wanted to do some hands-on research."

It took me a second to digest that and realize he didn't really think Olivia had killed Gold. He'd set out a simmering pile of manure to get me off his scent. Interesting. "I'll take that into consideration," I said, using a noncommittal phrase. Sheriff was an elected position, so technically, that made me a politician, even if I didn't still hold the office. That made it legal for me to use political platitudes.

He seemed satisfied and pushed back from the table. "Do you need to know anything else?"

Since he wasn't in the mood to make friends, with me or, apparently, his fellow travelers, I let him go. "Can you ask Olivia to come in next?"

He grunted something I took to be, "Oh, I'd simply love to."

As soon as he was gone, Louise poked her head from the pod. "It's too bad Deenie isn't here to gush and go on about how she *knows* it's got to be Sean who killed Gold."

I twisted in my chair to pin her with my focus. "Why do you think she'd suspect Sean?"

Louise stuffed her hands on her hips. "Deenie would say Sean obviously hated Gold."

"To be fair, I don't think anyone liked him, you and me included."

Louise pursed her lips. "Yeah, but Sean was holding back. There's something about his sister. I don't think she wanted to be an ornithologist."

"Why?"

She flashed a look that plainly said, *Duh*. "Because if your sister had a passion like that and you loved her enough to take a stupid trip like this at this time of year, you'd at least know how to pronounce *ornithologist*."

She was right. I hadn't picked up on that. "That's right. He said *or-IN-thology*. Not *orn-UH-thology*. Look at you. A regular Agatha Christie."

It looked like she tried to suppress a smug look.

I winked at her, even though I knew she'd hate it. "I mean, you were right when you said Deenie would suspect Sean. She'd be so clever to notice that."

She huffed and flounced back into the pod.

26

Olivia zipped in from the hallway. She tucked her black hair behind her ears and scowled at me. "I still think this is bullshit. But since you've already talked to everyone else, you might as well talk to me."

I stood and stretched. That movement, or probably Olivia's voice, brought Poupon from the pod. "I need to stretch a little. Get a cup of coffee."

She backed toward the door. "I can bring it to you. Cream and sugar?"

That seemed oddly helpful. "I want to talk to Deenie. See if she found what she was looking for on her phone."

"Oh." She stopped, and I nearly bumped into her. "I'll go with you."

Poupon and I continued into the freezing hallway. It was really getting cold out here. If the storm didn't let up and we didn't get dug out soon, we'd all be huddled in the library, maybe using those Bunsen burners for warmth. I hoped the generator would keep kicking out at least some heat.

The glow from the library lights filtered out to the hallway, looking almost cozy. I guess I was reaching for any comfort I could find. I hated not knowing what was happening with Baxter. It had been about twenty hours since I'd last talked to him. Carly and Diane would be there by now. Maybe they'd found Aria. Maybe they were already planning their trip home.

I'd need to figure out the best way to help Louise and Norm and their family. Not sure I could do much about Dad and Deenie. Olivia was the only person left to interview. Then I would've done all I could do and I'd turn my notes over to Zoe and Trey Ridnour from the state patrol.

Poupon and I would head home to snuggle in our warm house. Maybe I'd make my own pot of chili and cinnamon rolls. I was doing a much better job of keeping food around my house these days. And that would give me all that time to worry and stress over Baxter.

I stepped into the library to find Kenneth/Benjamin dozing on the couch and Joyce/Eliana in the chair next to him, a hardcover book open on her lap. I'd need to pick which names to use for them and decided on Kenneth and Joyce. Since they didn't know we knew and we weren't ready to reveal that, it made sense to keep things simple. Although I could always revert to Mr. and Mrs. Howell.

Anna sat close to them, huddled into her thick wool sweater with her hands tucked into the sleeves. Her knees clutched together and her shoulders drawn forward, she looked like she wished to curl into a hedgehog ball and hide away. It appeared that she and Joyce had been talking but stopped abruptly when I entered.

Sean slipped past me on his way out. "I've gotta hit the john."

Did he need permission or a parade? He got neither.

Aaron stood at the far side of the library opposite the windows. He'd been studying the bookshelf that lined that wall. Olivia walked to Binda's desk, where her notebook and pen rested. Ford lay stretched out on his cot.

I looked toward the back of the library. I couldn't see every inch of the room because of the shelves, but Deenie wasn't around. "Where's Deenie?"

Joyce blessed me with the disdain I'd come to expect from her. "How should we know?"

Aaron spoke up from across the room. "She said she was going to the restroom."

Olivia gave him an annoyed look. "I never heard her say that. And she wasn't in the science room."

Ford sided with Aaron. "I heard her say that too. Maybe she went into it from another classroom so she wouldn't interrupt your interview."

She was part of the interview process; she wouldn't worry about interrupting.

I quickly covered the floor in front of the three chest-high bookshelves to make sure she wasn't camped out on the ground, maybe hiding from the others. She wasn't at the table in back. "She came in here to check her phone. Where did she go?"

Anna glanced around as if surprised not to see Deenie. "She was here earlier. I don't know when she left."

There wasn't anywhere for Deenie to go that wasn't freezing cold, and even if she had left the library, she would have told me. I'd have seen her. And I definitely did not see her. My elevated heart rate must have alerted Poupon, because he perked his ears forward, a distinct spark of worry in his eyes.

Aaron meandered from the far wall. "Maybe she didn't want to disturb you and went to nap in a classroom."

That was ridiculous. And now my chest tightened in worry.

Sean opened the library door and slipped inside.

I spun toward him. "Did you see Deenie? Was she with Louise?"

He glanced at the others before talking to me. "Uh. No. Louise was working on setting up some kind of oven thing with the Bunsen burner and two pans."

Aaron perked up. "Uh-oh. I think maybe I should go help her." He rushed from the room.

I backed up, Poupon moving with me like a dancing partner. "You all," I swept my arm around the room, "stay here. No one goes anywhere until I get back."

Joyce folded her arms across her thin chest. "As if we'd risk freezing to death. It's cold enough in here as it is. Can't you turn up the thermostat?"

They could start burning the furniture, for all I cared. But not the books. Never the books.

I sped into the dim hallway and popped into the science room. "Deenie? Louise, have you seen Deenie?"

When I rushed into the center pod, Louise and Aaron were face-to-face. She looked as if she were guarding the dwindling collection of the green fuel cartridges, Bunsen burners and tubing, a Dutch oven and a cake pan, and who knows whatever else. "I saw this on a YouTube video about camp cooking."

Aaron assessed her supplies and spoke like a therapist calming a rooftop jumper. "You've got the right idea. I'm here to help you execute it without blowing us up."

She looked a little sheepish but still defiant. "It should work. You put the fire under here, and the cake pan here, and cover it all with the overturned Dutch oven, and it will bake."

"Um-hm." He reached in. "May I?"

She stood back.

"Have you seen Deenie since lunch? Did she come back here?" I sounded as frantic as I felt.

Louise watched Aaron work and said to me, "You would have seen her in the science room if she came back here."

"Maybe she came from a different room?" I repeated Sean's suggestion.

Louise looked over her shoulder at me, annoyed. "Really, Kate. I'm busy trying to get you people fed. If I'd seen Deenie, I would have told you."

Poupon whined.

He picked a bad time to need to go outside, but when you get the call, you get the call. I could check the classrooms on the way back. "Come on."

We jetted into the corridor and turned to the north, following the icy hallway to the outside door.

"Deenie!" My shouts echoed back to me in the empty school. Even though I'd spent chunks of my youth within these walls, both during and after school, I felt a creepiness now I'd never imagined back then. "Deenie!"

To my surprise, Poupon started to jog ahead of me. He let out a bark. A bark. From a dog who hardly ever made a peep, not even a growl when I nudged him off my couch.

He got to the door first and gave a single low whine while swiping his paw down.

"It's an emergency, huh?" I'd given him sloppy joe leftovers last night for dinner and a couple of eggs for breakfast. "People food not agreeing with you. Sorry about that."

I smacked the bar on the door and leaned hard, expecting the wind to give resistance. I nearly tumbled out.

Poupon barked, the sound spreading across the afternoon sky. But at least it wasn't swallowed up with the jet-engine roar of wind. Maybe more like a teakettle whoosh. The sky was still milky, and thick snowflakes dropped almost like rain. But I could make out the whole pirate ship and even the tall triangle of the swing set.

But holy moly, was it cold. Like nose-hairs freezing, lung burning, instant finger-tingling cold. "Hurry up, bud. Let's get back inside."

He barked again, a high-pitched kind of yelp that wasn't normal for him. It was enough to make me search around and look behind the door I held open.

"Oh my God!"

27

She lay on her side, lips blue, eyes closed.

"Deenie!"

Poupon barked again, this time putting up a loud racket.

I lunged back inside for the brick to prop the door open. It would be insanely ironic if I locked us out trying to help Deenie, and then we all froze to death. At least Louise would be right that someone got stuck in a snowbank.

Deenie had some weight on me, and she wasn't able to help me at all, but by sheer adrenaline, I was able to drag her inside. Poupon jumped over her and was inside before I kicked the brick loose and the door slammed shut.

He set up barking again. Loud enough it brought Aaron and Louise on the run. And behind them, others rushed toward us.

"Deenie was locked outside. Help me get her to the library," I shouted and shivered.

Deenie looked ghostly, and her breathing was shallow. Her skin felt icy. How long had she been out there? Long enough to get frostbite? Pneumonia? What if I hadn't found her?

"Good boy, Poupon. Good boy. Good boy." I kept repeating it under my breath as I slipped my arms under Deenie's frosty shoulder blades to lift her.

Olivia shoved the others out of the way and slapped a camping cot onto the ground. "It'll work for a stretcher."

"That's smart." This girl could act in an emergency. A natural leader and problem-solver. I'd seen her be kind to Louise and affectionate with Poupon. Even though she seemed to take a dislike to me, I found much to admire in her. Not in a let's-get-coffee-and-hang-out kind of way. Her intensity might be a bit much.

Aaron and Sean helped Olivia and me load Deenie onto the stretcher. It took Olivia telling Ford to grab hold for him to join us in transporting the cot to the library. The hallway had never seemed so long before. And cold.

I wanted to call Eunice Fleenor, the best EMT the world had ever seen. She would help Deenie, make sure everything was okay. With Eunice in charge, they'd rush Deenie to a warm, clean hospital, and she'd be comfortable in no time.

But we didn't have Eunice or an ambulance, and Anna didn't seem to be one to take charge, even if she did have medical training.

Kenneth hadn't moved from the couch where he'd stayed tucked in a sleeping bag. But the rest of the crew gathered blankets and sleeping bags and helped me wrap up Deenie. Anna and I pulled Deenie's arms out and began to rub her fingers.

Aaron nudged Sean, and they tugged off Deenie's tennis shoes and rubbed her feet.

I looked up from her face, which had a bluish tint. "How did she get locked outside?"

Louise hovered above us. "Is she going to be okay? Maybe we could get some hot broth into her. I have some bouillon in my supplies. I can heat water in the pod."

"It would be good to have something warm to give her when she wakes up. Thanks, Louise." Giving my bossy sister something to do would help her, and the warm fluid would be good for Deenie.

Someone draped a sleeping bag on my shoulders, and I twisted my neck to see Olivia above me. "You looked cold," she said.

Actually, I'd forgotten how frozen I felt, but when I pulled the cover around me, relief sank deep. Then I started to shiver. Maybe I ought to get some coffee, too.

Anna didn't make eye contact. She kept rubbing Deenie's hand. I let my gaze drift from each of them. Most looked away, like when Dad had gathered us all and asked who had ripped the gutters off the roof.

That had been the twins and Jeremy making a Ninja Warrior course. Jeremy, not more than a tot, had slipped off the roof, grabbed the gutter, and when it detached, rode it to the plank they'd laid across two sawhorses, broke that in two, and crushed the tomato plants underneath. After Dad determined the red goo all over Jeremy wasn't blood and guts, he'd started his investigation.

I pressed them. "Anyone? How did Deenie get locked in the storm without her coat?"

Finally Ford started to mumble, his expression sheepish, "I don't know how she got outside. But she…" He trailed off and glanced at the others.

"She what?" I demanded. Dang, I was tired of this bunch.

He took a half step back as if afraid I'd fly across the room and throttle him. He might be justified in that. "I gave her. Well, she asked. And I, like, I was happy to share. But maybe she's not used to it. And I kind of thought I shouldn't, but I didn't want to be like, 'I'm not going to share.'" Finally he stopped.

I couldn't help raising my voice. "What are you talking about?"

In her soft voice, Anna explained. "I think maybe he's saying Deenie asked for some of his weed, and maybe she had too much."

Ford nodded at Anna. "That's right."

It felt like maybe Deenie's skin warmed a little. I rubbed harder, getting angrier. "You're saying she got high and wandered outside?"

Ford glanced around as if searching for assistance.

"How much did you give her?" Olivia asked.

Ford bent over to his backpack and pulled out a small brown bottle. "It's a tincture. So, like, it comes out in a dropper. I take a couple of drops sometimes. It helps me relax. So. Yeah. If she took a bunch, then I don't know."

I couldn't see Deenie asking for cannabis and then sucking down a bunch. It wasn't that I was shocked she'd use some from time to time. She was hanging with Dad, who was a Vietnam vet. Mom was big into the hippie scene in the late sixties and early seventies. I hadn't witnessed my folks using weed, but it seemed a pretty good bet they'd enjoyed it in their earlier years, and with its new acceptance, I supposed they still did.

Although, for the record, I didn't give two beans for what Mom did these days.

Deenie stirred and gave a weak moan.

Louise rushed from the doorway, a steaming Styrofoam cup in her hand.

Aaron and Sean backed up. Anna and I kept hold of Deenie's cold hands.

Deenie's eyes pried open into slits as if they'd frozen closed. Her voice creaked out. "So cold."

I let go of her hand and rubbed her arms vigorously from her shoulders to her elbows.

She closed her eyes again and whispered, "Thanks."

Louise flitted above us like a miller moth I wanted to swat away. But she was worried, too.

Deenie worked her mouth, trying to speak, but the words were hidden in her throat. When she opened her eyes again, the pupils swallowed nearly everything, leaving a narrow rim of what should have been white but was pink.

Her confused glance started on Ford, then dipped to Sean and Aaron, round to Anna, over to me, then up to Louise. With a surprising lurch that at first I thought was a cough, she burst out with a weak bark of laughter. "Oh my God, Louise." She wheezed in a breath. "You look like a Christmas angel we used to have when I was little. And Mom..." She started laughing and couldn't finish the sentence.

How would Louise take being compared to an old Christmas tree angel in a way that seemed hilarious to Deenie? I braced for a sharp retort.

Instead, Louise leaned forward. "I've got some warm broth. Do you think you can take a sip?"

Deenie laughed harder. "See? Angel. I knew it."

Louise propped Deenie up a little and held the cup close to her face. "Here. Drink a little of this. It'll make you feel better."

Deenie looked up and gasped. "Oh my God. I'm so hungry. This is wonderful of you. You're such a good person. I love you. You know that? You're the most lovable person. Why don't you know that?"

She might have gone on longer, except Louise shoved the cup against her lips and Deenie sipped.

I glared at Ford. "How long will this take to wear off?"

Guilt spread across his face, and he popped his chin up to throw his hair out of his eyes. "No way of knowing. Everyone gets a different high."

Deenie pulled her head back, and Louise took the cup away from her lips. "You haven't had enough," Louise said. She spoke in a gentle voice I'd only heard her use with her kids. And then, only in their most vulnerable moments.

Deenie shook her head. "I'm gonna sleep now." She closed her eyes and lay back.

I shook her gently. "Deenie. Wait. Can you tell me why were you outside?"

She didn't open her eyes. "I was outside? Snowin' outside."

I put my thumb and forefinger, which had to be like ice cubes, on her chin. "Why did you go outside?"

Her eyes barely opened. "Outside?" She started to close her eyes, then opened them again. "Walk. She held my hand. Lily of the valley."

Louise sucked in a quick breath.

I ignored the absurd phrase that I knew jumped at Louise. Mom wore lily of the valley scent. "Did someone take you outside? Leave you there?"

Deenie wrinkled her brow. "Wanted...but. Then...and okay. Wouldn't give me the red sweatshirt. And that's..." She drifted off.

I wagged her chin. "Deenie. Red sweatshirt. Someone in a red sweatshirt took you outside?"

She didn't open her eyes.

Aaron sounded musing. "Isn't that interesting. A person in a red sweatshirt. This seems significant."

Anna tucked the sleeping bag around her. "Sleep is probably the best thing for her."

I slapped her cheek, not hard, even though I wanted to. "Deenie. Wake up. Tell me."

She frowned and seemed to struggle to open her eyes. "Oh, Kate. Something to tell you. Something. Podcast. Pendergast. Pendergast."

Olivia nudged me aside and plopped another sleeping bag on top of Deenie. "How's that. Nice and snug?"

I shoved back. "What, Deenie?" I waggled her chin again. "Pendergast podcast? What's that mean?"

She let out a tired giggle. "Not Jesse. Not James." She laughed, ending in a cough.

Sean's voice boomed, way too loud. "Louise, did you say we're having beans? Did you grow them yourself?"

Louise didn't answer.

All my concentration narrowed to the cot. "Come on, Deenie. Stay with me. Tell me this, and then you can sleep it off."

Anna tapped my hand off Deenie's chin. "She really needs to rest. You can talk to her later."

Ford was quick to agree. "It'll wear off faster if you leave her alone and let her sleep."

Deenie opened her eyes wider than she'd done before, a playful glint to them. "Ford. See? First clue. Archer. Jesse James. We should have known." She closed her eyes.

"Deenie!" I shook her, pretty forcefully. "I don't understand."

Joyce tugged my shoulder. "For heaven's sake. Let the poor girl rest."

Deenie worked her jaw again, not opening her eyes. She whispered, "Jesse." Her lips pressed together, and she let out another sound, like an engine putter.

And then she relaxed deeply enough I checked her neck to feel the pulse and make sure she hadn't died. She started her not-so-gentle motorboat snore, one of the most welcome sounds I could imagine.

I sat back, and Poupon sidled close to me. I figured he wanted a little affection and reassurance that I remembered him. Apparently, he'd reverted to his old ways of ignoring me. With that chewed and sloppy paperback, he stretched out as close to Deenie's cot as possible. He grunted and set the book between his front paws, lowering his chin to rest on it. Maybe he planned on guarding Deenie.

I scratched both his ears until his eyes closed. "You're the best boy."

Louise tapped my shoulder and trod toward the door. "I could use your help with the beans."

No. Louise needed no help with the beans. But she definitely wanted me to follow her out.

When we got back to the pod, the camp light had died. Aaron's battery-powered light bulb was barely lit. It felt colder, but maybe that was because my core temperature had dropped during the time I spent outside with Deenie.

Maybe I'd been mistaken about Louise needing me to follow because she went to the beans and lifted the lid. Steam poured out, releasing the scent of ham and onions. "There are two quart jars of peaches in the bag in the basket."

I gave her a disbelieving grunt. "You're a magician. Holding out on us, huh?"

She kept stirring. "I didn't know if we'd be stuck here another night. I was holding back the peaches and the rest of the peanut butter, and the cookies, just in case. But I think the storm is dying down. They'll be out to get us tonight. Probably not until after supper, though."

She might be right. On the other hand, assuming we'd be okay, they might wait until morning. I did not crave being locked in here another night with a murderer.

She settled the lid back on the beans and turned to me, casting a glance out the door to the science room. "She got it right."

I felt a pang of excitement. "Deenie? Got what right?"

Again, she looked to make sure no one was listening. "Archer house. It was Frank and Jesse James's safe house. So you've got all this Jesse James stuff."

"I forgot about Archer house. But we knew Gold has a Jesse James connection. And Robert Ford killed Jesse James. What's new?"

"The ghost screen mentioned Archer and the H. That's Archer Haven." She was getting worked up.

"I don't get it."

Frustration built. "Deenie flat out told you. What was the last thing she said? Think about it."

"Damn it, Louise. I don't want to play games. Just tell me."

She lifted her chin in a stubborn way. "Her last word."

I had to think. "Jesse. She said Jesse."

Louise shot me that cat-with-the-canary grin. "Not Jesse. She said Jessup."

Jessup?

28

The name only vaguely tripped a familiar bone. Louise was cranking up my impatience to an eleven. "What about Jessup?"

She ground her hands onto her hips. "He's that guy that killed all those people." She stared at me as if I ought to shout *Eureka!*

"You're going to have to be more specific," I said.

She picked up the Mason jar with peaches, golden half domes swimming in light syrup. "Jimmy Jessup was one of those cult leaders. Like David Koresh in Waco. Or that guy, the Ruby Ridge one."

I didn't know. Cult leaders weren't my specialty.

"Or Jim Jones in Guyana," she offered.

I didn't slap her, but I was low on patience. "Stop it. I don't know. Tell me who Jimmy Jessup is."

She set the peaches down and flashed her eyes at me to show she thought I was being unreasonable and spoiling her fun. "Okay, so this guy, Jimmy Jessup, he grew up super poor. Like poverty where he didn't have shoes or enough to eat. And he got warped, felt like the world owed him something. But he was genius smart. So he's watching the cult leaders. Like the Bhagwan Shree Rajneesh, remember him?"

"Louise!" I yelled. And then it hit me. "You're a true crime fan. Like Deenie."

Louise shook her head in protest. "I'm not like Deenie. I'm not obsessed. I've listened to a couple of podcasts, that's all. Nothing big."

"Jimmy Jessup. What about him?"

She toyed with the peach jar. "I really don't remember all the details."

I wanted to jump across the room and grab her by the throat until she spilled it all. "You seemed to be doing pretty well up to now."

She stepped to the bean pot and lifted the lid, letting the steam escape. "I only listened to the first episode out of five. The Jimmy Jessup stuff all happened when I was a really little kid. You might not have been born yet."

"Whoever this guy was, someone wanted him dead. If Jesse Gold is Jimmy Jessup—"

Louise interrupted. "He has to be. Jesse is Jessup, James is Jimmy. It's his clever and sick play on his name."

"Let's say he is. We need more information about him to figure out who killed him." I pulled out my phone. "Damn it. I don't know how to research stuff without the internet."

She slammed the lid on the pot. "I know how we're going to find out."

I had to run to keep up with her as we flew from the science room. We popped back to the library, and I checked on Deenie. She lay on her side, snoring away. I felt her forehead, not sure why exactly. But her skin felt normal, so I assumed she'd sleep off her high and be okay. Still, I sent Ford a crusty look.

He ducked his head in a guilty way.

The others seemed to be passing the time the same as earlier. Olivia scribbled in her Moleskin notebook. Joyce sat in a padded chair and read while Kenneth dozed on the couch. Anna held her rigid posture with her Bible open in her lap, fingers splayed on the pages. She might have been praying when we entered, but now her gaze followed us.

Ford and Sean played cards. And Aaron stood at the same bookshelf along the back wall, a hardcover in his hands. Like the others, he watched Louise hustle toward the back.

So, that's where she was going. I should have thought of that. I gave Deenie one more quick assessment, then beat cleats after Louise.

By the time I reached the far corner, Louise already had the thick *Time-Life* book on the table and was flipping to the index. It was the book about

US crimes in the second half of the last century. She ran her finger down a column. "Jes...Jes...Jessup. Here it is."

She quickly fumbled through the slick pages and found the spot, spreading it before us like a butterfly pinned to a corkboard.

I slid a chair next to her, and we pored over it together.

"*O-M-G.*" Typical Louise, using the initials. Saying *God* outside of prayer or reverence would be too coarse for her. She might have a lot in common with Anna. "This is so much worse than I thought."

A harsh query slapped the back of my head. "What are you reading?"

I jerked at the sound of Olivia's voice. I'd been so absorbed I hadn't heard her approach.

Louise paused, hand on the page to mark her place, and looked up at Olivia. "Did you know?"

Olivia's eyes flicked to the book, then back at us. "Know what?"

Louise sounded insulted that Olivia made her state it. "That Jesse Gold was really Jimmy Jessup?"

Olivia's puzzled look wasn't convincing. "Who? As far as I know, Jesse Gold is some rich, racist, misogynistic asshole. I've never heard of Jimmy Jessup."

I scanned the library for the others. Since most were seated up front, even though the shelves were only chest-high, I couldn't see them. But my glance was unexpected enough to catch Aaron off guard. He spun away and lowered his head to his book. But he'd definitely been watching us.

I slammed the book shut and stood, hoisting it under my arm. "I think the beans are burning." I nodded at Olivia. "We'll eat as soon as we can get the room set up."

If Olivia hadn't stepped out of the way, I was prepared to trample over her.

Louise nearly ran me over when I stopped to check on Deenie again before we hotfooted it to the science room.

Louise seemed animated in a way I hadn't seen her since we were kids and we sprayed shaving cream into Diane's hand when she was asleep. Using an eagle's feather Mom had given one of us, we tickled Diane's nose. When she slapped her nose, the shaving cream went everywhere. Since we'd used the eagle's feather, which gave us an extra foot of distance from her, we had a head start and were down the stairs before she woke up enough to realize what happened. That hadn't turned out so well for us. First, because Diane hadn't reacted satisfactorily. No screaming. No chasing. No mention of it at all.

And secondly, because she'd gotten us both back. Even as a teen, Diane believed in the motto that revenge was best served cold. When she slept over at a friend's, she'd hidden alarm clocks all over our bedroom. They went off every half hour or hour all night long.

Louise panted, excited to be on the chase. "Olivia so did too know who Jimmy Jessup is. You didn't interview her. But now we know she's the one. We just don't know why."

We slipped into the pod, and I laid the book open on the planning desk while Louise pulled the lamp closer, its glow now nearly useless. I said, "I doubt it's Olivia. She wasn't even born when Jimmy Jessup was doing his dirty deeds."

"But maybe she's avenging someone."

We both bent down and read, each of us gasping or whooshing disbelief as we came across more shocking news. In a matter of ten minutes, we both sat back. Louise wore an expression that had to mirror mine, horror and disbelief. Trying to comprehend the immensity of his crimes and come to terms with the fact that a monster, even a dead monster, lay a few yards away from us.

He'd gathered his flock of believers and taken them to pristine forestland he'd convinced a farmer to let them use. In this conveniently remote forest, they'd created their utopia and, soon after, their mass grave.

"I can't believe this," Louise said, her voice wavering, like a kid who's been spooked by a campfire ghost story. "I knew Jimmy Jessup grew up poor. And that he somehow convinced people he was sent from God to show them how to live in love and unity."

I looked at the door to his room. "He was such a vile, crap-stained, horror of a person. I can't believe he got so many people to follow him. To believe he cared about them."

Louise followed my gaze. "He told them what they wanted to hear. That someone loved and valued them and that they were chosen by God to teach the world how to live. Everyone wants to feel special."

Had Louise ever felt special? The second of nine kids. Not the smartest of us, not the most popular. Not the pretty one. She'd been with Norm since, well, I couldn't remember when they'd started being a couple, but it would have been so early she'd never have been romanced. As solid and devoted as Norm was to Louise and their kids, he was hardly a Valentino. And then Louise launched into motherhood by the time she was twenty, where she'd put all her energy into her children. She might feel she'd always been in the background. And maybe she was.

Now was not the time for psychoanalysis. We needed to concentrate on the life and death of the devil Jimmy Jessup.

A community of three hundred or so people without running water and sewer would damage pristine forest. "And then starting the commune in northern California. How did he convince someone to give him that land? I can't imagine the mess they would have made of it."

Louise sat back with a dazed look. "He got them there and created these rituals. Drinking the juice to symbolize their being specially chosen by the leader."

"How brainwashed would you have to be to tip back grape juice laced with poison and not think twice?"

"First of all, they speculate the people didn't know they were being drugged. By the time he killed them, he'd already purged those who weren't true believers."

The article said the commune had a meeting and exiled a hundred people. Since there were no survivors of those who'd stayed, the people who'd been sent away assumed the ceremony where Jessup poisoned them all was some kind of unity celebration.

Louise sounded amazed. "The people who they kicked out thought the victims were probably rejoicing because they, among all those on the planet, had the true calling. Congratulating themselves on their faithfulness to God and Jessup. He was so devious."

I nodded. "He must have hatched his plan all along because he never even asked them for money. Though, it looks like some of them handed it over."

Louise caught my eye. "Like Joel Klein. Who gave over a million dollars." She ran her finger down the book to find the quote and read, "His parents, Benjamin and Eliana, confirmed Klein donated over one million dollars to Jessup to create a water and sewer system." She stopped and looked up at me. "That scum Jessup had no intention of using the money for that."

Still thinking of them as Kenneth and Joyce, I couldn't help glancing at the wall separating us from the library. "They have a good motive to get rid of Jesse Gold."

"I don't know what I'd do if someone killed my son." Louise glowered like a mother bear assessing a hunter. "I think I'd be capable of murder."

"But so many others had motives, too." I tapped the book. "The kidneys. I can hardly think of that without getting sick."

Neither of us spoke for a moment, and maybe Louise was imagining the scene, too. What the investigators had pieced together after the fact was that one hundred and eighty-six adults and children drank their homemade grape juice spiked with cyanide. They would have almost immediately realized their mistake, but the poison acted so fast, most died of respiratory failure where they stood.

And that was not the worst of it.

Those who had been ostracized and sent away earlier grew concerned when they hadn't run into any of the faithful recruiting in nearby towns. Jessup had an established system for rotating cult members out into the public to convince others to join Archer Haven. Not seeing them in the towns raised red flags. But the exiled people were afraid to return to Archer Haven because Jessup tended to punish those who disobeyed. And his punishments were violent and painful.

After two weeks, the exiled followers were able to roust law enforcement to check up on their former comrades.

The cops arrived at the camp that had once housed three hundred men, women, and children in crude cabins and yurts, with latrines dug several yards away. The whole place was abandoned. Not a soul stirred.

It was several more days until the horror was discovered.

A mass grave, dug with a backhoe rented supposedly to dig a septic system, filled with those who'd been left behind. One hundred eighty-six people, including thirteen children under the age of fifteen. The children's bodies had been left intact. The adults, however, hadn't been granted that dignity.

Even after almost three weeks of decomposing, it was obvious that organs had been sliced from the bodies. Kidneys, livers, corneas. Those were the most common.

Jessup and his cohorts had done their research and used cyanide, which didn't taint the organs. They'd worked quickly, removing and carting off the coolers of precious cargo. The network for distribution had been established early, with a few small planes whisking the organs to various clinics outside of the state, set up where desperate people were willing to cough up life savings for a chance outside the legal limits of medicine.

It had been an intricate operation run with precision. And those at the top had ample time to leave the country before the damage had been discovered.

The scope of the investigation revealed an organ-harvesting ring that involved several countries and many hospitals. It was intricate and ingenious, with hospitals, and therefore recipients, having no idea where their donated organs originated. Officials never found all the organs, and many surgeries were presumed to be successful.

But some, because of the long delays in using the organs, or the health of the donor, or any number of complications, resulted in more tragedy.

"And they never found him," Louise said, her attention again drawn to Gold's door.

"Until now."

She lowered her voice to a whisper. "The Kleins lost a son. Aaron's wife died from a kidney transplant. Sean said his sister died because she trusted someone and wanted to help him with his dream. Anyone of them could have killed Gold."

I nodded. "What about Anna, Olivia, and Ford? Do you suppose they have a connection, too?"

Louise narrowed her eyes in thought. "Anna is from the same area where Archer Haven is. Ford?"

I couldn't draw a line from Jessup to either Ford or Olivia. "I don't know."

She swallowed, probably her stomach as queasy as mine. "How do you suppose they found him and got him to come on this tour?"

I tried to put things together. "Gold said he was here for a business deal. Aaron suspected a Medicare scam, and I found a file in Gold's things that might confirm that. But the bird-watching tour? I don't know."

Louise's forehead crinkled in thought.

"The article said the authorities concluded that in the weeks it took for them to figure out what happened, Jessup had likely used false IDs to flee the country. They eventually quit searching. But he's been on most wanted lists for thirty years."

"Vietnam," Louise said. "Aaron and Ford both mentioned that."

"Hey." Ford's voice shot from the science room. "Are we about to eat? Kenneth's getting hungry."

Louise and I both jumped up. My heart thundered, and for the first time, I feared for our safety. I didn't know for certain who'd killed Jesse Gold, but between us, we were closing in on answers. Or more accurately, a murderer. Maybe Deenie had figured out something and been drugged and forced into the dangerous cold to silence her.

If someone killed once, it might be easier for them to kill again.

Louise answered with a casual tone, as if she had been hiding her emotions her whole life and was good at it. "It won't be too long."

His voice floated back to us. "Roger."

I stared at Louise as if she were nuts.

She turned to the bean pot. "Well, we can't starve them."

"Just don't let them know what we discovered." I grabbed a stack of plastic bowls and counted out spoons.

She slipped on mitten potholders. "They already know we've figured out Jesse Gold is Jimmy Jessup."

"I know." We needed to figure this out fast. I couldn't risk the next victim being Louise, Deenie, or me. Or all three of us. It might be risky, but I needed more information. "Cover for me. I'm going to search their luggage."

29

Louise wasn't happy about my plan to snoop through the luggage, but I hadn't given her a chance to argue because I grabbed the cutting board holding Aaron's light bulb and lunged for the Levines' door. Or more accurately the Kleins'.

Poupon scuttled from under the counter to join me. He wasn't much of an investigator, but he provided me a drop more courage just by being there.

I wasn't surprised to find the Kleins shared one suitcase for the two of them. I guessed Joyce, a.k.a. Eliana, organized their travel and that she ran their lives like a four-star general. She'd have a smaller overnight case that would be easy to lug in. And at least one bigger bag for the bulk of their belongings. Assuming we'd only be here overnight, she'd have had them bring in only this one, leaving the bigger bags in the van.

Poupon sat by the door like one of those ceramic dogs you see on front porches.

The room was cold, and the tip of my nose and fingers tingled. Digging through other people's things gave me the heebie-jeebies. We Foxes might have grown up stuffed together like clowns in a circus car, but we respected privacy. Pawing through luggage was a violation I wouldn't do if I didn't think it was necessary to protect Louise and Deenie, and me and Poupon, as well.

Joyce was a fan of lotions. There were several bottles and jars for various parts of her body, including separate potions for feet, hands, eyes, and neck. A slinky black negligée surprised me. Then I felt ashamed I'd assumed an older couple wouldn't appreciate a little romance. A few changes of underwear for them both, socks, and a couple of sweaters, nothing incriminating.

Rummaging through their cosmetic bags, I pulled out two orange prescription bottles. Hadn't Joyce made a point of asking Anna to bring the orange sweater? There was no orange sweater anywhere. But one of the bottles was empty. I leaned close to the light to see.

Digoxin. Grandma Ardith had a heart problem and she took digoxin. If Kenneth needed this for his heart, why would the bottle be empty?

The other bottle, also for Kenneth, was Ambien.

Seeing nothing else interesting, Poupon and I started out of the room.

Wait. A Dixie cup sat on the teacher's desk. A thin layer of dark liquid pooled in the bottom. I hurried over and picked it up, giving it the sniff test. "Wine," I told Poupon, even though he didn't seem interested. Coupled with the footprint in Jessup's room, this shone an interesting light on Joyce.

We hurried from their room to the social studies room, where Aaron and Sean stayed. It was equally frigid, and I shivered. A hot mug of tea to wrap my fingers around would sure feel good right now. Not as great as getting out of this school and this impossible situation.

Poupon kept guard by the door again. He was turning into a pretty good deputy.

Sean used a duffel, not much bigger than a gym bag. His belongings were stuffed in the opening and spilling out the sides. Outdoorsy kind of clothes that all could use a few spins on the heavy-duty cycle. I didn't see anything pointing to him as a murderer.

Aaron's bag was airplane carry-on size. He used those net packing cubes. Everything rolled and fitted into the proper place. Underwear and T-shirts along with socks, two pairs of khaki slacks, two soft pullover sweaters, all in one side of the bag. I unzipped the other side and was not surprised to find a few *Popular Science* magazines. His bathroom bag of slick nylon contained the usual items. But along with them was a bottle of clear liquid. I unscrewed the lid and gave it a tentative sniff. Almonds.

Could that be some treatment for his hair? I stuffed it into my shirt pocket along with the bottles from the Levines' room. I hadn't reconciled myself to rifling through people's private things, and I didn't seem to be gaining any new information, but I had one more room to go.

"'Spose Louise can keep them occupied for a few more minutes?" I asked Poupon, who showed no interest in advising me.

"One more," I said, ushering him out of the social studies room and into the math room to paw through Olivia's and Anna's belongings. What a dumpster-diving raccoon I'd become.

Anna kept her clothes in a large, tapestried carpetbag type of carrier. Some flowy green-gray items that might have been scarves or skirts or tops, I couldn't tell. She stored her bathroom items in a quart zip bag, the kind that can go through airport security. Not much there, especially if you compared it to what Joyce brought. A faux leather zippered pouch about the size of my fist was at the bottom of her bag. I opened it, and my heart gave a nervous bump to find a vial of insulin and a handful of disposable syringes.

The same type I'd found in Gold's room after his murder.

Anna hadn't taken her sleeping bag to the library last night, and it lay in a heap. For no reason except frustration at getting more questions and no answers, I picked it up. Something rolled out, and I thought it might be a lump of clothes she used for a pillow. But it had more heft. I bent over to look.

"Okay," I said to Poupon. "This is interesting." I lifted Jesse Gold's camera case by the shoulder strap. "What's Anna doing with this?"

Olivia had a hard-sided suitcase covered in travel stickers. The clothes she'd worn yesterday were jumbled next to her bag, and the suitcase was closed. I lifted one side to see everything fairly neat and organized. Nothing extraordinary in her things, just clothes and cosmetics. With care, I eased one side over to close the bag.

"So far, not much to go on." I said it out loud, maybe hoping Poupon would come up with some insight.

He had no response, but that was typical. He did let out an enormous sigh to tell me he wanted to be home.

"If we make it out of here, I promise to let you sleep on the couch for a week." Not that he didn't camp on the couch whenever he wanted, but this time, I wouldn't harass him about it.

I pushed myself to stand and reached for the light I'd set on the floor next to Olivia's bag. Something caught my eye, and I crouched down again. Tilting my head to the side so I could get a better look at the sticker on the side of Olivia's bag, I leaned in.

"I'll be danged." The sticker featured tropical greenery, and in bright yellow letters splashed across, it said *Vietnam*.

30

When Poupon and I slipped back into the pod, Louise was stirring the beans. She turned to me. "I can't hold them off any longer. They keep checking on supper."

"It's okay," I said. I didn't know how I was going to proceed, but time was running out.

I grabbed a plate of sliced bread and started to follow Louise out of the science room. A sudden thought struck me. Last night as we were settling in for bed, two people had come into the science room. On a hunch, I scurried to the specimen shelf. In the dusky light from the overhead bulb, I spotted something. Thank goodness for Mrs. Brown's obsessive streak. One jar was slightly off center from the others. I snatched it up, opened the lid, and sniffed.

"Exactly what I thought." I pocketed the jar along with the other things I'd collected, making the front of my flannel shirt bulky, and took off for the library. Poupon, looking disgusted with his lot in life, trailed behind.

I set the bread on the table and went to check on Deenie.

With Deenie passed out in what I hoped was blissful oblivion, I patted her down gently. "Where's her phone?"

Louise cast her searching mom-eye on everyone. Joyce, Anna, and Kenneth were gathered on the couch and chair. Anna and Joyce both rose, maybe intending to help us with the food. Aaron and Olivia sat across from each other at a work table in the middle of the library. Ford and Sean slouched in comfy chairs close to the door.

Louise had five kids to perfect her withering stare that coaxed confessions. Unfortunately, it didn't have the same effect on the birders as it did on her children. Which is to say, no one coughed up any answers.

Joyce stopped a few steps away from us and folded her arms in a challenge.

I stood, getting tired of this bunch of yahoos. They acted as if they couldn't stand each other, and yet, they all provided alibis for everyone. And still, they were quick to accuse the next one of murder. I couldn't get a handle on their game. If there even was one.

Olivia, Ford, and Aaron had a connection with Vietnam, where Jesse Gold was hiding out. Anna had hid the camera case. Maybe she thought the tablet had been inside, but it had fallen out in Gold's room. Aaron, Joyce, and Kenneth all had clear motives.

Deenie's phone might hold some clue. We needed to find it.

The desk seemed as good as any place to begin the search. "Check there." I spoke to Louise and pointed to Binda's desk. I strode to the conversation grouping and ripped the cushion off the chair Joyce had been using.

She rushed to me. "What are you doing?"

I yanked the cushion from where Anna had perched. "Looking for Deenie's phone."

Louise raised her voice so I could hear it across the room. "Not here. I'll look in the card catalog."

Joyce fluttered around me, her voice shrill. "This is insane. You can't rip up furniture because your friend is careless with her phone. She misplaced it, like all people do from time to time."

I gently nudged her out of the way and addressed Kenneth. "Can you sit up, please. I'd like to check underneath you."

"This is an outrage," Joyce complained predictably. "He isn't feeling well. This is elder abuse."

Kenneth didn't change his bemused expression and made a feeble effort to sit up. I reached out to help him.

Joyce slapped my hand away. "Don't touch him."

Anna appeared by Joyce's side. "Let me help."

Joyce folded her arms again. It was a gesture as common to her as hands on hips was to Louise. Maybe when you experience so much frustration in life, you find your signature stance. All Joyce's indignation hugged into a tight ball of fury that was clear in her smooth, tight voice. "This. Is. An. Outrage."

I ignored her and rifled under the middle cushion and one end. Then waited for Anna to help Kenneth reposition himself so I could check under that cushion. Nothing.

Joyce took Kenneth's arm and, together with Anna, helped settle him. "Are you happy now?" It sounded like the pop of gunfire.

It wouldn't do any good to explain to her that if the whole troop of monkeys would start to cooperate with me, none of this would be necessary. Instead, I tried to open my mind, imagining likely hiding places, and did a slow three-sixty, considering the endless nooks and crannies of the shelves. One possibility dropped in front of me, and I walked to where Aaron had been standing earlier holding a heavy hardcover.

It took a second to home in on the section where he'd been and then notice one book slightly pushed out from the rest. I tugged it free. "Isn't this interesting?" I held up Deenie's phone.

Louise slammed the drawer of the card catalog she'd been searching. "What is it doing there?"

"I don't know. Aaron, what is it doing there?" I marched across the room, holding the phone up to him.

Aaron widened his eyes in a shocked expression. "I have no idea. I absolutely pulled that book out. It's an old examination of Darwin that I hadn't seen since I'd been in college. I was amazed a library would keep something so out of date. But I never hid that phone there. I can't tell you if it was tucked on the back of the shelf when I returned the book."

His eyes didn't flick around while he spoke. He seemed genuinely puzzled. Lying or not? I couldn't tell.

I was reluctant to accuse him or accept his explanation, so I made my skepticism plain. "I see."

Louise grabbed the phone from my hand, apparently not afraid I'd swat her for stealing it, which I wanted to do but didn't. She held the power button, and we stared at the screen as it booted up. She whipped her head to me. "What's her password?"

Why would I know her password? "Dad's birthday?"

She gave me a disdainful look. "Seriously?"

"Well, I don't know her birthday. I'm not a codebreaker."

The others hadn't offered any explanation of why the phone ended up there, who'd snatched it, or a password suggestion. Not that I'd expected any help. Even though no one acted overtly interested, I swore the air thickened with tension.

Anna, Joyce, and Kenneth weren't paying any attention to us that I could tell. Ford, Sean, and Olivia kept their eyes on us like we were performing the next installment of some TV crime thriller, maybe as if they'd like to turn the channel. Only Aaron edged closer and focused on Deenie's phone.

Louise slid the phone into her back pocket. "I'll hang on to this until she wakes up."

I hated for Louise to stow that phone. There was something on it that Deenie thought was important. And someone went to great lengths to make sure she never found it. If the murderer came after the phone, I'd rather they come for me and not Louise.

Louise clapped her hands, a la the kindergarten teacher, Mrs. Wilder. "Supper's ready. Let's eat."

31

Supper sounded as enticing as covering myself with honey and sitting in a red ant pile. And even if I did want to eat, the last thing I needed in my stomach was a mess of ham and beans. But here we sat, gathered around the library tables, steaming bowls of beans in front of us.

I'd speared a peach half onto my plate, and now I poked my fork at the shiny surface.

No one spoke, and we all stared at our food.

Anna broke the silence. "Shall we say grace?"

Louise brightened at that. "What a good idea. Would you do the honors?"

Anna deferred. "Maybe Aaron can."

He dipped his chin and let his gaze wander around the table to the others, giving them each a look of what appeared to be tenderness. "For this we're about to receive, we give thanks."

A buzz made me jerk upright, the vibration in my back pocket alerting me to a surprise phone call.

Everyone riveted their attention on me.

I pushed back from the table and slipped my phone from my pocket, glancing at the caller ID as I did so. I punched it on and held it to my face. "Zoe. I didn't realize we had signal again."

She shouted, the sound of a roaring engine in the background. "They just got the tower back online. So, hey, how are you guys holding up in there?"

I had my back to the rest, and I looked over my shoulder. "We're, well, we're hoping you'll get us dug out soon."

"Yeah. One of the county plows broke down already. But the other is going strong. She's going to plow the highways to the county line, but the school is next, I promise. Still, it's gonna be a while, I think."

The others made no bones about watching me.

I turned my back to them. "You might want to call Trey. There's been a death here."

"Shit," she fired back at me. "That's all we need. Cause?"

With a lowered voice, I said, "Unclear. But the sooner we can get the body to the medical examiner, the better."

Zoe sighed. "Okay. I'll see what I can do."

I hung up, and Olivia jumped all over me. "What did she say? Are they digging us out? How long?"

She must have heard Zoe's voice, at least enough to detect a woman on the other end. She had gathered the gist.

"They're working on it. A few more hours, I think."

Joyce looked relieved. "Finally. We'll get back to civilization. I, for one, cannot wait to get to a heated hotel with a hot shower. Kenneth will be ecstatic to sleep in a real bed."

Sean gave a nod to Louise, a smile breaking through his dark beard. "One thing I can say, though, is the food's been all right."

I was sure he meant to give her a compliment, but *all right* wouldn't sit well with Louise.

She surprised me again by acknowledging what he said in the spirit it was given and nodded back with appreciation. "Thank you."

Aaron didn't seem to share the relief of the rest of them. He studied me with a somber expression. "Will we be allowed to continue our tour?"

Louise snapped her attention to me, and we shared a glance before I said, "I've got the interviews. I'll give them to the sheriff and the state patrol and let them decide."

Ford's alarmed gaze flicked around the table. "But, you know, it looks like Gold gave himself an overdose. Right? Isn't that what you said?"

Aaron hadn't taken his eyes from me. He gave me the focus of an eagle zeroing in on a mouse. "No, I don't believe she said that."

Sean jumped in. "If you think someone killed Gold, then who and why?"

Louise couldn't help herself from correcting him. "Jimmy Jessup. He wasn't Jesse Gold. And we know you all knew him."

Way to tip our hand, Louise.

It was as if Mr. Freeze walked into the room and shot his gun. There was a definite scent of doom falling into the library. No one spoke or moved.

I smiled at everyone, hoping it would look unconcerned. We could do all the accusing and detaining we wanted to do after we were rescued. But we needed to survive this first. Not knowing who murdered Jessup and how desperate they'd be, we needed to play it cool.

I shrugged. "We're not law enforcement. Just three citizens, and Deenie won't remember anything. I don't even need to tell them I've interviewed anyone. We can let the authorities decide cause of death." I lifted my spoon as if I washed my hands of the issue. "And as you said, a case could be made for an overdose."

Olivia pushed her thick black hair behind her ears, and her intelligent eyes focused on me as if adding up a column of numbers. "Except you don't believe that."

Sean spoke louder. "What about the black SUV? The person in the red hoodie. They probably got into the school. Killed him. Then left."

I dipped my spoon into the beans. "Another theory." Threat grew around me like wolves circling a campfire.

Maybe Louise felt the tension building in the room. She sounded too cheerful. "This might be the best mess of beans I've cooked in years. The ham hock came from our Christmas ham, and I seasoned the heck out of that. My family, well, I don't know if I told you I have five kids—"

Anna interrupted. "I've been smelling these cooking all day. Such a comfort. I can't wait to eat." She filled a spoon and raised it, pausing while she watched me.

Maybe I was paranoid, but I felt everyone's eyes on me, as if weighing their next moves based on my actions. It felt downright creepy.

Sean used that same enthusiastic tone as when he wanted to convince me about the possibilities of Gold's death. "The food here has been awesome. We should dig in." Like Anna, he lifted his full spoon and focused on me.

I wasn't the queen who demanded no one could eat until I did, but they seemed to expect me to ring the opening bell, so I leaned over my bowl—a sure sign I was not royalty—and opened my mouth.

Before the beans hit my lips, someone slapped my hand and the spoon went flying. "Huh?"

Hot bean juice splashed my wrist and sleeve, and I immediately wanted to punch the attacker. Good thing I was an adult who could control my reactions.

Deenie stood over me, flushed, her eyes intense like bull on the fight. "It's poisoned. Like they did to me."

She sank into a chair next to me, panting as if she'd run a race.

Louise jumped up. "The ham was frozen. There's no chance it's spoiled."

While the others seemed paralyzed and looked at each other as if holding silent but urgent conversations, I reached into my flannel shirt pockets and deposited my treasures on the table. "Like maybe how Jesse Gold's wine was poisoned?"

Joyce slammed her palm on the table, face etched in fury. "You went through our things? How dare you!"

Deenie leaned her elbows on the table and propped her chin on her palms. She was slowly coming back to life. Her eyes had lost much of their dazed glint. "Poison worked on Gold, and it damn sure worked on me. Why wouldn't the murderer use it on you, now that you're getting close to figuring out who killed Jessup?"

"You were poisoned?" Louise asked. "We thought you used Ford's marijuana to get high."

Deenie glared at her. "Uh, no. I had a cup of coffee. And then it all got weird. Last I remember is thinking I should come get you guys, but I got lost."

Louise huffed. "In a circular hallway?"

Deenie shrugged. "I must have been hallucinating, because I swear someone in a red hoodie said they'd help. I'm sure all the talk of the red hoodie person put the idea in my head. And then, I guess I ended up outside."

Louise gasped. "Someone tried to kill you!"

There was a general round of denials, and Aaron spoke. "No one tried to kill you. Maybe you accidentally drank Ford's coffee."

Deenie closed her eyes, clearly not ready to fight about it.

I pointed to the items. "Ambien. Digoxin. Syringe."

Deenie reached for the specimen jar. "What is this?"

I smiled. "I think it's a cross section of some animal's artery."

She curled her lip in disgust.

"Open it," I said. "Give it a smell."

With a skeptical scowl toward me, she unscrewed the lid and tentatively sniffed. "I don't smell anything."

"You would if it were formaldehyde."

She gave me a puzzled look.

I picked up the bottle of clear liquid from Aaron's bag and started to remove the lid. "Not sure what this is."

Aaron shouted, "No. Don't touch that."

More gingerly than I'd picked it up, I set it next to the others. "What is it?"

Aaron shifted uncomfortably in his chair. Although he kept his face placid, I could sense his struggle to stay in control by the firm set of his jaw. "I distilled it from almonds. It's a potent poison."

Did that make him the murderer? Or was he a decoy? Or something else entirely? "Why would you have poison in your suitcase?"

He looked embarrassed. "I'm terrified of rats. I know it seems ludicrous, but I can't shake the fixation. When I was a kid, we lived in an apartment building in Chicago, and the rats would come in at night. Once I woke up with one on my face. When I travel, I set out poison. It's the only way I can sleep."

Deenie and I exchanged a look as neutral as we could manage. It wasn't looking good for Aaron. He was the last one to have contact with Gold that we knew about. The phone was hidden behind a book he was handling. And now this.

Louise gave him a compassionate sigh. "It's beyond horrible what happened to your wife. I'm sure the courts will take extenuating circumstances into account."

I held up my finger. "What about Gold's camera case I found in Anna's things?"

Anna threw her head back as if I'd hit her. "What camera case? I've got nothing to do with that."

"Sure you don't," I said with sarcasm, although I only had one guess why she'd have it. "You took the case because you knew Gold kept his tablet there, and you didn't want us to find out you'd been sending him death threats."

Louise's mouth dropped open. "So it's Anna?"

That would be too easy, though. "Not so fast. I'd like to ask Joyce a question. Why were you having a glass of wine with Gold before he died?"

Her jaw dropped open in a most inelegant Joyce way. "I, uh. I didn't get enough at dinner. I knew he had more, and so I asked if he'd mind if we opened another bottle."

Louise's voice showed her incredulity. "You drank with him? Alone?"

Deenie propped her cheek on her hand and said, "And then you killed him."

"That's preposterous."

I pushed my bowl away. "There's still something missing."

"Maybe this will help." Louise pulled Deenie's phone from her back pocket and set it on the table, pushing it to Deenie.

A little life came back in her eyes as she grasped it and turned it on. "Oh. I forgot about that. Wait 'til you hear this."

Olivia suddenly pushed back from the table. "Kenneth looks like he's tired. We should probably help him back to the couch."

Nice try. "He looks fine to me." And he did look fine. Actually, better than fine.

Deenie swiped, punched, then set the phone on the table with the speaker on.

Olivia made a grab for the phone, but Louise was quicker. She'd had nearly twenty years of keeping half an eye on her kids, who might reach for skillet handles on hot stoves, run in front of a charging horse, smack the sibling sitting next to them, or do any of a million stupid or unexpected moves.

You couldn't blame Olivia. She had no idea of how Mom Superpowers could translate into the world of murder investigations.

A jazzy tune heralded the opening of a podcast. "The redwood forests of California boast beautiful landscapes unrivaled anywhere in the world. They're also known for drawing more than their share of murderers. One of the most evil of these killers enticed over three hundred people to join him in his vision of a loving utopia. But his lies would result in the death and mutilation of more than half of those dreamers. And then he simply vanished in a puff of toxic smoke. What happened to the mourning families he left behind? And what became of this country's most notorious monster? Join me now and for the next four episodes of Crime Chronicles as we tell the tragic tale of the Butcher in the Redwoods, Jimmy Jessup."

Louise and I gaped at Olivia. Deenie eyed her with a cagey grin. The others glanced nervously around the room.

Olivia closed her eyes and inhaled and exhaled deeply in surrender as we heard her voice from the telephone speaker.

"This is Liv Pendergast. And this is Crime Chronicles." More jazzy music blared before Deenie reached up and tapped it off.

She pointed at Olivia. "I knew I'd heard your voice before. And I listened to that whole series on Jessup, except that was when I was going through a divorce and moving and nothing was sticking in my head at the time."

Louise pointed at Olivia. "I started listening to that, too. Only got through the first episode."

Deenie nodded enthusiastically at Louise. "Wasn't it great? I mean, how could you not have listened to more?"

Louise frowned. "I intended to get back to it, but I never seemed to find the time. So, now we know, Olivia killed Jesse Gold. But why?"

Deenie rubbed her forehead, maybe still a little groggy. "That's just it.

She's got no real motive, right? She'd want a good ending to her podcast, and if she murdered him, it would cause too much scrutiny."

Olivia flopped back in her chair. "Are you stupid? I didn't kill Gold. I'm a podcaster and a writer. I'm not a murderer."

"Says you," Louise shot back.

"I agree," Deenie said.

I should probably put a stop to all of this, but I was curious how the birders would react.

Joyce spoke up. "Of course Olivia didn't kill Gold. It was Aaron. As I told you earlier."

Aaron whipped his head to Joyce. "How could you say that? I didn't kill Gold. It was obviously Anna."

Anna gasped. "That's crazy. I have no reason to kill him. We all know it was Ford."

Ford snorted, as if she'd told a joke. It seemed a good guess that he'd been sampling his tincture again. "Gold probably deserved to die, but it wasn't me. I'm thinking it was Joyce."

Sean was combative. "Based on what? I would think it's clear to everyone that Gold was not murdered. He died of an overdose, administered by himself."

I held up a finger. "Except he was left-handed, and the injection was in his left arm, meaning he would have had to give himself a shot with his right hand."

Olivia spoke as though we were all idiots. "It was the person in the black SUV. The person in the red hoodie. Look around. None of us are capable of murder. We didn't even know Jesse Gold was Jimmy Jessup. And we all saw the SUV following us. All of us, even Gold, was suspicious of the person in the hoodie."

Louise's face was stony, obviously buying Olivia's story with the same faith as when the twins told her they weren't the ones who broke the kitchen window.

Deenie shook her head at the crew as if they all disappointed her.

I pushed back from the table. "It was clever of you all to manufacture the phantom SUV and red hoodie suspect. But I think you can admit to that fantasy."

Ford gave a grunt of protest. "Uh-uh. That part is the truth."

Before I could answer, there was a click and pop, then the lights in the library winked and went out.

There was a flurry at the far end of the table, like someone moving quickly. A chair tipped over, and Joyce screamed.

32

In the inky black of the library, it sounded like Louise jumped to her feet. "The generator isn't supposed to go out."

Without the juice supplying the library, it was darker than Wind Cave, a place we'd stop on our way back from camping trips to the Black Hills when we were kids, where the pitch black scared the crap out of Michael and Douglas, though they wouldn't admit it. I couldn't see a knife if it was thrust at my throat.

"I'll get the lamp from the science room." Deenie fumbled next to me. She knocked a bowl, and it tumbled to the carpet, splashing my jeans with beans. "Dang."

Some slight stirring and murmurs came from the others, but nothing that suggested anyone was making a run for it. I stood still, braced to intercede, feeling like I ought to sense if someone tried to sneak away.

The lights blinked back on, and Anna gasped.

Louise had that look on her face that made the twins cower in their sneakers—and scaring them was a feat.

Kenneth leveled a pistol at me, his vacant and benign expression replaced with sharp determination. "You should have let it go. Declared Jesse Gold's death an accidental overdose. You didn't need to dig into his identity or why I wanted him dead."

Deenie snapped her fingers. "I knew there was something up with you."

Louise agreed with her. "The way you tucked into the sloppy joes wasn't like the feeble old man you pretended to be."

Poupon showed the first inkling of interest. He had taken one of his quirky likings to Kenneth.

Maybe I shouldn't trust Poupon's judgment, but what else did I have to go on? "You're not going to shoot me," I said to Kenneth.

The others stayed in their places. It was possible they hadn't realized Kenneth had been faking his disability. But I doubted that. My guess was that they knew more than they were letting on. But him drawing a gun might be a twist they hadn't expected.

Joyce rose from her chair in solidarity with her husband. "I wouldn't test him, if I were you."

I started to speak, but the lights flickered again. Before anyone could take a breath, the lights went out, and we were plunged under a black shroud.

"For pity's sake," Louise uttered in irritation. "I knew the contractor the district used wasn't worth a darn. He promised us this generator was top of the line."

There was a bit more rustling at the other end of the table. Poupon let out a low growl. He might think I was in danger and wanted to protect me, but that would be a reach.

I used my most authoritative tone. "No one move."

Without warning, the lights popped back on.

Again, Anna gasped.

Louise's face grew even more threatening.

Deenie's eyes widened in surprise.

I wasn't all that shocked to see Olivia holding the gun on me.

She trembled slightly, which probably annoyed her. "Kenneth was right."

"You mean Benjamin," Deenie said.

Olivia flicked her gaze to Deenie. "Whatever. You should never have poked your nose into this."

"Are you going to shoot us?" I asked. "How will you explain that?"

Before she could shoot first and work out the details later, the lights popped off again.

This time the rustling was louder and more intense. The blackout didn't last long.

When the lights came back on, Louise held the gun pointing at the ground. She inspected it. "They didn't take the safety off." She shoved it in the front pocket of her baggy jeans. Exactly as I'd seen her do with items she'd snatched out of her kids' hands.

"That's because they were never going to shoot us." I spoke with a confidence I hadn't quite believed before Louise's action.

"How do you know that?" Louise asked.

"Because Kenneth and Olivia aren't killers. None of them are."

I was met with stony stares from the phony birders.

I could lay out the scenario, but not being a big golden-age mystery fan, the joy would be lost on me. "Deenie, would you like to do the honors?"

She seemed startled, gave it a second, then nodded with solemnity.

"Everyone, please be seated." I kept my eyes on all of them in case I'd read them wrong and someone actually would get violent.

Deenie's eyes sparkled, a good sign that she was coming back to life. While the others begrudgingly took their seats around the table, she stood and started to pace at the front of the room.

"Benjamin and Eliana Klein. Jimmy Jessup lured your son, Joel, into his plan, finagled a million dollars from him, and, in the end, murdered him with the others."

Eliana clenched her teeth and spoke in a clipped tone. "How did you find out?"

Deenie grinned. "Your real names? Listen, you should never underestimate Kate Fox."

The older couple clasped hands, Eliana looking like she wanted to shoot me, Benjamin with that mildly lost look.

Deenie continued. "Aaron Fields. Your wife tragically died from receiving a stolen kidney in an illegal scam."

Aaron's voice was a low rumble. "She had so much to live for."

Still pacing, Deenie stopped behind the man with the green beanie. "Sean Murray. I remember your interview for the podcast. Your sister,

Molly, had just graduated from high school. She was going to start college with the dream of being a social worker. But Jimmy Jessup convinced her that living at Archer Haven would give her the opportunity to change the world to a more loving place. So young and trusting. You and your parents didn't know where she'd gone, and you searched for her for months. It wasn't until her body was identified by the authorities that you knew what happened."

Sean dropped his head, his voice snaking out in a quiet mumble. "My parents never really recovered."

"Anna," Deenie said.

Anna jerked as if poked. She sat upright, her hands in her lap, clasped so tight it looked like they might shatter.

"Your father, Manuel Ortiz, owned the land where Jimmy Jessup located Archer Haven."

Anna's eyes shone with hatred in her pale face. She brushed her hair back and spit out her words. "Papa believed in the idea of an egalitarian society. He was happy to let Jessup have the land for his utopia. But after... when Papa found out what Jessup had done? It was more than he could bear. He took cyanide, the same poison that killed all those innocent people. He died a horrible death. And the state confiscated his land."

Deenie turned her attention to Olivia's challenging glare. "Liv Pendergast. Your fascination with true crime and unsolved cases drew you to the missing Jimmy Jessup. I'm not sure how you got involved with this."

Sean cleared his throat. "I can tell you. Liv interviewed family members of the victims. We met three years ago and had an instant connection."

Olivia's face performed an amazing transformation when she and Sean made eye contact. A glow of peace and kindness fell across her like a silk scarf. It was a part of her she'd hinted at when she'd pet Poupon or spoke with Louise. "Sean and I were married last year."

He didn't take his eyes off her. "And we have a daughter. Molly. Named after my sister. She's six months old now and is crawling."

Louise let out an *aw* sound. "Congratulations. Enjoy her, because the time goes by so fast."

Deenie tapped her chin and considered Ford. "I'm not sure how you fit in here."

Louise raised her hand. "Oh, I know. Ford is Jimmy Jessup's son. He's here because Jessup abandoned Ford's mother. With Jessup's money, she might have had better options and not died young."

Tears glistened in Ford's eyes. "You should have known her. She was so funny and kind."

"How did you know that?" Deenie asked Louise.

Louise patted Ford's hand. "In the *Time-Life* book, they said Jessup had a son named Dylan. Jessup left his family behind when he started Archer Haven. Ford said the same thing when you interviewed him."

Ford nodded. "I'm Dylan, but Mom changed my name to her maiden name because she never wanted anyone to know who my father was. He always had a thing for Jesse James, you know, naming that horrible place Archer Haven and then choosing Jesse for his alias. Ford seemed like a good twist."

Deenie looked them all over. "Every one of you had incentive to murder Jimmy Jessup. What I can't figure out is how you all ended up on this trip and who killed him."

Benjamin had slumped in his chair. He no longer wore that lost expression, but he looked every bit as weak as he had all along.

Eliana sat close to him, still holding his hand. "It was me. Jessup robbed us of our light. Stole so many good souls from so many loving hearts. I couldn't stand for him to survive any longer."

Olivia spoke up. "No. It was me. I started investigating for my podcast. One of Jessup's accomplices in the organ-stealing scheme, Dirk Black, got caught and convicted. He was being released, and he hoped that by talking to me he might get someone interested in doing a movie or something. Black is a real piece of shit."

Deenie added, "Oh, I remember him. He was so gross, talking about how he never planned the murders but was brought in after the fact. He made it sound like he was being heroic in helping fly the organs to different sites for the people who needed them."

Olivia curled her lip in disgust. "Black isn't very bright, probably the reason he got caught. He was with Jessup from the beginning. He was affiliated with the organ thieves, luring desperate people in developing countries in by promising them jobs and a new life in other countries. Then he and the rest of that gang tricked the poor people, stole their organs, and abandoned them. It goes on all the time. Somehow, Jessup found Black, used him to hook up with—" Here she stopped and swallowed, as if pushing down nausea. "Distributors, for lack of a better term. Dirk Black was the only one they ever caught."

It took me a moment to imagine the logistics of harvesting so many organs, getting them on ice, and taking them to clandestine clinics all over the country within hours.

Aaron looked ill. "According to Black, they used a veterinarian to do the extractions. He claimed the vet was from Mexico. Who knows? They never found him."

Olivia continued. "Black dropped a few hints that he might be able to contact Jessup. I didn't follow up with him then because I assumed he was trying to string me along."

"But something changed?" I asked.

She slipped her hair behind her ears, and her gaze softened when she looked at her husband. "I met Sean and learned about the devastation Jessup had caused. When the podcast aired, Eliana and Benjamin contacted me."

Eliana took up from there. "We brainstormed and finally came up with a plan to use Black to bait Jessup."

Olivia interrupted. "After so much time, Jessup got less careful, and with a few clues from that idiot, not to mention a lot of money the Kleins kicked in for bribes and investigators, we were finally able to track Jessup to Vietnam."

Louise surprised me by asking, "Is there extradition with Vietnam? I mean, why not go to the authorities when you found him?"

"No extradition," Olivia said.

Eliana's lip curled. "The government wouldn't give us justice, anyway."

I pointed at her. "You set up a phony Medicare scam to draw him in."

Eliana's mouth twitched as if she were tempted to smile. "I looked up scams about Medicare and imitated them. Jessup was sloppy about the details. He couldn't resist the easy money, though. We lured him to the States and told him the bird-watching tour would be our cover while we finalized the plans."

Deenie's mouth opened a bit, and she looked completely drawn into the tale. Louise slowly shook her head, practically mesmerized.

Aaron's bass took up the thread. "Before all of that, Olivia contacted me for the podcast."

Deenie looked thoughtful. "I don't remember you from the show."

He acknowledged that. "Out of an abundance of caution to protect my children. I didn't mind my name getting out, but I didn't want anyone near my family. They don't remember much about their mother, and I've tried hard to make sure their memories are about her life and not her death."

"How did you end up in Vietnam?" Louise asked.

Eliana broke in. "Me. When Olivia found Jessup's trail and located him in Hanoi, I contacted others and concocted a plan. Benjamin and I have nothing to spend our money on since we have no children or grandchildren. We sent Aaron over to get close to Jessup. And Dylan was there for support and backup. We had to get Jessup over here and to a place where his death would seem accidental."

Aaron said, "Using the Kleins' money, we bought off Gold's assistant, and I was able to get hired as his replacement. From there, it was my job to make the travel arrangements and get him to Nebraska."

Eliana gave a rueful chuckle. "We picked the most isolated place we thought we might convince Jessup to travel. We were going to take him to the top of the Scottsbluff Monument and shove him off."

Yikes. That seemed harsh. And not foolproof. But it wouldn't be hard to make it look like an accident.

Anna spoke with authority she hadn't demonstrated earlier. She said to me, "You already know there is no Flock Watch Tours. But Jessup bought into Aaron's supposed research and the fake website I set up. It was a matter of acquiring the van."

Louise spoke to Anna. "You're a caretaker for Benjamin."

Anna nodded. She cast a warm look at the Kleins. "For the past six months. He has good days and bad. But this trip has been good for him. Until now."

She smiled at Benjamin, then back to me she said, "If you accuse anyone of murder, it will ruin so many lives. Good people who have already been through so much tragedy at the hands of a monster."

Eliana sounded ready to fight. "I confess. I did it. When we couldn't make it to Scottsbluff, I decided to end it here. I wanted to drug Jessup's wine. But he threw it up. I was afraid enough poison hadn't gotten into his system, so I injected him with more to make sure he didn't survive."

Deenie looked dubious.

Louise said flat out, "I don't believe that."

I shoved my chair back and held my hand toward Deenie's chair to indicate she should sit.

Even though I hated Agatha Christie's detective Hercule Poirot's habit of dissecting the crime in front of the suspects, explaining everything in the end, this time it seemed inevitable I'd need to. "Eliana killed Jessup."

Louise gasped.

"And so did Aaron, Sean, Dylan, Anna, and Olivia. Even Benjamin had a hand in it," I finished.

Louise raised her eyebrows to encourage me to continue.

"None of you are stone-cold killers. Maybe the original plan had been for all of you to shove him off the monument and make it look like an accident. That way you'd all share the blame. But the blizzard stranded you here. Still, not one of you could face killing a human being, even one as awful as Jimmy Jessup. So, you all helped."

The group of people passed meaningful glances around, but no one made eye contact with me. Even Louise and Deenie locked eyes with each other, as if asking what they thought about my theory.

Deenie snapped her fingers. "That's right. And you all tried to pretend you disliked each other to keep us from figuring out you were working together."

"First, you all contributed some drug to his wine. But the combination made him puke it up. Aaron, as a science teacher, knew that if you injected formaldehyde into his veins, it would be like embalming fluid, and it would kill him. Painfully, and not quickly. But it would do the trick."

No one stirred.

"Anna, a diabetic, supplied the syringe. Sean stole the specimen jar off the shelf. Olivia replaced it."

Riveted by the explanation, Louise said, "Then who injected him?"

I looked at Dylan. "Eliana shared a glass of wine with Jessup. Only his was laced with Benjamin's Ambien. It wasn't quite enough to knock him out, so Dylan was on hand to hold him down while Benjamin and Eliana injected him."

Eliana straightened her shoulders. "I killed the bastard. I hired Olivia to find him, paid for Aaron and Dylan to go to Vietnam and set this up. I injected him with poison. No one else needs to be punished for this."

Aaron's calm, deep voice contrasted with Eliana's angry one. "Jessup was a monster. He murdered one hundred and eighty-six men, women, and children. And. He. Sliced. Them. Open. Like they were sausages. Who knows how many people died in his evil wake. He's destroyed countless lives. My children, who grew up without a mother. Anna, who was robbed of not only her father's companionship and love, but the legacy of her family's land."

Dylan's head bobbled up and down. "And Mom. Who he abandoned. And I had to be raised by an old lady who could have retired to her novels and sunshine but had to keep working to support me."

Sean's voice cracked. "And Molly. Who would she have saved in her life? She had so much love and wanted to make the world better."

Olivia slapped her hand on the table. "He mutilated people. Then collected a fortune and lived a life of luxury in Southeast Asia. He never gave a single cent to anyone to make their lives better, despite being obscenely rich."

Benjamin cleared his throat. It was such a startling sound, we all gave him full attention. He spoke slowly, and I thought it likely took a lot of effort. "What are you going to do about it? The right thing? Or the legal thing?"

Black: These people had committed murder. Revenge. Premeditated. Brutal. Wrong.

White: There is a law against murder. We live in a country of laws. No eye-for-an-eye barbaric behaviors.

Gray: Everyone here had been robbed of something beloved. Their loved ones had been murdered, dissected, driven so deeply into despair, they'd had no hope.

Black: Jimmy Jessup was a monster. There was no record of even one kindness he'd ever done.

My phone rang. The sound cutting through the thick silence, breaking the focus of nine pairs of eyes on me.

I jerked. My heart spiked and sent vibrations of alarm through me. Yanking my phone from my shirt pocket, I was surprised at what the caller ID showed. Before I answered, I slipped into the hallway and lowered my voice.

33

"Is everything okay?"

Dad sounded tense. "That's what I was going to ask you. They said Deenie is in the school with you and Louise."

And a baker's half dozen of murderers, a dead body, and one unhappy dog.

My brain skipped from that to Dad and Deenie. "What is wrong with you?" I didn't give him a chance to respond before I launched in. "How could you be anything but loving and supportive of Deenie? She might be the best thing that ever happened to you. She's authentic. Not a deceptive molecule in her. She's a damned treasure. Doesn't demand anything from you. And for whatever reason, this woman has fallen for you."

He coughed. "For whatever reason?"

"Okay, that might have been uncalled for. We love you and think you're great. But Deenie is younger than you—"

His voice was dry. "Thanks. I wasn't aware of that."

Maybe I was being all Louise-judgy and sticking my nose where it didn't belong. No *maybe* about it. I was aware of the irony of lecturing Dad when I was often annoyed with my family for sticking their noses into my love life. Nonetheless, damn the torpedoes. "Sorry. But why wouldn't you reassure her? She doesn't deserve to be treated like that. To put her heart out there and have you stomp on it. At the very least, rise to the occasion and reassure her what she means to you."

There was a moment of silence. "I see she told you about the feather."

"A feather, Dad." I had stalked down the corridor far enough that I believed I could risk raising my voice a little. "Let. Mom. Go. She walked out on you. On us."

Quietly, in that sad voice that had broken my heart right after Mom had left, he said, "How would you explain that feather in my bed?"

I threw my hand in the air and dropped it down to smack my thigh, wishing I could slap something, maybe even him. "Who knows? But Mom isn't back in the Sandhills stalking you. And even if she were, what difference does it make? She made a choice, and that can't be undone."

"You don't need a moment to think about what you'd do if she came back?"

I wanted to shout but didn't. "She's *not* coming back. It's stupid to think about. We've had three years to reconcile that. Dang it, Dad, the whole country, or at least everyone who watches CNN, came to terms with the kind of person she is. So, no. After she rejected us, I'm not wasting any time thinking about what I'd do if she suddenly had second thoughts and wanted to be back in our loving embrace. By the way, have you forgotten she's a fugitive?"

I could picture him listening and weighing everything I said. After a second, he responded. "You're not usually so black and white. I've always known you to consider all angles. And that's what I had to do this time."

Oh, really? Right now he wanted to bring up black and white and where gray entered into the equation? When I had the fate of all those people in the library to consider. "Deenie is a good woman."

There was a smile in his voice. "That's what I know, too. I'm sorry it took me a while to figure that out. Do you think it's too late?"

I thought about how down Deenie had been. "My guess is that she's in love with you. But you're going to have to win her back."

I'd made it all the way to the metal door.

"Would it help if I dug her out of the school?"

I stopped in the cold hallway. "Where are you?"

"Outside the north door, where Barkley told me he let you in."

I slammed my elbow into the bar and shoved with my shoulder, letting in a whoosh of frigid air.

Dad grabbed the edge of the door and yanked it away from my shoulder, throwing me off-balance. "Where is she?"

I stumbled backward as he rushed by me into the building. And then I nearly fell over with shock when Norm lumbered past me as well.

I knew it was Norm because I recognized his oil-stained insulated coveralls and his Fredrickson's ski cap. Other than that, he was completely wrapped up with only his eyes peeking out.

I glanced out into the gloomy evening. The wind was calm. A mound of snow showed where the pirate ship was grounded next to the swings. I had a sudden chill thinking about the killer topiary in *The Shining*.

Ahead of where I stood, the bank where I'd seen what might have been a trail into or out of the school was completely crushed from Dad and Norm's assault. Dad's old Dodge was stopped a few yards away, with an old car hood rigged to the front grill to make a kind of low-rent snowplow. The evidence of two men worried about the women they loved and determined to get to them. It warmed my heart, even as ridiculous as it looked.

Good thing they'd made it to the school when they had, because that rickety jerry-rigged contraption wasn't going much further.

Stars were popping into the night sky. Unless there were clouds, we got a show every night. Another one of those things I wasn't willing to give up to move to a city, even with Baxter.

On the still evening air, the rumble of engines sounded. The good people of Grand County were digging out. No doubt they'd be checking on the elderly and making sure everyone had heat and plenty to eat. In Grand County, there could be jealousy, backbiting, and mean gossip, but in a crisis, this community showed up for each other.

Like the Foxes.

My phone buzzed with a text from Stormy saying he'd have the van repaired soon. Good thing he'd dragged it to his shop before the worst of the storm, and apparently, it didn't need parts he didn't have on hand.

I trotted down the corridor, trying to catch up to Dad and Norm. I wanted to witness the shock and happiness when they surprised Deenie and Louise.

In my mind, I'd seen the two women rush into their men's arms. There would be tears and kisses and the warm feeling of being cherished.

Not exactly the scenario that played out as I rounded the corner into the library. Deenie was backing up as Dad approached, and Louise stood with her hands on hips, casting a wintry glare at Norm.

The seven tourists knotted together. They didn't speak, didn't touch. Barely seemed to look at each other. No matter what their justification or the consequences, they'd killed someone. For most people, that truth would sink sharp teeth deep into their souls.

Norm whipped off his ski cap and lowered the balaclava over his face. His sparse light-colored hair stood in wispy spikes. "Hon. I was worried."

Her face was firm. "I'm okay. Who's with the kids?" She was awfully combative for a woman who'd told me her kids would be fine alone.

He looked lost, a state I figured he navigated in a lot. "David is sixteen. Esther is fourteen. They're capable of watching the twins. You taught them that well."

Hands still on her hips, she seemed to soften a tad bit.

He took a step closer, as if wooing a wild animal. "I knew you'd be fine, but can you blame me for wanting to get to you? Nothing could have kept me away. What if you didn't have heat or enough to eat?"

She let her arms drop. "I don't need you to save me."

He stepped closer and didn't say anything, just opened his arms.

Louise walked into them and laid her head on his chest. His arms clamped around her, and he bent his neck into her. It was as if they'd shut the door on the rest of the room.

Deenie had her back to the card catalog. The look on her face showed a washing machine of emotions. Shock, surprise, anger, trepidation, and a fair amount of general pain. "Hank." It sounded accusatory. "What are you doing here?"

He stopped, maybe realizing he might seem threatening. "I'm sorry. I'm sorry. I was wrong. I'm sorry."

She cocked her head as if listening for something else. "About what?"

He seemed surprised by her question. It took him a second. "I'm sorry I didn't understand immediately what a treasure you are in my life."

Treasure? Isn't that what I'd said? He might have needed my help to get him there.

When Deenie didn't respond, he kept going. "I should have told you right then. You are an amazing woman, and I don't deserve you. But if you'll give me another chance, I promise to make it up to you."

With a lost look, Deenie glanced up at me, then to the people at the table all fixated on her, and finally to Louise and Norm, still in their clutch. She returned her attention back to Dad. "I've come to the point in my life where I don't want to make excuses for the person who is supposed to have my back. I'm not willing to give space to someone who doesn't understand my worth as a woman, a partner, or a person."

Dad didn't take another step toward her, for which I was thankful. At least he understood that much. "You shouldn't have to. And I have no right to ask you to forgive me. But that's what I'm doing. I know I insulted you by hesitating. That was wrong. Even if you don't give me a second chance—and I won't blame you if you don't—you should know what a fantastic woman you are. Smart, funny, gentle, with an outlook on life I only wish I could gain. These last months with you have been some of the happiest of my life."

Her face remained neutral.

For Dad, I wanted Deenie to declare she forgave him and for them to fall into each other's arms. But for Deenie, I wanted her to be with a man totally devoted to her. Did I want her to take the risk on a man raised in a different time? A few months ago, he'd broken my heart in a similar situation, when he hadn't responded by supporting me right away.

It turned out he'd assumed I knew he loved me no matter what, and he'd been working through his own stuff. But I wanted Deenie to have a man who wouldn't need to process his own feelings before understanding he needed to be a fortress for her, too.

Deenie's eyes softened. "I love you, Hank. I gave you my heart. And that meant something to me. If you need to stop and think before you can give me the same in return, then that tells me all I need to know."

Dad's head dropped. "Deenie. I was wrong."

She nodded sadly. "Yeah. You were. But I'm not willing to let you be wrong with my heart again. I'll get over you. It won't be easy. But I refuse to be someone's second thought. Ever again."

My phone buzzed in my hand. Zoe. I punched her on and turned from the rest. "Dad and Norm got to us. How is it looking out there?"

She let out a whoosh. "It's a mess, as you'd imagine. The second plow is up and going. Since they got the cell tower repaired and electricity back on, everyone can hunker down and wait for the plows. Kids aren't having any trouble getting out and about."

Snow days were the best. It was as if the world paused for play and hot chocolate. Blanket tents in the living room, epic Monopoly games, Jiffy Pop by the bushelful. Not exactly the kind of retreat we had going at the school right now. "Stormy said he'd have the birders' van ready for them in a couple of hours. I'll send Louise and Deenie home and wait with the rest of them here."

"What about the dead guy?"

"Still dead. I've got depositions from everyone."

"I need to make sure there's no emergencies with the live folks out here, and I'll be there as soon as I can.

What was I going to do about the murder of Jesse Gold? Those people in the library had been through so much. They'd lost people they loved and needed. If Jimmy Jessup's death wasn't justified, then I didn't know what was.

My phone vibrated again. When I saw the ID, my heart bounded in my chest, and I couldn't answer quickly enough. "What's happening?"

Carly's voice sounded unnaturally calm. "How is everything up there? We haven't been able to reach you since yesterday."

"Blizzard knocked everything out. How about you? I was talking with Baxter, and we got cut off. I haven't heard from him. Don't have a message or anything."

"Yeah. So, he's not here." Her words fell like a cement block.

My guts twisted. "What do you mean?"

She inhaled, and a tropical bird cawed in the background. "He was supposed to be at the airport. But when he wasn't there, we went to his hotel. His stuff is there, but he never came back."

No. I couldn't be hearing this. Baxter had to be in his hotel. He was waiting for Diane and Carly. He might be frustrated and angry, but he was safe. He had to be.

Except that's not what Carly said. Fear sawed at the edges of my control. Where could Baxter have gone? I dug deep to keep myself from falling apart. I replayed our last words and forced myself to pull together. "He said he found a lead and he was going down the coast. I don't know where exactly he was headed."

Voices from the library crept into the corridor, and I retreated further around the curve.

Carly repeated what I'd said, and Diane spoke, her voice coming to me. "Tell her to sit tight. And I mean to stay the hell at home because she can't help us down here. Not yet, not now. And we might need her there."

Carly started to repeat Diane's words, and I interrupted her. "I heard. There's no way I can sit around here. You know that. I'm heading to Denver as soon as I can get out of this damned school. And I'll be on my way to Chile."

Carly spoke with authority and power I hadn't heard before. "You anchor your ass down. We can't do what we need to do if we have to babysit you."

Diane must have taken the phone, because the next thing I heard was even more shocking than Carly's orders. Diane actually sounded kind. "Look, babe, I know you're worried. But you're going to have to trust us. If we think you can help at all, we'll get you down here. But we don't know who we're dealing with and what they want. We don't even know if Baxter is in any trouble. He might have lost his phone or something. The important thing is not to panic."

"Too late," I said, my stomach a swirl of acid. "I'm giving you two days. Then I'm coming down."

Diane bit back at me. "You don't give me a deadline. Sit. Stay."

I started to argue, but she cut me off.

"Do you even have a passport?"

"I..."

"Yeah, didn't think so." She let her victory sit a second. "If you can help, we'll get you here."

Damn it. Damn it. Damn it to hell and back. "Call me. Keep me updated."

Carly came back on the line. "We'll do what we can. This is the kind of thing we do. And sometimes we can't call. We've done this before. A lot of times. We're good at it."

Diane spoke from what sounded like a few feet away. "We've got to go."

Carly said, "We love you, and you love him, so, you know, we'll bring him and Aria home."

The connection ended. And I felt as though my stomach had been ripped open and all my innards splashed onto the sickening orange carpet.

How could I cool my jets here in Nebraska when Baxter might be in danger in Chile? They'd given me an impossible mission. Even if Diane made a good point about a passport, there must be something I could do to get there.

A mumble of voices made me look up.

Louise and Norm were walking toward me. His arm was around her waist, and her head drooped onto his shoulder. She looked exhausted, pale, and for the first time, terrified.

She had a dreadful battle ahead. She'd need warriors by her side. Sisters and brothers she could trust to care for her family, to sit with her when she needed support. I had a job to do here.

Just because I wanted to be in Chile fighting for Baxter didn't mean that was the place I needed to be right now.

I squeezed her hand as they passed. "I'll pack up your stuff and bring it by later."

"Thanks," Norm said as they continued to the door. I'd never thought of him as a rock, but he was about to be put to the test. Somehow, I believed he'd rise to it. But if he didn't, I'd be there to fill in the gaps.

Deenie trudged down in their wake. "Can you catch a ride home?"

"No problem." What could I say to her? I loved Dad and wanted him to find love and happiness. But I respected and truly liked Deenie and admired the way she prioritized herself. "Thank you for going through this with me."

She stopped and gazed back at the library. "What are you going to do about them?"

Man, I wished I knew.

She must have seen the battle on my face. "He was an evil man. And those people? They're good people. He nearly destroyed their lives. Haven't they paid enough?"

What about the law? The one I'd sworn to uphold? I couldn't answer, and we stood silent for a moment.

She reached out and hugged me, her body comforting and her grip strong. "You'll do the right thing." She started to walk away. "Call me, and we'll get together soon."

Dad may have lost his new love, but I'd gained a friend.

Zoe and Deenie spoke briefly by the door, and I waited while Deenie left and Zoe strode down the corridor toward me.

Dad shuffled out of the library looking like a whipped dog. He didn't make eye contact with me while he passed, just held up his hand. "Don't say it. I messed up."

He looked so forlorn it nearly tore a hole in my heart. "I still love you."

He hung his head and kept going. "Thanks for that, Katie."

Zoe watched him for a few steps, then gave me a questioning raise of her eyebrows.

I waved it off. "A lesson learned, I guess. So, let me introduce you to Jesse Gold, a.k.a. Jimmy Jessup."

34

I didn't offer any theories while Zoe inspected the scene. The room had stayed cold enough, but the smell was overwhelming, and it'd take some heavy-duty solvents and cleaners to make it fresh again. The lights were back on, and the overhead fluorescents didn't help Jessup's bluish complexion and agonized expression.

Zoe zeroed in on the syringe, checked his luggage, examined the injection site, and did all the things I'd done, including noting the wine stain, the opened bottle, and the vomit.

While she took notes on everything, I told her the history of Jessup and Archer Haven. I didn't include the relationship each traveler had with him.

"He was about as bad as they come, huh?" She stared at him.

Somewhere around sixteen hours after his death, even in the room's cold temperature, he resembled a dead trout lying on the damp mud of a riverbank.

Zoe was sharp. I didn't think I'd be able to sell her on the idea of suicide. But she didn't give me the chance to try when she said, "He didn't kill himself."

"Why do you say that?"

"He was left-handed."

I hadn't told her that.

"You can tell by his trimmer." She pointed at a tiny pair of scissors in his bathroom kit.

Well, I'll be. Grand County had one smart sheriff.

She mulled that over. "Looks like there would be more than a few folks who'd like to see him dead. But how many would follow him to the Sandhills and find a way inside a school in a blizzard?"

"It's a mystery, for sure."

She pulled off her gloves with a snap and assessed me. A twenty-five-year-old mother of a toddler, ranching partner, best friends with Carly and my youngest sister, and one of the keenest minds I'd ever known. "I guess I'd better meet his fellow travelers."

The crew sat in their usual places around the table. I made the introductions, using the names I'd learned when I'd met them at their van, just over twenty-four hours ago.

Zoe asked each of them where they lived and why they'd joined the tour. She didn't take notes since she knew I'd already covered this in my interviews. The cogs and levers turned and chugged in her head. What conclusions she drew I could only speculate.

My phone buzzed with Stormy's number. I slipped out to the hall and answered. He'd finished the van and left it outside in the plowed parking lot. He asked me to collect payment.

When I returned to the library, Zoe was leaning on the desk, arms crossed. She gave the whole group a skeptical gaze. "You're all claiming alibis for each other. And since no one knew Jesse Gold previously except his assistant, Aaron Fields, and you all claim to not know he was Jimmy Jessup, you're all saying you're innocent."

Some nodded a little, most watched her with nervous faces.

"So, if you didn't kill him, and he didn't kill himself, who do you suppose did it?"

Olivia took on her role of group spokesperson. "There was a black SUV that had been following us for the last couple of days. It was at every stop."

Seriously? They were going with that tired ploy?

Zoe's eyebrows shot up, and her focus sharpened. "A black SUV. Did you see who was driving it?"

Ford jumped in, maybe too enthusiastic. "A person in a red hoodie. Maybe a woman. We don't know."

Zoe nodded. "A woman. That makes sense with the small footprint in the wine."

It felt like everyone held their breath while Zoe thought. After a few seconds, she turned to me. "Who do you think did it?"

Dang. The moment I'd been dreading. The decision I hadn't decided. Except I must have decided, because I opened my mouth and out it came. "The back door had been propped open several times. And the snowbank looked like someone might have come in or gone out. I think it's possible someone entered and left the building. Maybe during the time Jessup would have died."

The tiniest tidbit of a twinkle lit deep in Zoe's eyes. She knew me. Knew lying wasn't my strong suit. And she'd probably heard the hesitation and the lack of definitive words I'd used.

But she pursed her lips and nodded, as if accepting every word. "Makes sense."

Maybe. A strange, tangled, coincidental kind of sense. But justice might be a little gray sometimes.

A clatter of keys and a grumbled "No, no, no, no" heralded Principal Barkley's entrance into the library.

I didn't have a chance to say anything before he started in. "Look what you've done. There's food and beds and everything is a complete mess. Janice is on her way in, and it's going to take her hours of overtime to get this place ready for our students tomorrow."

Janice being the janitor who, with help from me, would have the school tidied up in less than an hour.

But Dean Barkley hadn't seen the dead body in the meeting space. I wanted to be standing a ways back when he discovered it.

The tourists dispersed to gather their belongings and load up the van. I imagined they'd want to put as much distance between them and this schoolhouse as they could.

Zoe called Eunice Fleenor to bring the ambulance to collect Jessup.

I took the liberty of starting the cold van so it could heat up and stood outside as the others filtered out.

Sean and Olivia walked with their arms around each other, peaceful, if with sad and tired expressions on their faces. Dylan wandered out, blinked at the dark sky a few times, then stopped and gazed at it, probably mesmerized by the stars.

Aaron came up behind him. "I'll drive." That seemed like a good plan, since Dylan appeared lost.

I stopped Dylan before he climbed into the van. "Was there really a black SUV and a woman in a red hoodie?"

Dylan's eyes looked glassy. "Oh, yeah. Only, like, one time. At a rest stop. But, like, how could she be stalking anyone while wearing red. That stands out."

Not in Nebraska, where Go Big Red was our way of life.

"You might want to dip south and hit the interstate," I said to Aaron, waving an arm at the accumulated snow. "It's likely the roads will be more traveled and clearer."

He nodded and opened his mouth as if he'd like to say something, then shut it and shook his head. I took it to mean that after planning, executing, and trying to cover up murdering a monster and being allowed to walk away, there weren't words. I agreed and nodded back.

Anna walked out with her bag slung over her shoulder and rolling the Kleins' bag. Her face was wet with tears, and her shoulders shook every few steps. She stopped in front of me while Aaron loaded the bags in back. "It needed to be done, but it doesn't bring them back."

I gave her a hug, even though she didn't seem to want it. She already knew what I'd discovered after my sister's death: nothing brings them back or makes the pain disappear forever.

Benjamin and Eliana were the last to load up, mincing their way across the snowy path, holding hands. Eliana paused in front of me. "I suppose I should thank you. But you put us through so much while you battled your conscience. The decision should have been apparent from the beginning."

"Have a safe trip," I said in return.

I did the Sandhills thing of standing in the cold and watching them drive off, but I didn't offer a wave. I'd be glad to never see or hear from them again.

I went inside and started collecting Louise's food and supplies.

Poupon plopped down in his favorite place under the planning area in the back of the pod.

My brain was stuffed with images of a jungle and Baxter being prodded along a narrow trail by a khaki-clad gang member with a gun.

Staying in Nebraska would be impossible.

I tripped over something and looked down to see the soggy paperback Poupon had been carrying. I guess he didn't need it for comfort now that the tension-filled air from the Archer Haven group had dissipated. I owed Binda and the school a new paperback, and I read the cover to see what I needed to get.

I nearly lost my breath when I saw the cover. Agatha Christie. Who knew Poupon was a mystery buff? But the title was what stopped me. I read it, then stared at my sleepy dog, who gave me a knowing look. *Murder on the Orient Express*?

He shut his eyes and started snoring.

35

With the ambulance gone, the tourists-slash-murderers on their way to anywhere not here, and Principal Barkley inspecting the school, Zoe and I shoved the last of the sleeping bags, cots, and kitchen supplies in the trunk and back seat of her cruiser. There was hardly any room left for Poupon. But he gladly jumped in anyway. His look very clearly said "Good riddance" to that whole experience.

I climbed in the passenger seat, and Zoe cranked the heat. We drove in silence for a bit, watching the highway shiny with black ice and the four-foot banks on either side. Now that the moon had climbed high, everything had a quiet, blue glow. Frosty and killing cold, but pretty in its way.

I fought with myself to let it go. Accept that the whole sordid episode could die and never be resurrected. But I opened my mouth. "Thanks for that. Back there."

Zoe glanced at me, then back at the road. "For what?"

"For going along with the person in the red hoodie. Those people all seem a little off, but they're good people, and they've been through a lot."

Zoe whoofed out a breath. "Yeah, they've been through a lot. Getting snowed in at a school and then having someone die. And discovering you were sharing a bird-watching trip with a mass murderer. And finding out you're being stalked and the killer was right there. Man, that'd be something to have to get over."

I waited. "But the black SUV. Going along with that. Someone in a blizzard. That was… well, just thanks."

She gave me a puzzled look as we turned the corner and drove up to Stormy's garage so I could drop off the check from Olivia, who I was sure would be reimbursed by Eliana. It would have been awkward for Eliana, who was supposed to be Joyce, to write a check.

My hand on the door latch fumbled when I caught sight of a black SUV inside Stormy's open shop door. My mouth dropped open, and I turned back to Zoe. "What is that?"

She eyed it. "My guess is that it's Jimmy Jessup's killer's rig."

Now my heart started thundering in my chest. "Oh?"

"Found it stranded in a snowbank on the highway heading north. Not far from your turnoff, actually. No footprints, but with all this wind and snow, that's not surprising. We ran the plates. Turns out it's a rental from Chicago. Some woman rented it using a false ID. We'll sweep it for prints, but I doubt we'll find any. You were right. Jimmy Jessup was a bad guy. I don't think anyone is going to be in a hurry to find his killer."

Feathers. Someone in a red hoodie leading Deenie outside. A woman from Chicago. I refused to allow any of these beads to string together into one awful necklace.

For me, that big sinister black SUV had carried Jessup's killer to the Sandhills. It was a mystery I never wanted to think about again.

36

Zoe dropped Poupon and me off at my little house, and we waded through the drifts to the front porch. I shed my jacket and boots by the front door, glad the heat was on and the place seemed cozy.

Poupon headed straight for the couch, and I didn't say a word when he climbed up and stretched out with a sigh of contentment. There was a touch of jealousy in my bones as I envied him being happy with his world.

I had a hard time deciding if I was more hungry or tired as I slouched to the kitchen in my socks and two-day-old clothes. Both of those conditions came second to my need for a hot shower. A girl can only stand the same underwear for so long.

Leaving my clothes in a heap on the bathroom floor, I climbed into the steaming spray and let it do its best to wash away the trauma of the last twenty-four hours.

My insides churned with worry about Baxter. Were he and Aria abducted by the same people, and why wasn't there a call for ransom? Or were their disappearances unrelated? I could trust Diane and Carly. No question I could. But it seemed impossible for me to stay here while Baxter could be in danger.

And what about Louise? Tomorrow I'd force her to sit down and tell me exactly what the doctors said and help her figure out treatment and care for her family.

I reached for my shampoo, but when I squeezed it out, the bottle was conditioner instead. With my mind still on Baxter, I set the bottle down and absently washed my hand, then started the process again. But when I looked down to see the thick glob of conditioner in my palm again, and not shampoo, I paused. Yep, the conditioner bottle was on the shelf in the shower where I always kept the shampoo. And the shampoo bottle was on the corner lip at the end of the tub, where I never set it. That was weird. I wasn't OCD, but I lived alone, and I tended to do things the same way. Routine. Spices in the same location in the cupboard. My favorite fluffy socks rolled on the right side of the drawer. Phone on the end table in the living room. Habits. And I kept my shampoo and conditioner in their regular spots.

Oh well. Maybe I'd been distracted last time I showered.

I finished up, wrapped a towel around myself, and plodded to the bedroom for my softest hoodie and sweatpants. But when I whipped open the drawer where I expected to find my black hoodie with the vibrant rainbow across the front, there was only the lesser Husker one I'd inherited from my brother Douglas when it shrank in the wash.

And I swore my sock drawer looked a little light, like maybe missing a couple of pairs of black socks.

Had one of my siblings been here and not told me? Carly, the usual culprit when things went missing, had been gone as long as I had. Ruthie was in Lincoln at school, and Esther, who wasn't old enough to legally drive, had been snowed in at home.

Honestly, I was too tired—and did I mention hungry?—to stress about another mystery. I'd just solved a murder, and my brain needed a rest.

I shuffled to the kitchen, hoping that Louise had shoved the bacon we'd been cooking when Zoe called into the fridge. If not, I'd be dipping a spoon into peanut butter.

But only enough to stop my stomach from grumbling until I could sleep, which I hoped to do until well into tomorrow. That is, if I could stave off worry about Baxter and Louise and second-guessing my decision to release seven murderers into the world.

Bless Louise's heart. I found the bacon in a plastic bag and started nibbling without warming it up. I wandered to the sink so I could stare out at the darkness and the moon shadows on the drifts.

The peace of the quiet Sandhills settled around me, and my shoulders started to melt from my ears. We'd be okay. Carly and Diane would find Baxter and Aria and bring them home. Maybe they were already on their way. Breast cancer wasn't a death sentence, and we'd get through that, too.

The bacon hit my system, and for the first time since we'd been blown back into the schoolhouse by the storm, I started to relax.

And that's when my eyes caught the slightest hint of gray on my windowsill. It looked like a small dust bunny at first. But as my eyes focused, my heart slammed into my ribs.

I backed away, the bacon now a salty glob in my throat. My earlier reassurances that all would be well seemed like a joke.

A downy puff of a feather, no bigger than my pinky nail, nestled in the corner of the sill.

SCORCHED LINE
Kate Fox #12

When her estranged mother becomes the target of a killer, Kate must decide whether blood truly outweighs betrayal.

Marguerite Fox is back.

Three years after vanishing without a word, the woman who shattered Kate's family has returned to the Sandhills—and this time, someone wants her dead.

A shot fired. A chase through open country. Suddenly, Kate is forced to do the unthinkable: face a past she thought was buried. With her siblings on edge, threats circling closer, and trust wearing thin, protecting her family might mean protecting the one person she can't forgive.

But Marguerite has secrets buried deeper than prairie roots—and she's not done making deals. As loyalties shift and old wounds rip open, Kate must choose between justice and family... before someone else makes the choice for her.

Get your copy today at
severnriverbooks.com

30% Off your next paperback.

Thank you for reading. For exclusive offers on your next paperback:

- **Visit SevernRiverBooks.com** and enter code **PRINTBOOKS30** at checkout.
- Or scan the QR code.

Offer valid for future paperback purchases only. The discount applies solely to the book price (excluding shipping, taxes, and fees) and is limited to one use per customer. Offer available to US customers only. Additional terms and conditions apply.

ACKNOWLEDGMENTS

This book owes its very existence to Dame Agatha Christie, the Queen of Mystery. I admit my knowledge of the books of the Golden Age of Mystery is limited. But something about *Murder on the Orient Express* has always intrigued me and it was a pure joy to use it as inspiration and Sandhillize it. Every mystery writer owes a debt to Agatha Christie and I would hope she'd accept this book as my humble thanks.

I dedicated this book to Kate Fox's readers. When Kate first popped into my life, I'd hoped this tale to last longer than my previous series run of three books. In a fit of optimism, I gave Kate eight siblings so that I could feature one sibling in each book. Because you've been so faithful, I was offered more books. I thought I'd be done at book 10—this one, which had a very different story planned. That seemed like an acceptable achievement, though I was sad to leave Kate's world. And then, you all made it possible for me to play around in Kate's world a little longer. I am forever grateful for that.

To Joy Brown, whose peonies I will never forget, thank you for all things science teacher in this book. It was fun catching up.

If you ever feel the need for the truest, funniest, smartest, most supportive friends ever, simply become a mystery writer. This community is full of the world's best folks. I'm calling out Erica Ruth Neubauer and Jess Lourey as the crème de la crème. Traveling, writing, dissecting books and the business, but mostly, being the most fierce support all through life I could ever imagine. There isn't a thank you big enough.

If you're a reader of acknowledgements, you'll recognize my constant thanks to developmental editor and dear friend, Jessica Morrell. She's simply the best. And is responsible for me looking far better than I deserve.

All the good people at SRP make everything happen. To Julia Hastings who keeps me on track, Catherine Ferrell who knows how to create magic on social media, and to Mo Metlen, who's warmth and humor I deeply appreciate, thank you for all you do. To Amber Hudock, keep those titles coming! To Andrew Watts, it's always interesting to see what you've got planned next! Seriously, I have a stellar publishing team.

For the most outstanding agent in the biz, a huge thank you to Jill Marsal. Smart, savvy, tolerant of my outbursts and blue language, and seemingly ever-present, thanks for navigating this voyage.

I thank my daughters in every book, and you know what? They've never helped me write a single word. But they are on every page. To deserve these two, as Maria Von Trapp sings, "Somewhere in my youth or childhood, I must have done something good."

Speaking of good...thank you to Dave. This is a crazy career with ups and downs that happen often from one minute to the next. I'm so lucky to have a partner who keeps me laughing, and can ride the thermals alongside me.

ABOUT THE AUTHOR

Shannon Baker is the award-winning author of *The Desert Behind Me* and the Kate Fox series, along with the Nora Abbott mysteries and the Michaela Sanchez Southwest Crime Thrillers. She is the proud recipient of the Rocky Mountain Fiction Writers 2014 and 2017-18 Writer of the Year Award.

Baker spent 20 years in the Nebraska Sandhills, where cattle outnumber people by more than 50:1. She now lives on the edge of the desert in Tucson with her crazy Weimaraner and her favorite human. A lover of the great outdoors, she can be found backpacking, traipsing to the bottom of the Grand Canyon, skiing mountains and plains, kayaking lakes, river running, hiking, cycling, and scuba diving whenever she gets a chance. Arizona sunsets notwithstanding, Baker is, and always will be a Nebraska Husker. Go Big Red.

Sign up for Shannon Baker's reader list at severnriverbooks.com